AN ARTIST'S MODEL

She was the apotheosis of indolent Oriental pou-
lence, draped in gold-cloth harem pajamas, languidly
tapping cigarette ashes into a tray on the mosaic table
beside her, and smiling at a man who was working at a
painter's easel near the edge of the pool . . . And she
was not Rosa Philipous, unless Rosa had had a tint job.
This was a lush, mature woman, heavy-hipped but with
enough height to balance the Slavic squatness, with a
square-jawed Tartar face beneath a wealth of ash-
blond hair expertly arranged in a heavy roped threaded
with flowers—a photograph out of *Vogue*.

She abandoned the cigarette, rose to her feet at the
sight of our little procession and came forward, hand
outstretched to greet Maggie. The artist set aside his
palette. His back was to me before he also got to his
feet, but he didn't need to turn around. I knew that
copper-brown hair, the close set of those ears, the flick
of those slender, masterful fingers setting a brush into
its jar . . .

The artist was my ex-husband, Kai Penberthy . . .

Elsie Lee

The Spy at the Villa Miranda

ZEBRA BOOKS
KENSINGTON PUBLISHING CORP.

ZEBRA BOOKS

are published by

Kensington Publishing Corp.
475 Park Avenue South
New York, NY 10016

First Zebra Books printing: June 1987

Printed in the United States of America

I

When the divorce papers arrived, I'd have said I hoped never to speak to Kai for the rest of my life, let alone depend on him for my very existence a scant two months later. Bess brought the envelope when she came in from the Embassy, and I abandoned my contemplation of the Seine boats. "Here we are," I said, triumphantly drawing out the stiff paper, "and if I never see Kai Penberthy again, tell him hello from me."

Bess giggled faintly, but her face was troubled. "Don't sound so bitter, Siri. You loved him once."

"Did I? I must have, or I wouldn't have married him, would I? What a difference five years makes."

"Yes. In both directions," she remarked, kicking off her shoes with a sigh. "Time is a pendulum—five years from orange blossoms to disenchantment; but who knows what the future holds?"

"If you're suggesting I'll be back to orange blossoms with Kai in another five years, the mere idea repels. Why must my pendulum be on a ten-year cycle? I don't mean to wait so long, I assure you, quite apart from the fact that the one who's got him now won't be letting him go in five years—or any other time interval." I could hear her chuckling in the bedroom while I looked at the check for five thousand dollars attached to the lawyer's letter.

I hadn't wanted to take any money. "Why not, Mrs. Penberthy?" The lawyer was six feet four, resembled a stalk of bleached Belgian asparagus, and was named (most improbably) Josiah Tubby.

"I don't need money. I'm an able-bodied woman with no children; I can support myself. I don't believe in alimony for women like me. If my husband wants a divorce, he can have one; he can pay for it, that's fair, but I won't be bought off to salve his conscience." I was growing excited, insulted. "I won't be put in the position of an albatross, dammit. Neither he nor his next wife is ever going to be able to say, 'If it weren't for Kai's alimony . . .' Nothing doing! If you put in any provision, if I ever get a check, I'll tear it up. That's final."

Mr. Tubby cleared his throat and fussed with a paper on his desk. "That is not precisely the situation, Mrs. Penberthy. Apparently you did not understand; I represent your husband's grandfather, Mr. Marcus Penberthy. The divorce action will be handled by, uh, Simon and Seidel"—he studied the paper, then dropped it distastefully—"and I see no provision for alimony. However, Mr. Marcus Penberthy has instructed me to arrange for a, hmmm, modest settlement to you. I have asked you here today merely to agree on what payments will suit you best. Tentatively, he has suggested five thousand every six months for five years, but if you would prefer a lump sum, I am empowered to draw you a check."

I stared at the lawyer. "You mean," I asked

6

incredulously, "that Kai isn't even making the gesture of paying me off, he's managed to con the Aged P into doing *that* for him along with giving him an annual income? I might have known! The answer is double *no*."

Tubby's lips twitched faintly. "I'd better read my instructions from the Aged P," he said blandly, picking up another paper and ignoring my blush of embarrassment. By the time I was pulled together, he was saying, "... quit that job, get away to think ... wasting herself on a career ... Kai's fault, artistic introversion, can't see the woods for the trees. Give her fifty thousand any way she wants it—five thousand semiannual for five years or lump sum. She won't make ducks and drakes of it, so don't hem and haw. I want her to have it." Tubby eyed me over his half-spectacles. "The last sentence is underscored, Mrs. Penberthy." He laid aside the letter and sat silent, waiting. When I said nothing, he asked, "What disturbs you? Why do you hesitate?"

"Can he afford it?" I asked bluntly. "I mean, that's a lot of money, Mr. Tubby, on top of subsidizing Kai."

"Afford—!" He choked slightly, then recovered himself. "Yes—or he wouldn't suggest it. Your husband's income is a trust, administered by Mr. Penberthy and myself, but not paid from Mr. Penberthy's private funds."

"I see. I didn't know that." I was still uncertain. True, Marcus had no heir but Kai, and I knew he'd approved of me. But nothing I'd seen in the huge old Marblehead house had led me to suppose that he could give his ex-granddaughter-in-law fifty grand. The place was stuffed with clipper-ship trove, but more than half

7

shut-up. I distinctly recalled the day Marcus installed a second bathroom. It was on the ground floor, and its construction rivaled Kai's first major picture sale in importance. I looked at Mr. Tubby. "What ought I to do?"

He pursed his lips. "I think you should accept enough to permit you to go away for a year. That will be five thousand today and another five thousand in six months. Look at it this way, Mrs. Penberthy—Marcus wishes to give you a chance to start a new life. You do not, of course, need money—I understand you command a high salary. I suspect your employers will prefer to give you a year's leave than risk your transferral to a competitor." Mr. Tubby twinkled frostily. "The alternative is *status quo*—but if you will forgive plain speaking, I do not think it will be comfortable for you during the period of the divorce action and subsequent adjustments to a second Mrs. Kai Penberthy in a social world you formerly, uh, adorned by that name."

"No," I agreed sickly. "I'm . . . everyone is dreading it—being forced to sort of take sides, remember not to ask us to the same party . . . And we're still bound to fall over each other all the time."

"Exactly. That's what Marcus wants you to avoid, and I may say I agree with him." He sat up briskly, hauling forward a huge ledger-checkbook and writing as he talked. "In a year the social aspect will be an old story. You will either return to your current position or find another. Some of your former friends will have dropped out of sight, moved, or changed jobs, no longer be so close as formerly. You will have new friends to replace them—it's a natural process in New

8

York. I am not, of course, privy to all Mr. Marcus Penberthy's reasonings," he remarked prissily, "but I think I may venture to advance the theory that his offer is not intended either as, uh, buying you off or saving his grandson's face. In fact, it's something I assure you he can well afford for a young woman he likes. If you reject it for suspicion of ulterior motive, you will be ungracious—and he will be deeply hurt."

"Yes. The nicest thing about Kai is his grandfather. Thank you for explaining."

He nodded. "In a year, if you feel no more need to rest and reshape your life, you may refuse further payments. Mr. Penberthy will be quite satisfied to know he's helped." He tore the check neatly from the ledger and handed it to me. "Where will you go?" he asked, leaning expansively back in his chair. "A cruise around the world? Do you have friends in foreign parts whom you might visit?"

I was looking at the check: Pay to the order of Sigrid Quain Penberthy. "I don't know. I hadn't thought of going away at all. I have an old school friend with our Embassy in Paris," I said absently. "Mr. Tubby, do I *have* to be Mrs. Penberthy?"

"I'm afraid it's your legal name—unless you petition the court for permission to resume your maiden name."

But this second check was still Sigrid Quain Penberthy, and when I went carefully through the divorce decree, there was no word about names. In a way, it didn't matter. I was Miss Quain in business; when I renewed my college passport, I said I was divorced and left it at that. After all, I nearly was; I'd signed papers, and the lawyer said there was never a problem when there were no children. If you asked for

9

your maiden name, the judge always said yes. It didn't matter, it was just . . . odd. Even if it was a separate paper, why hadn't it come at the same time as the decree?

I looked at that again. "Sigrid Quain Penberthy having refused to fulfill her marital promises, the court deems the petition of Marcus Kai Penberthy VI for dissolution of the marriage to be just, and the petition is granted and it is so ordered."

The date was only two weeks ago; strange it had taken so long, when Kai had left town the day after revelation. But perhaps he'd had to reestablish New Mexico residency. "Lucky I kept the shack, isn't it? Even the name is suitable—Truth or Consequences." The odd gold-flecked brown eyes had sparkled wickedly, and I'd been too stunned by the whole situation to watch my words.

"You have the truth, and I get the consequences, as usual."

"But you have truths of your own, haven't you, Siri-biri-bin? Someone always has to take what's left—it's the way life is."

"I never knew you to take a leftover in your life, unless it was minced *filet mignon*. But I'll agree it's lucky you kept the shack," I said evenly, "because no matter what you do, I'll never divorce you on New York statutory grounds, and frankly I haven't time to go to Reno right now. When are you leaving?"

"As soon as I finish packing," he said after a moment. I could hear quiet movement, drawers opening and closing in the distant bedroom. Then I spread out my evening's work in the study and forgot him. The wrap-up presentation for Wells, Atherton's

10

plummiest new client *had* to be ready next day, no matter if the roof had just fallen in on me—and at least the task covered my numbness.

"You don't really give a damn, do you?"

"Would it matter if I did?"

"Oh, definitely yes," he said. "Male egotism, no doubt, but one would wish to create a misted eye, a tiny tremble in the voice, possibly even the semblance of pallid melancholy—some crumb of assurance that one would be remembered for as long as it takes from the front door of this pad down to street level. But then, you are not one to pander to masculine infirmities, are you?"

"Make your mind easy," I said grimly. "I can assure you, you'll be longer remembered than regretted."

"Glad I made an impression at all." A key ring landed on the desk before me with a muted jangle.

"What's this?" I asked, startled.

"Keys to the love nest, what else?"

"But . . . what about your things? The studio, the paintings . . . How will you get in?"

"I shall never need to get in. The packers will dismantle the studio and remove all traces of masculine occupancy tomorrow, via the superintendent's key. If they miss anything, you can throw it out. If you should ever need me, give a shout. Don't know why I say that, must be dancing-school manners. You haven't needed me in years, if you ever did. Good night, sweet princess, and may the mating call of tigers lull you to sleep each night. May the bird of paradise molt in your typewriter, and *la gazza ladra* expropriate your second-best wig on opening night at the horse show."

He's drunk, I thought with half my mind, while I

11

stared at the solid-gold latch key. I shouldn't have spent the money for a housewarming present and thought of the weary hours I'd tramped about town to find an apartment with northern exposure for the studio. I was suddenly shaking with inner fury. Three *months!* My feet still ached in memory. I'd had to find a job before we were properly settled in order to pay for the remodeling—and it meant so little to Kai that he could throw the keys on my desk and walk away forever? What the hell had he thought *I* wanted with a seven-room apartment complete with atelier? Before I could ask, the front door had closed with soft finality.

Bess came out of the bedroom, switching on lamps. "Will you stop brooding and get dressed?" she asked politely. "It's over, it's over, and too soon to examine the evidence. We're due at the Granets' in half an hour."

"Sorry. I forgot." The check and covering letter had slipped to the floor. I retrieved them and tossed them on the bureau while I rapidly stripped, showered, and dressed. It was when I finished with the lipstick and dropped it onto the crackling paper that I saw a postscript.

"It was my understanding you had intended to ask the court's permission to resume your maiden name. Since it is not mentioned in the decree, I took the liberty of ascertaining whether your request had, in fact, been made, or if there might have been some error in transmitting your instructions." I smiled to myself at Mr. Tubby's unconcealed distrust of divorce lawyers—and stopped smiling at the next sentence. "It appears, however, that the application was made in proper form, but that Mr. Kai Penberthy (who was of course present in the courtroom) entered an immediate *caveat.*"

There was more, but what it boiled down to was that for reasons unknown, since the entire divorce was his idea, Kai had first shed me very legally on grounds of desertion—and subsequently objected (equally legally) to my shedding his name. Why? I was more bewildered than angry, until Bess called, "Aren't you ready? Hurry up—we'll be late." I tossed the letter aside—I'd worry about it later. *What's in a name? A rose by any other, etc.*

All the same it was . . . disconcerting, if only for its total petty unimportance, because Kai was never petty. It was one of the tiny maddening things about him, that he knew when he'd been had, could be infuriated by other people's small meannesses, yet refused to retaliate by so much as a word or a glance. He'd splutter it out of his system at home, and next time he met the guy who snitched our cigarettes or stuck us for cab fare, Kai ignored the whole thing. So if Kai had stuck me with his name, it wasn't meant as a pinprick— he had some valid reason. But why on earth did he want *two* Mrs. Penberthys? Not even New York was big enough to hold both of us, particularly if one was me. . . .

II

A dinner at the Granets' was always memorable, even though Sidonie had more money than sense and Jean-Paul possessed fewer wits than wallets. Tonight was a tasteful blend of Music and International Finance. The musicians had wives. Presumably so did the tycoons; but one was surfing in Hawaii, and the other was making an African wildlife film with a white hunter commissioned to acquire two okapis, a cheetah, and a baby rhinoceros for a zoo in South America. Bess drew the Hawaiian one and got off to a flying start with instant agreement on the general nastiness of poi. I got the Lady Brett husband, and after a few exploratory gambits, we settled to a comfortable discussion of archaeology—not that I know anything about this, but all the more reason to listen, because apparently Mr. Jonas did.

Troy, Dr. Mallowan's book, and the true interpretation of the Golden Fleece, lasted us through dinner. When we removed to the salon for coffee, Mr. Jonas was right at my elbow with more facts and figures. He was so obviously enjoying the chance to ride his hobby horse that I hadn't the heart to say I couldn't care less where Odysseus really went, and after a while he remembered it was a dinner party. "That's enough about me; now let's talk about you, Miss Quain."

"What did *you* think of my performance?" I murmured irrepressibly.

He laughed. "You're too polite a listener," he apologized. "If Anya, my wife, were here, she'd have been signaling an hour ago, 'Gyorgy, stop boring that good child.'"

"I wasn't bored," I told him sincerely. "I like hearing new things. You've given me a lot of ideas. I may use them differently, but they'll come in handy sometime."

"Ah? How? Are you a writer, or do you work at the Embassy too?"

"No, I'm in advertising. That is, I'm taking a sort of, uh, leave of absence," I said evasively. "When I get back—well, I'll have a job, but I'd like to have a few aces up my sleeve that would get me the promotion I may have forfeited—if you understand what I mean. It sounds a bit muddled."

"On the contrary, it's perfectly clear. You are in the position of an honor student who has lost a few terms, you will be readmitted without question, but perhaps you will be demoted a grade unless you demonstrate conclusively that you have done your homework during your absence." Mr. Jonas nodded calmly. "If you think of using prehistoric legends in an advertising campaign, they will fit best with travel, of course, but you should not overlook any importer, Miss Quain. Cosmetics, perfumes, spices, jewelry—those are obvious. But the box of salt we buy for ten cents or the cheap tin pie plate? Five thousand years ago, the tribe that controlled a salt deposit was supreme. And the espionage to discover sources of tin . . ."

He drew out a pocket notebook and gold-mounted

pen to write busily, while I controlled a gulp of respect. Whoohee, he was sharp! "I was vaguely thinking of one of the oil companies that make documentary films," I said in a small voice, "I'm not sure how Aeneas or the Odyssey would tie in—"

"They don't," he interrupted authoritatively. "Early man had no use for petroleum as such; he used olive oil—fish oils in the north—and Odysseus was the bear who came over the mountain, just looking to see what he could see. All the good bits of the Odyssey were in the Atlantic," Jonas added casually, "so he may have been after tin."

Somehow he'd got my mind into high gear. "Who cares? Get a good amateur yachtsman with seagoing boat, start him at Troy, and let him follow Odysseus, filming all the places he can fuel today."

Jonas tore the sheet from his notebook and handed it to me. "Here's some research to go on with—and if you can tie oil to a prehistoric voyage," he chuckled, "I'll hire you myself, Miss Quain. How long will you be in Europe?"

"Six months or so." I shrugged, tucking the paper into my purse. "I'm tackling Scandinavia this summer; I'll drive to Copenhagen and take whatever local boats I can get for fjords and such."

"You'd be better in the Greek archipelago, if you're seriously planning a campaign."

"Perhaps, but I've been there, Mr. Jonas." I thrust aside the memory of the two months on which Kai had spent half his annual income the first year we were married.

*　　　*　　　*

16

("How *could* you! How will we pay rent or utilities, we can't afford tunafish, let alone hamburger, and you hate them both! . . .")

("I'll do some illustrations, Serious Siri.")

("But you're meant to be an Artist, that was the whole point.")

("The *point* was for you to be a young and carefree bride, twining vine leaves in your Celtic curls and dancing amid Attic splendor. Didn't you enjoy it?")

("You know I did—but—")

("There are no 'buts,' dear heart." . . .)

"I loved the islands," I told Mr. Jonas firmly. "I'd like to go back sometime—but this summer I'd rather see Scandinavia. I've never been there, you see, but now that you've started me thinking, I expect I'll find some good leads in Vikingland." . . .

But in the end I went to Greece instead of Denmark, and everything that ensued was really the fault of Mr. Jonas.

Paris in May is even better than Paris in April, no matter what the songs tell you. Too often in April it's rainy, or a late frost kills the chestnut blossoms overnight. The apartment was cozy and warm; there was a daily *bonne à tout faire* named Agnès who had a light hand with an omelet . . . I had the place to myself from nine to five or later, and more than enough social strings to the bow to prevent repining. I cashed Marcus

17

Penberthy's check. I didn't really need it—I hadn't spent all the first one, and the firm, as Tubby had predicted, was giving me "royalties on past work" to make sure I'd feel obligated to return. Even what I'd forced Bess to take as a share of household expenses was a pittance.

"Why should you pay anything? The apartment's here, I have Agnès with or without you, and she hasn't enough to do as it is. She's forever wishing I'd have a *salon* alternate Tuesdays and Thursdays so she can demonstrate her command of *la cuisine*. You'll be a godsend, particularly if you can think of people to invite to dinner."

But I cashed the check, because I thought the Aged P would be happier, and I wrote him a progress report. I'd written once to say I was safely in Italy, met amusing people on the plane, had hired a car to view the Leaning Tower before it overreached itself, and so on. Three months later when I collected accumulated mail at Bess's apartment, there was no acknowledgment from Marblehead.

Still, I wrote . . . skimming lightly over my journey from Rome to Paris, impressions of the château country, life with Bess, projected tour of Scandinavia. I said nothing about the divorce papers or Kai's objection to my resuming my maiden name. Intuitively I knew he didn't view divorce lightly; neither do I, if it comes to that. And in not acknowledging my first letter, I felt Marcus Penberthy had silently set our relationship—he liked me well enough to think of my bruised ego, but it would be foreign to his social code to continue the acquaintance. It was I who'd nicknamed him the Aged P, on our first visit to Marblehead, and

18

the morning we left he'd handed me a book—a first edition of *Great Expectations* from the family library.

"You've forgotten your Dickens," he said austerely. "Let this refresh your mind, Siri. Any resemblance is purely coincidental."

"Absolutely," I agreed. "You haven't a draw-bridge. . . ." He was still laughing when we drove away—but I'd been wrong. Marcus Penberthy did have a drawbridge, and clearly I was meant to stay on the other side of it. I understood, but it was a pity.

The days slid past unnoticed while I concentrated on the books on Jonas's list. Some I could buy; others proved to be rarities only to be consulted in libraries. I had no idea what I'd do with the material, but it was good to get my teeth into something once more. The farther I went, the more I understood Mr. Jonas's enthusiasm—because his name was open sesame! One glance at the spidery handwriting of the bibliography he'd given me, and heads of museums or libraries welcomed me deferentially. They didn't even ask where I'd got the list. They all knew that writing, and for the first time I realized it was European, remembered he'd had a faint accent despite flawless colloquial English.

"Who'n hell is that Jonas? Allah himself?"

"He's the Rumanian version of old Mr. Five Percent," Bess said, astonished. "Didn't you know? He owned half of Ploesti before the war, saw the handwriting on the wall, and traded it for a finger in every oil rig in the world—or something. His wife is minor Balkan royalty, and there's a playboy son. The real name is Ionascu."

"Good Lord," I said, appalled, "and I thought he was an American butter-and-egger—not Texas, he was too

19

literate, but maybe one of the Dakotas."

Bess snorted helplessly at my face. "Don't let it get you down," she advised. "He told Sidonie Granet he'd never had such an enjoyable evening in her house before, and now that he knew what was available, he wouldn't come again without a guarantee she'd maintain the standard."

"How rude," I said indignantly.

"Rich people are," Bess said with a shrug, "particularly Europeans. They're much more impressed by money than we are, actually. The instant they have five bucks in their jeans, they go out and insult all their neighbors. Hadn't you ever noticed?"

"No. I never knew any rich people."

She looked at me strangely, but all she said was, "Can we put off Copenhagen for two weeks? Mrs. Ambassador is splitting the reception this year."

I said it didn't matter when we left, which it didn't to me, but I'd reckoned without tourists. One thing after another was sold out, booked solid. The Paris travel people were soothing. There were always cancellations; once on the spot I'd find local trips not big enough to be handled in Paris. I did insist that they get hotel space, but since we didn't care which end of Scandinavia we began with, that was no problem. I got some upper-echelon introductions to colleagues of Paris librarians, replenished my wardrobe at the Galleries Lafayette, and was set to go—when Bess came in one night and said, "Would you like a job for the summer?"

"Depends on the job, and what about our trip?"

"Do it later, if I can get away at all, which looks more and more doubtful. The job is chauffeuse-companion to an American woman, Mrs. Corwin. She wants

20

someone to drive her to Greece, take her sight-seeing for two months. She came surging in this afternoon, evidently old family friend—the Ambassador took her off to the family rooms for a drink when he'd finished signing things, but she was talking away all during . . . and what she wants is a young woman to drive while she looks out the window."

"Why me? Why not an accredited courier? I don't speak a word of Greek, Bess."

"I don't know 'why you'—except I liked the woman, Siri, and you have been to Greece, plus this research kick. I didn't say anything—it was just an idea, and I didn't know how you'd feel. If you're set for Scandinavia, why don't you go on your own? I'll meet you, and we can come back together, but I know I'm stuck here until mid-August—and by then, Mrs. Corwin will be going home."

"Yes, I see it might work rather well, depending on how much free time I'd have. Money isn't really an object."

"I know—but I think it is for her," Bess said slowly. "I got the impression she hasn't too much. Someone's lent her a house and paid plane fare, but the rest is out of her own pocket. His Excellency suggested a professional courier, and she said the reason for a woman was to share hotel rooms en route. I forgot that, Siri—but it's only a few days. You have your own room when you get there. I don't know . . ." Bess frowned thoughtfully. "Maybe it was a fool idea. Forget it, Siri. Do as you planned."

"No, let me think overnight. She may already have someone anyway." But if Bess Rawson was sufficiently impressed by Mrs. Corwin that her first thought was to

21

send me along because I didn't need the money, the woman must be A-okay. That wasn't the problem; if I wanted a private room, I could pay for it. The problem was memory. Too true I'd been to Greece. Perhaps Mrs. Corwin meant to visit parts I hadn't seen—but if we went to Delphi or the islands or the Parthenon at night—could I stand it? By morning I'd decided there was no time like the present for exorcising the past. "If your Mrs. Corwin thinks I'll suit, I'll go."

Margaret Corwin was sixty-five, gray hair styled for easy home care, travel suit inexpensively becoming for about twenty pounds overweight. She had a crisply authoritative voice with a New England accent, and I could see why Bess had liked her at once. For myself, I wasn't so sure; I didn't think she was sure either. It was no part of my plan to bear-lead a middle-aged female who automatically treated me like a junior file clerk. I sat in the Embassy family living room and mentally kicked myself for quixotry while she conducted a probe worthy of J. Edgar Hoover.

"Miss Quain?" she repeated regally, when Bess had introduced us and departed. "It's an unusual name. Tell me about yourself, where d'you come from, where did you go to school?"

"Originally in Minneapolis, where I was born. I got a scholarship to Mount Holyoke—Miss Rawson was my roommate. Quain is French-Celtic—my father was a distant relative of the famous Irish surgeons."

"Irish? Where'd you get the Sigrid?"

"My mother's family was Norwegian. I was named for her grandmother."

22

"Your father is a doctor?"

"Was a doctor. He was killed at Anzio, and my mother died in nineteen sixty."

Mrs. Corwin nodded brusquely. "After college, what?"

"I worked for an advertising firm in New York."

"Why'd you give it up, what are you doing in Europe? Miss Rawson says you've been here for months—what are you living on? Why aren't you married, raising a family—or are you engaged? I don't want to find myself high and dry because you suddenly go off to get married. Why d'you want to go to Greece anyway, when you've already been there?"

"I don't know that I do," I said deliberately. "It appears we are at cross purposes, Mrs. Corwin. I'm sorry to have wasted your time. Miss Rawson thought that it might be more comfortable for you to have someone who needs only basic expenses and that I might as well research in Greece instead of being alone in Sweden until she's free to join me for the trip we planned. But I think you'll do better to hold to your original idea of a young student. I'm a good driver, but I don't speak Greek, you know, and I would want some time to myself."

"Pish, tush!" she snorted impatiently. "If you mean I'm an impertinent old woman and your business is yours, say so, Miss Quain."

"That's the general idea, Mrs. Corwin."

"I am as much on trial as you, Miss Quain?"

"Yes," I said baldly. "My reason for revisiting Greece is irrevelant. All that concerns you is a guarantee of my good character and a safe-driving certificate, both of which the Ambassador's secretary can supply."

23

"Good," she said unexpectedly. "I like a young woman who can keep her mouth shut. I assure you nothing could be more boring to a retired English professor than girlish confidences." She grinned wickedly. "Well, you will suit me—if I suit you, when shall we leave?"

"Why, you fraud," I protested. "You mean that inquisition was a put-up game?"

"Hadn't you better find out what *I* don't want to talk about?" she countered blandly. I was suddenly in perspective, seeing why Bess had liked her.

Poker-faced, I said, "Unnecessary. *I* would never ask such rude personal questions."

"No, you're too young. There's a trick to impertinence that requires age. I," she stated, "will teach you how."

"Thank you," I said politely. "The one thing I wanted for Christmas." Bess came back then and stared at us, sitting there laughing like fools. "It's all right—the summit conference has produced a meeting of minds, except for starting date." I sobered and turned to Mrs. Corwin. "When did you want to leave? I can be ready any time."

We settled for nine A.M. three days later. I gathered Mrs. Ambassador was a former pupil of Mrs. Corwin's, and from her determination to retain the professor by subtle wiles and stratagems for days, weeks, months, *forever,* I had all the character reference I needed for Mrs. Corwin. The "no questions" rule was observed on both sides, but Bess contributed a few details. Mrs. Corwin was Dr. Corwin, Radcliffe emeritus, widowed with children— number, age, and sex unknown. One day we came face to face as I emerged with a sheaf of introductions from the Bibliothèque Nationale. We exchanged polite greetings and parted, but presumably she asked Monsieur Launelle about me.

Otherwise, I knew nothing beyond our travel route and a final address that was apparently about thirty miles from Athens. Dr. Corwin said she understood there was a view of Euboea, but whether Villa Dresnatinko was rented or loaned, and who owned it, I had no idea. I asked about clothes. Simple and comfortable, one dinner dress for emergency. Dr. Corwin asked if I played bridge. Yes, but not for money. The Ambassador broadcast the news of our imminent descent upon the *Oikoumene* and furnished us with triplicate copies of impressive references for any inquisitive police en route. Mrs. Ambassador turned up a couple of friends in France and Italy who, after her noted roughshod technique, would be *delighted* to shelter us overnight, thus saving hotel bills.

Everything was *en train,* when I went on a final errand, and passing a major art gallery I faced a single elegantly gold-framed portrait in the window—a girl, harmoniously disposed on the corner of a *fauteuil.* She is reading an obvious love note that came with the box of flowers on the floor before her, and her face is virginal yearning, with a wealth of gold curls casually caught aside by a tortoise-shell comb. The young curves of her body are tastefully draped in a brilliant-green chiffon peignoir that exposes part—only part—of one leg. And how well I knew that picture!

It was Kai Penberthy's portrait of Sondra. The robe was mine. He'd always used my clothes closet for color

25

props, and that had created major crises. Once, a model's deodorant failure had made my only evening dress unwearable for a crucial business dinner; once, I'd innocently discarded a pair of faded slacks before he finished his picture. All part of the growing failure of our marriage. "I *don't* mind your borrowing my clothes, but if you want to paint them, why not have me wear them and save model fees?"

"I'm not great enough yet to paint you, my First Magnitude Sirius. Who could reproduce the moonstones of your gray eyes fringed with shadows, or the straight black Japanese brush stroke of your eyebrows when you disapprove of me? I shall spend the rest of my life patiently working up to the masterpiece— Penberthy's *Portrait of His Wife*. But no one will ever see it, no vulgar eye shall rest upon you until I am dead. You are special. . . ."

"I'm not nearly so special as my rather limited wardrobe, sweetie, so if you could think to ask me first?"

He'd asked for the green peignoir, I remembered. He gave it to me for my birthday, which is July 14, and two months later he asked, "May I borrow back that thing I gave you on Bastille Day?"

Stupidly, because I was thinking of the need for new sheets, I asked, "What thing?"

"The bathrobe, of course. Did I give you anything else?"

"I don't know, did you? Take it, of course; I've plenty of others." The robe had been in my closet when I made a grim tour of the apartment after Kai left. He must have replaced it that very day; it was hanging

26

prominently in the front—an expensive bit of froufrou from Maloof, but I could scarcely bear to touch it. I slammed the closet door and stamped off for a drink that was far too large, because my hand was shaking. I went around the place again, and I . . . oh, never mind. I did what any woman does—I broke some things, and I wept, and I had another drink, and finally I took the green peignoir into Kai's studio and folded it very neatly into a tissue-paper package on top of his palette. I tied it with black ribbons; at the time it seemed subtle.

Just as the sight of the second Mrs. Kai Penberthy's portrait in a Paris gallery was subtle torture. He couldn't paint *me;* he'd done nothing but a few sketches, probably discarded by now. I wasn't a beautiful artist's model, but why couldn't he have been honest, said "I adore you, Serious Siri, but you aren't worth painting when I'm so busy"? Well, he wouldn't have any trouble painting Sondra, and all the sweet talk about no vulgar eyes resting on me . . . he didn't have to care how many vulgar eyes rested on *her.* She was beautiful—and dammit, my legs were still better than hers!

I turned away blindly, catapulting into someone leaving the gallery. "Oh, *pardon."*

A male voice said, *N'importe,* mademoiselle Quain." I looked up, and it was Mr. Jonas. "How nice to see you again!"

"You, also." He smiled at me, then nodded toward the display window. "What do you think of that?"

"Why—it's very good, of course—" I began automatically, and caught myself. "Not that I know much about painting . . ."

27

Jonas moved forward for another critical appraisal. "They want a thousand for it. Do you think it's worth that?"

"Yes—it'll double in a few years."

"Ah?" I could feel his keen eyes on me. "You know this Kai Penberthy?"

"He's shown several times at better New York galleries, has a minor following, I believe. Are you going to buy it?"

"I wasn't," he said surprisingly, "but after all, perhaps I will, if you think it's a wise investment."

"Heavens, don't rely on me," I protested. "I told you I know nothing about art."

"You've a good eye, though. I agree it'll appreciate in a few years." He abandoned the picture and smiled at me. "How are you, have you time for a drink?"

"I'd like that. I meant to ask Sidonie Granet for an address, to let you know the progress of research. I can't thank you enough for starting me off."

"Have I made a convert?" He sounded pleased, grasping my elbow lightly and turning me away from the portrait. "The Ritz—or would you prefer the Café de la Paix?"

"The Ritz will do nicely, thanks, but only one drink, because I must finish packing. You'll never guess—but I'm leaving for Greece tomorrow morning!"

Mr. Jonas was suitably astonished. "You must tell me all about it."

"Oh, I shall," I assured him. "Rather more than you wish to hear, no doubt." I'd completely forgotten that he was one of the richest men in the world. He was merely someone I was happy to meet again—not that he looked like much in daylight. He wasn't much taller

28

than my five feet five, and despite twinkling dark eyes and pleasant voice, his face was sharp, almost ugly in repose. It didn't matter what he looked like—he was loaded with charm, and he was a most appreciative audience as I poured out my discoveries. "Then this trip turned up," I finished, "and it seemed meant. Bess can't leave now, but by the time I get back she'll be free—so we're off tomorrow."

"Who's 'we'?" he asked, smiling. "Where do you go, specifically?"

"We're Doctor Corwin, who's a retired college English professor, and myself. I drive, so she can look at things. We're going south, through the new tunnel— I'm dying to see it, but it's a bit frightening, too," I said parenthetically. "I keep thinking, suppose it caves in on top of us?"

"It won't," he assured me. "You'll enjoy it."

"If you say so. Then, we work our way across Italy and down the Adriatic coast to Greece, where she has a house for the summer, the Villa Dresnatinko, some-where near Athens." I was leaning forward for Jonas to light my cigarette, my eyes on his hand, and suddenly the fingers clenched so tightly on the lighter that I thought he'd crush the slender gold case. Then he relaxed, spun the wheel, capped the flame when the cigarette was glowing, and dropped the lighter into his pocket casually.

"Villa Dresnatinko? I've heard of it. Near Oinón, isn't it?" he said calmly. "The bathing is good, but you must beware of the rocks and riptides. Tell me about this Doctor Corwin—how long will she be there, how did you hear of her?"

"Through Bess Rawson. The Ambassador's wife was

a pupil of Doctor Corwin's." I made a good story of our interview, and Mr. Jonas smiled occasionally, but I had a feeling he wasn't entirely with it, despite the intentness with which he listened.

"So you don't know how she comes to have this house for the summer, whether it's loaned or rented?" he asked when I'd finished.

I shook my head. "Not my business. All I need know is that she has a house and a car. I do know the car is rented—the International Auto Club arranged it, and I had to fill out insurance papers. Otherwise—no questions and no unwanted confidences."

"Sounds restful, but a bit dull to be cooped up with a strange woman and have nothing to talk about."

"Oh, I expect there'll be lots. You're a strange man, and look how we talk! It's prevention of boredom, actually. I don't want to hear about her problem pupils, and she doesn't care about my past either."

"Have you a past, Miss Quain?" he asked lightly.

"Of course. Doesn't everybody?" I lowered my voice dramatically. "I'm really Secret Agent double oh six and a half disguised as a remittance woman, and all this research is only a cover for Operation Cowboy, which is a scheme to corner the market in elephant saddles. You won't tell anyone?" I asked anxiously.

"Not even the head of C.R.U.S.H., in which organization I happen to be chief mahout," he assured me. "Why are you only a half?"

"Because I ride an elephant."

"Tchk," said Mr. Jonas apologetically. "I should have thought of that myself, but I'm not really a very good agent. I can't even remember the password."

"That's the easiest," I told him kindly. "Mahootma,

30

of course. What else?" I chuckled at his face and finished my drink. "I hate to leave, but I must. I'm so glad we met again, Mr. Jonas. I did want you to know how you changed my life, but I kept forgetting to ask Sidonie—and now I needn't feel guilty for not writing."

"But now it is more than ever important for you to let me know how things go," he said swiftly, drawing out the notebook and scribbling. "This address will always reach me, Miss Quain. Please do not hesitate to wire or telephone at any time of day or night if I can be of assistance." I thought he was merely continuing the gag, but his face was oddly grim as he handed me the slip. "Commit it to memory, write it anonymously in the back of your traveler's check folder if you must, but destroy this at once. The password remains the same: Mahootma." I must have looked startled, because his face relaxed slightly. "I can't help but feel a bit responsible, Miss Quain. I'm glad my chance words were stimulating, but I hadn't anticipated such enthusiastic followup. Now I find you're off to Greece, planning several months with a total stranger who has cleverly persuaded you to ask no questions. I shouldn't like you to encounter an uncomfortable situation, that's all."

"That's kind of you, but what on earth could happen to me—aside from a personality clash? In which case, I pack up and move. I've enough money, our Ambassador's alerted the Embassy in Athens, and I'm loaded with credentials for local officials."

"Good, but what I had in mind was red tape. Perhaps a refusal to permit you to use research sources." He shrugged ruefully. "Sometimes one comes up against a petty satrap who won't honor anything short of a message from the angel Gabriel, which can be infuriating when time is limited. I have some small influence here and there, that's all." Mr. Jonas rose, smiling easily. "Keep the address, Miss Quain, and if there's any minor frustration, please use it."

"All right. I suppose you'd like me to eat it after I've memorized?"

"No, I wouldn't—it is not the best quality paper," he said apologetically. "You might burn it and scatter the ashes from the taxi window as you pass Père Lachaise. *Au revoir,* Miss Quain."

"A bientot," I returned automatically, "and thanks for the drink."

I found Mr. Jonas's slip last thing that night, when I was organizing my handbag for morning departure. The address was in the 13th arrondissement, which is down by the river and not particularly classy. In fact, when I consulted the street map I could scarcely find the place. It was a tiny cul-de-sac, a single block tucked near the wharves, but there was a telephone (Grange 6005), and the cable address was Geejay. For Gyorgy Jonas, I thought—simple to remember as well as the phone, which was Secret Agent 006½ slightly reversed. I smiled to myself at our foolishness this afternoon. How quickly Jonas had played up, caught the nonsense! No matter how rich he was, he was "real homely" as New Englanders put it—which brought back how we had literally run into each other.

A feather for Kai, if Jonas bought the portrait of Sondra. I had a snide regret that I hadn't queered the deal. Couldn't do it, of course, but I hated to think of

his innocently paying a thousand bucks for the portrait
of my ex-husband's mistress. If he found out, I thought
he wouldn't like my silence. Not moral rectitude—ugly
as he was, I'd bet Gyorgy Ionascu had never needed
money to get any woman he fancied. I found him
madly attractive, and not for any father substitute
either! Lucky he was older, married, completely out of
my social world; lucky I was leaving tomorrow, or I
knew I'd use that address with a trumped-up excuse to
see him again. But even if we never met, I didn't want to
lose his approval. Impulsively, I dashed off a note.

> You asked if I knew Kai Penberthy, and I
> deliberately misled you. I'm sorry. He is a first-
> class artist, and his work will be a good
> investment—he is also my ex-husband. The
> portrait is Sondra, his second wife. I thought you
> should know. Yours till mahots'mon 006½

I sealed the envelope, stamped and addressed it, and
dropped it into the mail chute before I could vacillate.
I'd easily remember the address, but grinning at his
nonsense about Père Lachaise, I scrambled the numbers the way Bess and I had used to pretend coding
in college days. I forget *why* we developed the kick—
something to do with her father being a complex
computer pioneer—but we baffled Gizmo, and Mr.
Rawson made us a test team. We had to be cleared by
the FBI and were ordered not to let play interfere with
exams, but for four years whenever we had time we
amused ourselves.

The best code was the simplest: add six to all
numbers and deduct the day of the week; add one after

every tenth number, deduct two after the twentieth, and so on. If you made Sunday equal zero on thirty-day months, one for thirty-one day months, and minus two for February—and picked a letter code from a standard college text—you could be damned confused. Gizmo had never heard of Rupert Brooke, for instance, and burst a gasket in frustration. So did Mr. Rawson; Bess merely widened her eyes and said, "I had no *idea* cryptographers were supposed to be only high school graduates, Daddy."

After that we had a ball thinking up goodies for Gizmo; so did Mr. Rawson, until we realized it was no good using ordinary literacy. Then we became sneaky. Gizmo lived chastely in the bottom of the Pentagon behind a door guarded by marines. When Bess heard that, she said, "Oh, poor Gizmo!" and hunted out a fruity passage from the *Decameron*. In Italian.

When Gizmo finally got it, he didn't know what it meant—and when Mr. Rawson (who did) explained, Gizmo got so excited he popped six buttons. Or it may have been the programmers, but as Bess said, "How did *we* know cryptographers took vows of celibacy?"

"They don't," said her father, "and if it's all the same to you, don't give them any ideas! This is a test program, not a bi-quinary bordello."

The last time we flummoxed Gizmo was with the Lord's Prayer in Middle English, which is worse than Chaucer's "Whan that Aprille with his shoures sote," because it comes out looking like runes. When Gizmo got it, neither he nor anybody else, including Mr. Rawson, could entirely believe it. They ran it through three times, until some of Gizmo's more inaccessible condensers melted from the strain, and Mr. Rawson got us out of bed at one A.M. to say "Kamerad! What have you loused us up with this time?"

We really had, too. Fortunately the General was married. He said, "Women are anyone's secret weapon. Lucky the commies made 'em sexless as well as classless, but we mightn't get such a break next time. You better reprogram everything for irrationality, Rawson." All of which got Bess's father a million more dollars for research and five years at hard labor—or so he maintained.

Chuckling, I translated Mr. Jonas's address into our original code, for which the basic sentence was "T 4 2 & 2 4 T, mi 4 U & U 4 mi"—except sometimes we spelled it out, or counted spaces, and various other refinements. We called it Squarawb and could do it in fifteen minutes even if we forgot which day or month it was, which occasionally happened if we were in a hurry. In these last months we'd reverted to it for all notes on the kitchen bulletin board, although Agnès was as uneasy as the cable operator who delayed Bess's marriage congratulations until someone in CIA said, "Rawson? Oh, my God, are they testing again?"

So I put it in my book under S for Secrets, and for good measure I put it in Bess's address book under E for Emergency. It came out of scrambling looking unusually innocent. I left a kitchen note for Bess to scan E, added the warning "Remember he's married and if he ever isn't, I get first crack." Then I tore the slip into tiny pieces and flushed them down the whooha, giggling to myself while I removed makeup and got ready for bed. Bess was already asleep, and I tiptoed about in dimmed lights finishing final packing.

When I went to put some final instructions about

laundry and cleaning on the kitchen board, I heard a peculiar *click* in the darkened living room. From the kitchen a long shaft of light fell across the hall entrance, and I distinctly saw the knob turn gently. For a moment I was petrified, until I saw the night chain in place. Then I thought it was the upstairs tenant, who was inclined to gad about and come home stoned in the wee hours. His wife seemed not to care what he did, provided he didn't wake her. I stalked over to the front door and said sternly, *"Qui est là?"* expecting a whispered apology from Monsieur Bernaud.

Instead, the knob was released sharply, there was another click, and then total silence for an eerie moment. Someone had hastily withdrawn a key and was standing in the hall waiting . . . but for what? I was half-frightened, half-furious, foolishly tempted to throw open the door and confront the intruder, but with my hand on the chain I knew it was silly. I asked again, insistently, *"Qui est là?"* Pressing my ear to the crack, I thought I could hear stifled breathing beyond. Suddenly, there were footsteps pattering lightly down the stairs into the distance. Whoever had tried to enter the apartment had made good his escape—but why should anyone want to get in? It might be a chance sneak thief hoping for a door that wasn't chained against a picklock, but somehow I felt it was purposeful.

This was a remarkably safe neighborhood. Our concierge was on duty until midnight, when the street door was locked; the apartment keys were individual, but each opened the lower entrance. It was only a simple affair meant to keep out stray cats, dogs, or drunks who couldn't recall where they lived—all of which raised an even more disturbing point.

Anyone might have a key to open the street door, even accidentally, but our intruder's key had turned *this* lock. I remembered now that Monsieur Bernaud's key wouldn't go all the way into this slot. So whoever it was had come with a key to Bess's apartment . . . and he was a stranger, or he'd have known there was a burglar lock and a chain. Yet, *why* this apartment?

I lit a cigarette and sat in the dark living room, considering possibilities. The concierge was unlikely— she'd been here for thirty years, and if she had a fault, it was a tendency to mother young tenants. If anyone had even asked for a key, we'd have heard of it, with censure for forgetting to tell her; she would have satisfied herself on the most minute details of the affair and accompanied the asker in person if necessary, standing uncompromisingly over him until the job was finished, even if Agnès was there. She did have extra keys for each apartment, aside from her concierge ring, but the one time I was locked out accidentally, she'd shrugged comfortably and said, "Eh, it is simpler to let you in myself, Mademoiselle Quain, than to get the duplicate from the bedroom closet. Only one flight, after all."

No, *nobody,* no matter what the excuse, could have got the extra keys out of Madame Durey for long enough even to make a soap impression.

The building owner was equally unlikely. He probably had a set of keys for his property, and he lived on the top floor, but he felt himself far too grand for mundane affairs. Everything was left to Madame Durey, from rent collection to complaints. Anyway, I remembered that he and his wife had gone to Cannes the day after Easter. The hideous *fin de siècle*

37

appartement, decorated by maman in 1900 and never subsequently altered (including a Turkish room *pour le smoking),* was closed until October.

Who else could get a duplicate key? Someone with access to the Embassy. There was a board file for every home, kept in His Excellency's private study, ever since a courier left the diplomatic pouch in his flat while he went to get his shirts from the laundry—and on the way back got his leg broken in a street accident. So there was a possibility. Not too good a possibility, though. It presupposed someone who could get into the Ambassador's study unquestioned—and that Bess's job involved something more than secretarial work. Well, that could be; I'd just been using Squarawb—and Bess had always been better at it than I. She might be doing some sort of special code work. But why would anyone suppose she had such stuff in her apartment? And if it was espionage, the spies were damned clumsy trying to sneak in when we were there. But perhaps they were desperate. . . .

Come to think of it, the apartment was well nigh impregnable. Agnès was there from eight to four every day and stayed late if we had guests; I was in and out, with no fixed schedule; Madame Durey was finished with her duties by four, enjoyed a tisane in her easy chair set strategically to observe the passing show. Nothing and no one could pass her unnoticed. She smiled politely at visitors, but she *saw* them. Anyone resembling a worker or tradesman was instantly challenged and dispatched to the service entrance. At six o'clock when she went to prepare dinner, Monsieur Durey had returned from his respectable job with le Metro and took her place in the easy chair, enjoying his *petit verre.* The Durey's door was always open; they ate, played cards, watched television in such a position as always to see who passed. The service doors were even worse, bolted top and bottom, to be opened only from inside.

I knew I was avoiding a final explanation—that Bess had a lover who'd mistaken the date of my departure . . . and why should I be startled? Bess was my age, twenty-seven—and I was no stranger to sex—but my mind said instantly, *It's not the sort of thing she'd do.* No, that wasn't putting it the right way. Bess was no virginal prude, merely selective. In college she said, "Benefit of clergy? From what I've seen, men need it more than I."

What Bess would not do was jettison a lover because I was here. Discretion, yes; oblivion, no. He'd have been around, I'd have met him however casually, but in nearly three months I'd seen no sign of partiality, no constant escort. Could she, would she, dissemble to me? If so, I thought, I must have noticed some change in our old uninhibited relationship—but in a way I had, though I'd unconsciously accepted it as maturity. We could still say anything we wanted to say without fear of misunderstanding—but I knew I hadn't *wanted* to say much of my marriage. Similarly, Bess's responsible position required silence occasionally . . . but why silence on personal affairs?

No, I couldn't believe that Bess had changed so much in five years as to take a lover she wouldn't acknowledge, no matter for what reason. Good heavens, could it be His Excellency? I held my breath in horror, then went limp with relief at the realization that he of all people knew best that I was still here. Dr.

39

Corwin was staying with his wife; he was not only privy to every detail of our departure but had had so many well-meant extra thoughts for our comfort as to be downright nuisancy.

A member of some congressional group? I rejected the idea at once; any congressman I ever saw would need an act of God as well as benefit of clergy.

Perhaps an international tycoon like Mr. Jonas, where there'd be the dual complication of a wife plus Bess's Embassy position that could lead to embarrassment in diplomatic circles? In the end I stubbed out my cigarette and left no word of an intruder on the bulletin board. If Bess could deny herself for three months, maintaining a blithe front of contentment in order to convince her closest friend of normalcy, it seemed tactless to let her know "all is discovered" in the final hours.

III

The car was not the utilitarian Volkswagen I'd expected. It was a Karmann Ghia, painted Schiaparelli Pink. Heaven knows where the auto club ever got such a rental, but it stood festively before the Embassy, with Dr. Corwin's luggage already loaded and its lessee trotting about proudly, holding a cup of *café au lait* and dunking a croissant between peeks to be sure the car was still there. She was attired in a miniskirt of mingled blue-purples in abstract design over grape-colored tights—and I only hope my legs will look that good when I'm sixty-five.

"The years I've wanted to be as comfortable as my students!" she exclaimed happily. "Come in, come in, child. Have some coffee, try one of these buns. Delicious! The French should stick to the kitchen and hire someone to run the country . . . *anyone* can run a country, look at some of the presidents we've had. No, no, no!" She dashed away, *"Not* in the tonneau, that's my skirt if we have to be respectable. Put it in the back seat, please."

Dr. Corwin was cock o' the walk, a kid going to camp for the first time, corny as Kansas in August,

41

totally natural and unaffected. She didn't care who knew this was a Dream Realized, she was an absolute dear, and the entire Embassy was smiling over her. His Excellency took me aside to deliver three more letters of introduction and a list of helpful hints copied from *What to See in Greece* (which I already had).

"Thank you *so* much," I said earnestly.

"It's nothing, nothing," he said hurriedly—because The Car was waiting, sitting disdainfully in black splendor behind the gaudy Karmann Ghia, with the effect of a flared nostril in its bonnet. "You've got maps? Make Vienne for lunch—I've ordered at la Pyramide for you. They'll be ready whenever you get there. And here"—he thrust a wad of notes into my hand—"for the tips. They'll put the bill through to me here. Have a good trip, call if there's the slightest difficulty."

"Oh—thank you so much, it really wasn't necessary—"

"Not at all, not at all," His Excellency muttered. "Want Maggie to have a good time, enjoy herself. Take care of her, will you?"

"So long," I said automatically, stuffing the money into my handbag and preferring not to think of the lunch he'd ordered. It was bound to be *tout à fait comme il faut,* complete with bottle of "an unassuming little wine, but rather nice for informal moments." With luck, we'd reach Vienne about one—but rather later than sooner, and the Pyramide would require at least two hours—*at least*—meaning we might get going again around three, but undoubtedly rather later than sooner. All of which meant we would *never* get to Grenoble, find our way through the morass of handwritten directions accompanied by a pencil map on the back of a used envelope, and reach our hosts in time for tea.

Now that the Ambassador had departed beaming with satisfaction over his little surprise (which I devoutly hoped would be the last time he loused us up), I still had to cope with Mrs. Ambassador. "You *will* take care of Maggie, won't you, Siri? I don't *at all* like her wandering around by herself in these foreign places," she fussed in a series of staccato exclamation points. "I begged her to wait until I could go with her— only two weeks before the boys return from school, a mere three *days* before they're off hosteling, but she was absolutely *determined* to leave at once. I don't know this *person* who's lent her the house, can't even *find* the name in the alumnae list—Rosa something, but Maggie says she can't remember the married name, except Greek and unpronounceable . . . and she's managed to lose *everything* but the address, which is *typical* of Maggie."

I thought Dr. Corwin was crazy like a fox, but I assured Mrs. Ambassador I'd manage discreet supervision—and would she please telephone Grenoble that we might be late in arriving? "Why?" she demanded. "I *gave* you a map."

"Yes, but your husband has ordered lunch for us at Vienne."

"Oh? What a good idea! Isn't that sweet of him, how Maggie will enjoy it. Now, don't tell her, just let it be a lovely surprise!"

"I'm sure it will be. If the luggage is stowed, I'm ready when you are, Dr. Corwin."

It was another twenty minutes before the final kisses

and hand wavings were behind us. Dr. Corwin settled herself in her seat with a deep sigh of contentment. "We're off to see the Wizard," she remarked. "What a relief! Really, Elspeth—a dear girl, one of the sweetest natures and tiniest intellects I ever met! George is a darling, too, but so exhausting. I can say anything I like about anyone," she inserted parenthetically, "because I never say anything I haven't already said to a person's face. You needn't worry when I sound scurrilous, Miss Quain."

"Then I shan't, particularly when I agree with you," I chuckled, "but you're not rid of them yet. I wasn't supposed to tell you, it was to be a lovely surprise, but the Erinyes of hospitality are still with us."

"What *do* you mean?"

"George has had the happy thought of bespeaking *déjeuner* for us at la Pyramide."

"Oh dear!"

"Yes, I thought you'd better know. We can make it by one if we go straight through, or we can stop to phone a cancellation, but the place is still three-star."

"I'm only bothered over what he's ordered. I go straight to sleep if I eat too much at midday." She debated briefly. "We'll go," she decided, "but you can phone about the menu. *Paté campagne,* I think, with an omelet and salad—perhaps some fruit?"

I left her looking over the maps; when I returned to report what the Ambassador had selected, she groaned. "I wonder what else they've got lined up for us," she pondered, eyeing her purple tights morosely. "Such earnest good people, but Elspeth will treat me like a witless Wamba until I have to assert myself—like these pants. I never in the world meant to buy pants, let

44

alone this color; I was looking for a comfortable travel skirt, but the instant I paused—just to admire the designs—Elspeth was so horrified that I couldn't resist. Then she was bound I should get black, so I got these," she finished defiantly, "and now I look like an opium dream."

"Nonsense, you look just right—comfortable and ready for adventure. Elspeth was jealous, her legs aren't as good as yours."

Dr. Corwin laughed. "That's consoling—but I should have got black."

"That's where you're absolutely out," I said firmly, keeping an eye out for a route intersection. "Black is only for young people, it points up young fresh skin and hair. Older people need color, lots of it."

"You sound very authoritative," she said after a moment. "Where'd you get this theory?"

"From an artist," I told her impersonally. "D'you mind looking for the turn to Melun . . . ?"

By the time we reached Vienne I was thoroughly pleased with the trip. Dr. Corwin had a keen sense of humor, a quick eye for passing scenery, and total efficiency with maps. We never missed a turn, nor even needed to slacken speed for an interchange. We talked casually or were comfortably silent. There seemed plenty to say without personalities or impertinent curiosity. Dr. Corwin was thinking of writing a book. "Not another scholarly tome," she confided. "I've done several of those. What I really want to write is a piece of trash that will go into ten editions and sell to the movies—not merely for money, but to see if I can

45

do it."

"You know you can do it," I scoffed. "In your secret heart you're kicking up your heels and hoping to shock everyone—particularly Elspeth."

"She's not the only sincere Radcliffe graduate, but I'm afraid you're right—I would like to shake 'em up a bit."

"Excellent for the liver," I agreed. "Any idea of a plot? If I can help, let me know. I'm researching prehistoric legends, might run across something useful for you."

"I thought you were in advertising."

"I am, but I've got interested in the possibility of explaining old familiar stories in modern terms tied to present-day business." I gave her a bit of Jason, Theseus, *et al.* while we finished lunch.

"It sounds fascinating. What got you started on it?"

"A man I met at a dinner party. I think, if you're able to move, we'd better get rolling for Grenoble. You can burp in the car."

After that, Dr. Corwin called me Siri; I think she was hardly aware of accepting me as honorary pupil. The friends Elspeth had bullied into putting us up for the night were bewildered but game when we rolled into the driveway about five. They blinked once, as she crawled out of the car in her miniskirt, muttering, "Tchk, I knew I shouldn't have got pleats for traveling, one simply sits them out . . . Oh," graciously, "Mrs. Arthur, and Mr. Arthur—how do you do? So kind of you to take us in. If you could pretend I am incognito until I change clothes, I shall look entirely respectable, I assure you. This is Miss Quain, who is traveling with me."

Mr. Arthur attempted gallantry. "You would always look respectable, Dr. Corwin."

"How *dull,*" she sniffed, while we were all shaking hands politely, "and in any case *not* suitable for bishops."

"I'm afraid we don't know any bishops," Mrs. Arthur murmured uneasily.

"Good—or were you so misguided as to invite some professors to dinner?" Dr. Corwin stared at them suspiciously.

"Well, as a matter of fact, we did, but they couldn't come—such short notice, summer holidays . . . Elspeth even called Professor Dorlant personally, but he couldn't change his schedule . . ." Mrs. Arthur's voice trailed away apologetically.

"Hah! That's lucky," Dr. Corwin stated grimly. "The last time I saw Fatty Dorlant, he had the impudence to question my translation of *'cilz doulx baisiers oste et rebute'!* Him and his white lace doctoral nightgown from the University of Bologna—and so fat he had to walk by himself in the Harvard graduation procession, wasn't room for anyone else. Oh, are those my bags?" as a sturdy youngster trotted past her. "I'll go along with him, shall I? Wash up and change, be down in fifteen minutes." She surged away, calling, *"Prenez garde!* Don't jiggle the makeup kit, you'll spill the face powder."

The Arthurs stared after her dazedly for a minute, then turned to me. "Forget everything Elspeth told you," I told them gently. "Relax, let it flow over you, and enjoy— make the most! It's not likely to come your way again."

"If you say so, Miss Quain, but Elspeth . . . I mean,

there's tea ready, or hot bouillon if Dr. Corwin would like to rest in bed before dinner . . . or a tray if she's too tired to come downstairs . . ."

I'd had a few private instructions from Bess. So I said succinctly, "Dr. Corwin will descend in fifteen minutes. She will appreciate two very dry martinis served rather quickly, followed by a third and possibly a fourth, depending on how long to dinner. She enjoys food, but is neither gourmet nor gourmand. After dinner she favors an orange liqueur with coffee—Grand Marnier, Cointreau, Curaçao, what have you—and she is not averse to a nightcap. Possibly two . . . or three . . . or more, depending on how stimulating the conversation. Brandy and soda."

Mr. Arthur eyed me impassively. "Who does the driving?"

"I do—and I can keep up with her any night," I told him sweetly, "except that I prefer Scotch and Benedictine. Don't tell Elspeth."

"Scout's honour," he assured me. "Well, well! This sounds like fun."

It was more than fun, once the Arthurs got over Elspeth's instructions. Dr. Corwin was a born charmer with an indefinable gift for young people. She both amused and influenced them, yet was never anything but herself. She neither wished to be "one of the girls" nor condescended to them. When she wished to communicate with a younger generation, she simply moved laterally from her maturity to theirs, and often though I observed the phenomenon in later weeks, I never ceased to be amazed at the results. I thought that, given time, even the sulkiest problem child would respond to her, while from young adults she evoked the best they had of heart, mind, even soul.

In the space of two martinis, she had our hosts completely captivated, begging us to stay a month, two weeks, just a few days, please, *please!* Dr. Corwin laughed—anyone likes to be liked—but she was firm. Our plans were made, we must leave tomorrow. Then Mrs. Arthur asked diffidently if she was too tired to meet neighbors who might drop in later. Dr. Corwin's eyes twinkled. "Not at all, they'll take the curse off an evening of professorism."

Mr. Arthur burst out laughing, until his wife said indignantly, "Stop laughing, John, it was *your* idea—but now they may as well come to dinner." In the end, I think she called her friends, who called all their friends. A stream of cars arrived, everyone brought whatever she was having for dinner; all the menus were different, there wasn't enough of anything to go completely around, which made the results even more fun. The boys cooked an assortment of meat, fish, and chicken on the back-terrace grill; the girls heated ragout and *pot au feu* in the kitchen. Dr. Corwin was in the thick of everything, naturally. "Siri, get the bag of oranges we bought in Vienne—I'll make a salad."

It was dark enough to need a flashlight. I ran upstairs to get it, came down, and found my way to the barn, where the handyman had stored our car. The flagged path was shielded by high shrubbery behind the kitchen, until you suddenly debouched into a cobbled farmyard, and turning the torch this way and that to pick out the Ghia among guest cars, I caught motion. The light focused briefly on a swarthy face, a figure

49

transfixed beside the yawning barn door. Then it disappeared, fading back into the shadows. Probably another farmhand. I had no idea how many people the Arthurs employed, but it had already emerged that they had a modest stock, plus chickens. I got the oranges and went back to the house without seeing the man again.

The impromptu party finally ended, regretfully, about one A.M., and by then I was quite ready for bed. Elspeth's master-minding made tomorrow's drive only about two hundred miles, and the Arthurs were escorting us to lunch near Turin, so I wouldn't need to be alert for road signs. I could still use some sleep. Yawning, I undressed and got ready for the night. The room was comfortable but unexpectedly chilly— someone had left a casement window open at the rear, looking over the kitchen extension to the farmyard.

Someone had also moved about my overnight cases. I thought the maid might have done it when she turned down the sheets, but when I opened the makeup box in search of toothpaste, there was no doubt that the girl had also been inquisitive. I woke up enough to check, but nothing was missing—merely misplaced, and the jar of cold cream appeared to have been stirred with a stick. When I examined the suitcase, I thought it had been disturbed, yet not so disarranged as the makeup. Curiouser and curiouser—but somehow revealing by the very things that weren't touched. Not clothes, which might interest a country maid . . . not perfumes or junk jewelry tossed carelessly into a side pocket— but powder box, cold-cream jar, shoes in the closet; I knew I hadn't left them tumbled across each other like that.

There was no doubt the room had been searched, but for what? I was wide-awake now, noticing. The maps for later stages of the trip had been unfolded, and two had been slightly crumpled in refolding and stuffed into the pocket anywhichway. My handbag looked as though it had been dumped out on the bed and everything replaced at random—yet passport and money were there. Quite a lot of money, in fact, left from the roll His Excellency had given me for tips in Vienne. The searcher was not a thief—but also not a servant girl seeing what ma'amselle had brought with her.

My mind flashed back to last night's intruder in Bess's apartment; yet what possible connection could there be? I had thought of a lover for Bess, but this altered matters. Was she under surveillance because of the Embassy, and was I being searched for my association with her? It seemed a long way to trail me, unless it was a farflung operation with local people in Grenoble who could be alerted for work on the spot— and how could they have known where I was going when I left Paris this morning?

Dr. Corwin, I thought suddenly. She'd been a guest at the Embassy—perhaps we were both being checked. That argued a similar search of her room. I felt sure she would spot it, but if she had any inkling of the cause by reason of her Embassy visit, she'd say nothing. I wouldn't either, unless she opened the subject. I wasn't especially frightened—mostly I was damned annoyed at having to reorganize my handbag. When I discovered a large, greasy thumbprint obscuring the A's in my address book, I was *furious*—until it began to strike me as funny. Clumsy oafs! What was that TV program

51

where the man kept saying, "Sorry about that, Chief"?

I couldn't take it seriously, but on the chance that it might mean something to Bess, I decided to phone tomorrow morning—ostensibly to let Mrs. Ambassador know we were safe. I'd mention the search as an amusing incident, and Bess could take it from there, if it had to go anywhere.

IV

Morning brought not counsel, but increased bewilderment. John Arthur greeted me with relief when I came down. "Don't want to upset Dr. Corwin, but apparently we had a prowler last night," he said. René doesn't think anything's gone, but he ran into someone at the barn when he came home. He sleeps in the loft, no business to be out, but he's courting." John smiled faintly. "Lilly wishes he'd cut the cackle and get to the barns so she could latch on to Jeanne for upstairs maid," he remarked. "Thing is, René knows this place like the palm of his hand, doesn't need lights to slip back without waking us—and as much as he could see, the man was a stranger. He cut and ran, of course. René thought it was someone looking for a place to sleep. We do occasionally get Gypsies—they'll take anything they can carry, and the man was darkskinned—but René hasn't heard of Gypsies recently. I think you'd better check, Siri."

"Of course." I went out to the car, feeling an uneasy quiver along my spine. It was beginning to be not funny after all. I'd seen a small, swarthy man when I went for the oranges . . . and my room had been searched. Now

I remembered the open window, and he'd have figured that was my room from the light on and off, followed by my appearance with the flashlight headed for the barn.

I pulled up the trunk lid expecting—I don't know what. But the bags were all there. At least, I wasn't sure how many Dr. Corwin had, but I felt they were exactly as the Embassy boy had stacked them, neatly piled in one half of the tonneau. The other half had been equally neat-packed with my cases—and they were still there, but two were upside-down.

After a moment, I tried the lock on Dr. Corwin's top bag, and when it opened easily, I flipped up the lid for a peek. Pristine tissue paper, exactly as the Embassy maid had left it. Steadily I drew out my own top bag, and although I don't pack like a ladies' maid, neither do I fold my clothes quite *that* carelessly.

Thoughtfully, I righted and restacked my bags. No question which belonged to whom—all the bags had handle tags. And only mine had been disarranged. That threw me back to Bess for the connection with the Embassy, or Dr. Corwin's bags would have been searched too. I closed the trunk and went back to the breakfast table slowly, trying to decide what best to do. Call Bess without being overheard, of course. Now that everything I owned had been inspected, it must be known I had nothing illicit; they were barking up the wrong tree, I'd be left alone from now on—but Bess had to know, just in case . . .

"Everything's there. I think René's right," I said cheerfully. "It was a hitchhiker looking for a shakedown." I was looking at Dr. Corwin as I spoke, and her face was unclouded.

"What are you talking about?"

"John said René bumped into a stranger lurking about the barn late last night." I sat down casually and attacked the fresh strawberries with gusto. "Home-grown? Mmm, how d'you get them to grow so big?"

"Lilly goes out and speaks to them every morning," John said, "but I have to speak to the broccoli. It won't mind her, for some reason."

"Of course not. Broccoli is a masculine vegetable," Dr. Corwin said. "She won't be any good with apples, either." But she gave me a long speculative glance before returning to her own breakfast.

I ate and drank mechanically, considering a new possibility—was she on some sort of secret project for our Embassy, or even from the State Department, for which I was to be cover? Perhaps the whole bit—from Bess's casual "Would you like a job?" through the interview and these stopovers in private homes—was a cloak for diplomatic maneuvering. I recalled Mr. Jonas's "She has cleverly persuaded you to ask no questions." I thought if I had any undercover work, I'd entrust it to Dr. Corwin unreservedly—but why wasn't I equally trustworthy? For a split second I felt deeply hurt; Bess should have known I could be told anything at all—then I reversed. Perhaps it was the subtlest flattery *not* to give me a hint. If we got through, bully for us—and if anything developed, Siri would figure it well enough to play up unquestioningly.

Bess had still better know how quickly we'd been traced. Unfortunately I got no chance before we left; neither was there a moment unobserved en route. It had become a sort of royal progress, with John and Lilly Arthur leading the way, but two other couples had decided to come too, making three cars in all, plus someone's daughter who wanted to know how to get into Radcliffe. Her name was Andrea and she rode with us; after fifteen minutes of Dr. Corwin, Andrea was undetachable as a limpet in the rear seat. Natch. Every so often we stopped and everybody switched cars, except Dr. Corwin. She sat comfortably where she was, smiling sweetly, and permitting the populace to argue over who was to drive her the next twenty miles. I have been on some harebrained excursions in my day, but never such an insane safari as that trip from Grenoble, up and through the St. Bernard tunnel, thence to Turin. At one point I was driving a Rolls-Royce, without the faintest idea which buttons were for what—but eventually we arrived at the restaurant.

Also eventually, we had a delicious lunch served alfresco with a view of pink tile roofs tucked about a hillside below us. I enjoyed both view and food, although the gourmet consultations between the men on the Perfect Menu and the Right Wine reminded me (unwilling) of Kai's wicked pencil sketch of four women splitting the check at Schrafft's. . . .

There was still a hundred miles to reach Elspeth's arrangements for tonight. At two, I suggested we'd better get going, but it was nearly three before we could shake our escort in a joyous honking of horns, waving of hands, and blowing of kisses as we turned east from the intersection. Dr. Corwin drew a long breath and exhaled gently.

"Cheer up. Something says the Valmontes will be entirely different," I said, "and we'll be in bed by midnight—if not before, due to boredom."

She snorted. "Hah! We'll be playing bridge until

Carlo wins, even if that's six A.M."

"Oh? In that case, would you like to catch forty winks, Dr. Corwin? I can perfectly cope with maps and directions."

"You seem able to cope with anything," she said after a moment. "I think perhaps—after we've left the Valmontes—you should call me Maggie . . . unless you find the name as offensive as I do, but one has no choice in such matters."

"No. That's how I got stuck with Sigrid."

"Suits you, though—particularly the nickname Siri." She shifted about comfortably, closed her eyes, and said placidly, "Now you had better tell me why the prowler upset you. Was anything damaged?"

Lucky I'd meant to call Bess and had a story ready! I said, equally placidly, "No, but not thanks to me. I'd left the trunk unlocked."

"Who expects thieves when staying at a private home?" she countered. "Why d'you think it wasn't a hitchhiker, as you told John?"

"Because I saw a swarthy type near the barn when I went to get the oranges. I supposed it was another farmhand, but there's only René, and John says they do get Gypsy camps occasionally."

"Strange he'd wait so long that René caught him."

"I scared him off, first—and with the amount of milling about, he probably didn't dare try again till the party was over. He wouldn't know René slept in the barn or was sneaking out after hours to see his girl." I shrugged and added experimentally, "He'd been into the trunk. Your bags were undisturbed, but the top of my pile was upside-down, as though he'd got it out and thrust back any old way, to avoid René."

"Hmmm." Her eyes were still closed, and she sounded sleepy. "Oh, well, no harm done. Don't feel negligent, Siri. If you'd locked it, he'd only have broken open the trunk, and those things are expensive to repair."

"Not half so expensive as replacing two complete wardrobes," I said dryly.

"The insurance covers," she murmured, suppressing a yawn, "unless you've something valuable. I got two thousand for each of us, but if you have furs or jewels . . . Have you, Siri? Have you something irreplaceable that I don't know about in your luggage?"

"No. I've nothing beyond the usual family trinkets and a mink jacket bought second-hand three years ago," I said evenly. "And I have a personal floater policy to cover those."

"Good." She was apparently asleep. I continued driving, mechanically catching the turns for Milan and pondering. How peculiarly she'd phrased the last query. "Have you something irreplaceable that I don't know about?" How would Dr. Corwin have any idea what I had, replaceable or not? For all she could know, I might be carrying the Mixo-Lydian crown jewels that I never wore because they were too gaudy—and what the hell difference did it make to her?

It was revealing, though. Bess could have told her I had no valuables. And it would unsettle her to hear of possible robbery, if I was right that some cloak and dagger was afoot. The last thing Maggie Corwin would want was anything unsuspected in my luggage to draw the attention of professional thieves! Should I have told her the whole story, given her a chance to organize her plans? If she knew that my belongings had already been searched, it might alter things. The safest place now would be in my bags. Had she expected such quick action from . . . Mr. Jonas's invention C.R.U.S.H.? I smiled to myself, but it was as good as any other name. Perhaps she'd also been searched and was wondering about me, but news of a prowler should be enough to alert her.

The only valuable thing I had was my engagement ring—three flawless diamonds conservatively appraised (and insured) for three thousand dollars despite the old-fashioned cut. Legally, it and my wedding ring were mine despite divorce. Kai hadn't asked, but if I'd had a scrap of decency I'd have offered to return them. The diamonds had been his mother's, and the heavy chased-gold ring was a family heirloom. Every Marcus Kai Penberthy wedded his wife with that ring. If there happened to be a living Mrs. Marcus Kai Penberthy, she took off the ring to be used during her son's wedding ceremony and got it back later, to wear until her death transferred it to the daughter-in-law. Kai's mother never got to wear it—she died before the Aged P's wife. Kai had the diamond circlet his mother had worn pro tem., but when he wrote his grandfather he meant to marry me, the old man had insisted Kai must have the family ring.

It had meant putting off the wedding for a week. We'd intended to go to City Hall with a couple of friends. I think Kai had forgotten about the ring, but when he was reminded he suddenly reverted to pure Penberthy—not that he would admit it. I knew he was rarin' to go, chomping at the bit with each succeeding day, but we had to wait for the ring . . . and finally an elderly mulatto in Pullman uniform turned up at the front door. "Thomas, as I live and breathe!" Kai said astonished. "Come in, man. Have a drink . . . this is Miss Quain. I'm going to marry her, did you know?"

"Yes, sir, Mr. Kai." Thomas grinned broadly, fumbling in his pocket. "And this here's what you need. Your grandfather give it to me this morning in Boston, first day he could get in—we've had a bad snowfall. Anyways, here 'tis, and I wish you the very best, Mr. Kai, sir." Thomas ducked his head at me politely. "Happy to make your acquaintance, Miss."

"I'm equally happy to make yours," I said. "I'd begun to think it was all a joke and Mr. Kai never meant to marry me at all."

"Oh, no, Miss!" Thomas sounded shocked. "Mr. Kai wouldn't never do that."

No more had he. He'd found a pleasant peaceful side-street church, and his face was unexpectedly mature when he slid the ring into place. I had the fanciful notion of some private vow not mentioned in the ceremony. Later, when we'd left the friends who were our witnesses, Kai stripped the glove from my hand in the taxi and contemplated the ring. "Siri Penberthy," he said. "If you run it together the right way, it's Serendipity. Darling Serendipity, you are well and truly married."

Which was one reason I'd kept the rings. I wouldn't wear them, I wouldn't be the mother of Marcus Kai Penberthy VII to hand them over for his bride, but no second wife should get them through divorce. Sondra wouldn't care. She'd have wanted the diamonds recut and reset, and she'd be much happier with the diamond circlet than a hundred-and-fifty-year-old gold ring. When I got back to New York, I'd give them to Mr.

Tubby to be held in trust for Kai's son, if he ever had one. I wondered, not for the first time, what would have happened if I hadn't miscarried twice in twelve months, so that the doctor firmly told us to wait another year. . . .

"What are you thinking to make you look so sad, my dear?"

"Personal matters," I said. "If you're awake enough, Doctor Corwin, could you get out Elspeth's map and watch for the cutoff?"

The Villa Delizia lived up to its name; its owners did not. They were pleasant, they seemed languidly happy to see Dr. Corwin again, and they were gracious to her traveling companion; but delightful they were not. Carlo Valmonte was rich, desiccated, middle-aged, and pompous. His wife was equally rich but shaped like a corseted cow with a vague smile. We were greeted and dispatched to our rooms for a change to clothes suitable for tea on the terrace. The conversation was principally English, in deference to Miss Quain, whose Italian was rudimentary. Miss Quain sat self-effacingly in the corner, speaking when spoken to and portraying depressed gentility struggling against adversity, humbly anxious to please, grateful for every crumb of social notice. I was Joan Fontaine in *Rebecca*—not so pretty, of course.

The Valmontes were highly approving, but the third time I leaped from my chair to light Dr. Corwin's cigarette, she muttered, "You're overdoing it!" I thought she probably knew the characterization better than I, so I subsided and enjoyed the tea, which was

61

delicious but skimpy. Four people—exactly eight tea sandwiches, four slivers of pound cake, and four one-inch squares of sponge. Carlo got an extra sandwich; his wife ate only one, and he scooped her second off the plate before anyone realized. Dr. Corwin paid him back by giving me her piece of pound cake. Rather ostentatiously, "Miss Quain has been driving all day, and with her figure she can eat anything, don't you agree?" Signora Valmonte nodded, unhappily. I thought for a moment that her husband was tempted to say *he* wasn't overweight either, but even if he could have used that piece of cake, *noblesse oblige* prevented that statement.

That was the way it went. After tea we were kindly dismissed to rest and dress for dinner at nine, aperitifs at eight-thirty. This seemed a good moment to phone Bess. I asked Signor Valmonte's permission to call Paris. "I should like to report safe arrival to the Ambassador's secretary."

"Si, si, certamente." He led me into an octagonal morning room and pressed various buttons to give me a private line. "Please to convey our pleasure at seeing Doctor Corwin ... and yourself, also." He bowed politely and departed, while I got through to Bess. She was still at the Embassy and sounded fagged to death.

"Siri, I meant to call you, but there hasn't been a minute."

"Call me? Why?"

"What did you do with the paper for Mr. Jonas?" she asked. "His secretary showed up yesterday—and perhaps you told me, but I forgot. I'm sorry, Siri, but the receptions have been worse than usual this year."

My fingers gripped the phone painfully to cover the pounding in my heart. "Bess, I hadn't anything for him but a private address. I put a note on the board. *You didn't tell her I had it?*"

"No, because I only saw it when she'd gone." Bess's voice was alert. "Siri, what's up?"

"I'm not sure. Your end first, everything you can remember."

"Let me light a cigarette." I could hear the lighter flick, the first inhale-exhale. "She was youngish, small Levantine type, dark eyes and hair . . . shell-pink nubby silk suit from Chanel, pumps dyed to match, gloves, straw hat—she was pale pink all over except a deep-rose-red handbag. I remember thinking she looked damned expensive, but when she said Jonas, I suppose his secretary gets enough to afford Paris boutiques."

"I expect so."

"I got home about four—somebody failed for the Embassy dinner, and I had to pinch-hit. I just missed Agnès, met her at the corner, in fact. When I got upstairs, there is this girl standing at the door, so I said, 'Were you looking for me?' and *she* said, 'Are you Miss Rawson?'"

"I remember now," Bess said suddenly, "she was badly rattled, Siri. When I came upstairs, she drew back a step and turned away. She expected me to go on up to another apartment, and when I didn't she was caught off-balance. Anyway, I said I was Miss Rawson and who was she, what did she want? Frankly, I wasn't too polite—I thought she was collecting for something, and I was dying to get into a tub to relax before starting

63

the ratrace again."

"Of course." I could visualize Bess's small, indomitable red-haired figure, and I'd bet the caller was rattled. "Go on."

"Well, then she said she didn't want me but my roommate."

"Didn't she ask for me by name?"

Bess paused. "No," she said slowly. "She knew Miss Rawson lived in that apartment and had a guest, but when I showed up, I don't think she knew which of us I was . . . and I'm not sure I ever mentioned your name, Siri. First I said you'd gone on holiday and what name should I give if I heard from you—and then she started a positive catechism, Siri! When did you leave, where had you gone, when would you return—that sort of thing, as though she didn't believe you weren't there. So I got a bit uffish myself and asked 'What's it to you?' or words to that effect.

"Finally, she said she was Miss Philipous, and Mr. Jonas had sent her to pick up a paper he'd given you. It was very important, he had to have it, where could she reach you? I thought," Bess finished, "it was a magazine article, something he might have lent you for this research. Anyway, I said I knew nothing of it, you hadn't left anything with me, and if it was vital you could be reached at the Arthurs' in Grenoble. I'm sorry if you were ducking something, Siri, but how could I know?"

"You couldn't, particularly as I don't myself. Listen, I don't know what it's all about, but somebody tried to get into your apartment the night before I left, and my room and my luggage were searched in Grenoble." Bess caught her breath while I detailed events. "First I

64

thought—forgive me, sweetie—you had a lover who'd
got my departure date mixed . . . and then I thought it
was diplomatic hanky-panky . . . But this doesn't fit
anywhere, Bess. Jonas never gave me anything but a
private address, in case I needed help with museum
directors in Greece."

"How . . . peculiar," she said. "Siri, I don't quite like
the sound of this. Shall I phone Jonas?"

"No, not yet," I said slowly, "but don't let anyone
know you can reach him—and if you have to, the
password is Mahootma. Don't forget that, I didn't put
it in your book. Bess, to the best of your knowledge,
there couldn't be any cloak-and-dagger bit between the
Embassy and Doctor Corwin?"

"There isn't," she said, "but I'll make sure. No, don't
argue. Even if there were something I don't know, it's
gone haywire, and the sooner the Ambassador knows,
the better . . . not but what it's probably some mistake,
but with anyone as internationally rich as Jonas, you
never know. I shall tell everyone at this end, and you
should do the same. Then if you happen to have an
accident, there'll be very inconvenient questions from
all directions, see?"

"Yes. I think you're right. I was only not saying
anything because I thought perhaps Doctor
Corwin . . . Although I didn't know why you'd think
you couldn't tell me, but I didn't want to louse up
anything."

"You've been reading too much Le Carré," she told
me disapprovingly, "and I don't have a lover. At least,"
she added gently, "not at the moment. Have a good
trip, Siri." There was a faint click, and the phone went
dead. I pressed the proper button to open the circuit,

and after a moment's reflection I turned off the desk light. Something said Carlo Valmonte saw no reason to illuminate untenanted rooms.

A six-foot passageway connected my room with Dr. Corwin's. There were double closets on one side and a bath on the other. My overnight case and makeup kit were emptied, resting smugly in a corner, and I couldn't find *anything*. The small bottle of Cabochard was deemed worthy of display upon the dressing table, together with my toothbrush and a bottle of roll-on deodorant. The larger bottle of Chanel Number Twenty-two was in the medicine chest, and the tube of toothpaste cuddled shyly next my eyebrow pencil. I thought that if I had time, I could enjoy analyzing the placement of my belongings as determined by the Italian servant mentality, but the call to Bess had brought us to seven-fifteen. Dr. Corwin's door was closed, the bathroom was tidy, but damp towels said she'd already bathed and was out of my way. I filled the tub, soaped and sloshed mechanically, trying to make sense of Bess's story.

Not Jonas, of course. I could imagine—barely—his carrying on our gag to the extent of a mysterious phone call, but he would never have frightened me by sending anyone to Bess's apartment. Anyway, he knew I was leaving Paris next morning. No, this was for real. Somebody thought Jonas had given me an important paper—it could only be someone who'd seen us together at the Ritz, seen him give me the notebook sheet, and subsequently trailed me to the apartment. Easy enough to see which door I entered, to identify the tenant as Miss Rawson, but how had they known I was a visitor?

From Bess's words, they hadn't—but if they'd watched, they'd seen us leaving together for dinner, and next day the girl had said "your roommate" . . . I wondered why they hadn't tried to get in as soon as they saw us leave; then I remembered my original estimate of the impregnability of the apartment. Remembered, too, that Madame Durey had been gossiping with a friend in the hall itself, in chairs drawn outside to enjoy the pleasant evening air while Monsieur Durey enjoyed TV . . . and Bess and I had come home just as she was saying good night to her pal, locking the main door for the night.

A watcher would have seen Bess's light go out, then allowed time for us to fall asleep, not knowing that I was padding around in the darkness with final packing . . . But I hadn't seen the man, I'd only scared him away. Why had he left so completely—why hadn't they seen my luggage being placed in a taxi next morning? That was a major booboo. Had they been hanging around all day, waiting for Agnès to leave, only to find I'd been gone for hours? I snorted involuntarily. Of all the inept, *clumsy* . . . C.R.U.S.H. must be a bunch of rank amateurs. Didn't they realize, if I *had* an important paper, the first thing I'd do would be to report the attempted entry and Grenoble search to Jonas?

One final combination—Dr. Corwin and Mr. Jonas? Both connected with some undercover work through the Embassy—she might be carrying out something initiated by him or concerning him, and it was pure idiot chance that I knew them both and would appear

67

to be a link? . . .

On that note, I climbed out of the tub, patted dry, and went into my bathroom. Dr. Corwin was comfortably ensconced in the easy chair, smoking a cigarette. "Oh, sorry," she said. "I came to be zipped . . . I didn't think. Are you prudish?"

"No," I said, ignoring my nudity. "Are you some sort of spy?"

She choked slightly and hooted with laughter. "No—I was beginning to wonder about you."

"Good heavens, why?"

"There's obviously something on your mind"—she shrugged—"and the Embassy was so determined to send you with me. Get dressed, child, and tell me as you go."

I began to explain, but at first it said nothing to her, either. "Who *is* this Mr. Jonas?" she asked finally.

"He's really Mr. Ionascu," I began, and that rang the bell.

She sat up sharply and stared at me. "Eleazar Ionascu?"

"He called himself Gyorgy. His wife's name is Anya."

"That's the older brother," she muttered absently. "Go over it again, Siri—not that it makes sense, unless it's mistaken identity." She listened intently while I filled in details. When I got to Bess's caller, she sighed heavily. "I think I get it—and I wish I didn't."

"Rosa Philipous is Mrs. Eleazar Ionascu, and she's insanely possessive about her husband. I gather he gives her ample grounds. The thing is, the brothers look much alike; I only met Gyorgy once, at Rosa's wedding, but I remember it was hard to tell them apart.

68

She's exactly the sort to have Zaro trailed and go make a scene about it. So the detectives trailed the wrong Jonas."

"I see. I suppose the attempt to break in was a detective hoping to find us in bed together, but why the search in Grenoble?"

"Looking for love tokens." Dr. Corwin shrugged. "She's capable of anything, that girl—but not for love! Her family was desperately poor, and Rosa came up the hard way. She hadn't the money to use her exchange year when she got it, but she was determined to be educated so she could help the parents—and then the mother died while she was in Cambridge." Dr. Corwin reflected silently for a moment. "I suppose she'd always have developed like this—money was really her only goal. When she caught Zaro she hit the jackpot; money *and* society. She'll never let him slip through her fingers! If I know Rosa, she's got him by the short hairs, tied in financial knots, and every extra bit of evidence helps her draw them tighter." She stood up with a sigh, presenting her back to me. "Zip, please?"

I pulled it up and fastened. "Well, as a case of espionage this was a bust. I never knew my Mr. Jonas had a brother, let alone met the man. I'm glad it's all so simple."

"Simple?" Dr. Corwin echoed. "That's what it isn't, Siri. If she turns up, I can try to convince her it's a mistake, but if I don't succeed, you may have to take the next plane leaving Athens and going anywhere at all."

"Why waste time on me?" I asked, bewildered. "Surely, she'll get back on his track, and when I'm never in the picture again, why should she turn up in Greece?"

"Because it's her house," Dr. Corwin said, surprised.

"Villa Dresnatinko belongs to Rosa Philipous?"

"To the Ionascu family. Apparently they share the main house for vacations, and there are guest cottages. Rosa offered me one as a retirement present." Dr. Corwin wrinkled her nose. "She loves playing Lady Bountiful—but I've never explored Greece, so I accepted. That's why she's likely to turn up; in fact, she said she hoped to see me in August. I thought at the time that I'd have six or eight weeks first and could afford to leave if I couldn't stand her. This puts a different face on it, of course. We'd better go down to dinner and think later."

But following Dr. Corwin sedately down the curving marble stairs, I was thinking now. No wonder Gyorgy Jonas had "heard of the Villa Dresnatinko"—he might be turning up too. But why hadn't he said it belonged to his family, and why had he thought I might need his private address in order to reach him "day or night"? The farther I went, the more incomprehensible . . .

V

It was after two before the final rubber was ended. Carlo Valmonte and I were the winners by a narrow margin, which he would have liked to increase with another rubber, but Dr. Corwin firmly refused. "You've *won*, that's enough, Carlo. I want Miss Quain fresh for driving tomorrow, and due to all those floods, we're having to go roundabout to Trieste."

Carlo agreed, but that wasn't the end of it. He was sufficiently pleased with my card skill that he insisted upon going over the auto-club route and giving me a number of useless suggestions for alternate bypasses. Fortunately he marked them with a red pencil. The auto club had used blue, so he didn't completely louse up the maps, and I was able to thank him with suitable humble gratitude, while Dr. Corwin coped with Signora Valmonte's incredibly vague recommendations for a lunch stop. By the time I got to bed, I was too sleepy to think, and next morning took on somewhat the air of a departing crusade.

Everything unpacked the previous evening was repacked while we were at breakfast. Various minions came and went, delivering communiqués on road and

71

weather conditions, filled bottles of water and coffee, placement of maps in the car. The flashlights had new batteries; the old ones were only three days old, but it's good to be on the safe side, isn't it? The Valmonte chauffeur reported a check of air pressure in the tires, replacement of a spark plug, and full tank of petrol. A picnic basket was on the rear seat; please not to overturn, the wine corks had been loosened.

In honor of the occasion, Signora Valmonte had descended for breakfast. This was a distinguishing mark of attention, but no blessing. Whatever Carlo hadn't thought of occurred instantly to his wife, and we had to wait while someone chased out to the hothouse for a basket of fruit, someone else rounded up all the cigarettes in the Villa Delizia and swamped our lighters with fluid. The Signora personally cut a bouquet of roses, the ones she could reach on the terrace wall without bending over. This led to redoubled efforts on Carlo's part, and for a while he was in favor of sending a Valmonte car with driver and mechanic to accompany us as outriders, but Dr. Corwin had the happy inspiration of pointing out that Valmonte would thus be minus a car for two full days before the escort could return.

We got away at last, leaving the Lord of the Manor, flanked by His Lady and surrounded by Serfs of the Desmesne, all waving dolefully as though they never expected to see us again—and as far as I was concerned, they never would. We drove rapidly, silently, the ten miles to the main road. Then Dr. Corwin said, "We made it. They haven't sent anyone with us, thank goodness."

"Thank goodness, although a yard of tin might have

been fun."

She laughed appreciatively. "This is Italy, not England. I don't think they ever had coach roads or tollgates here."

"Guelphs, Ghibellines, and private *banditti*," I agreed. "I think I'm in the wrong century, anyway. Would you look at those defaced maps, Doctor Corwin—use the blue marks if you can still see them."

"Maggie," she murmured absently, poring over the route lines, "and don't be Jane Eyre again, it doesn't suit you. We're looking for a left fork onto Twenty X. ... I've been thinking," she went on, after we'd made the turn, "and I believe I should write Rosa when we reach the villa, saying I've arrived safely and isn't it a small world—my traveling companion is doing a job of research for her brother-in-law Gyorgy. Never mind if it isn't accurate, it'll alert her to check up on the mistake. Bess may not have mentioned your name (though I'll bet she did without realizing), but Rosa can get it easily enough, and it's not a name to forget. Bess *didn't* say you were headed for Greece; we'll chance that the searcher concentrated on you and failed to report who you were with, so I won't mention your name either."

"Yes—I expect that's a good plan . . . although if Rosa's behind this, how could she get a searcher in Grenoble so quickly or tell him whom to search?"

"The detective agency, of course . . . and equally of course, she does have your name now. The man did your room first, he was told to look for a *young* woman. You came tripping out to the car, and he nipped upstairs. And your name is plastered over everything, including a passport. Ergo, he searched the

73

car bags labeled with the same name. We forgot that—but perhaps he still didn't say the name on the other tags. Calculated risk, I think. Are you going to write Mr. Jonas?"

"I'm not sure," I said evasively. "In a way, I don't know him that well. To accuse his sister-in-law of having me followed or searched . . . Frankly, I can't think how to put it, Maggie. He may know all Rosa's peculiarities—I doubt anything gets past him—but he mightn't care to hear this from a relative stranger."

"Yes—you've got a point." After a moment she said, "There's still something you haven't told me, isn't there, Siri? I don't wish to pry, but you'd better say whether or not I should write to Rosa at all. Are you . . . emotionally involved with this man?"

"Not in the least," I told her emphatically. "He's double my age and married, I've only seen him twice, he's never said a word to be misinterpreted. I'm not in his world at all—but I can tell he likes talking to me, and I *value* him. I don't want . . . oh, any sense of strain if we ever meet again."

"I see." Maggie dropped the subject, but I didn't think she was convinced, and in the end I did write Gyorgy Jonas, because I had nothing better to do.

We made Trieste by five o'clock, taking turns at the wheel and going straight through without stopping except for petrol. The Valmonte picnic basket was far more ample than their formal table, perhaps because it was packed by the cook, who didn't give a damn about waistlines. We checked into the hotel, and about ten minutes later Maggie tapped on my door. "Siri, could you amuse yourself this evening?"

"Of course. What's the matter, aren't you feeling good?"

"Never better, but as it happens"—she gave me an exaggerated simper—"I have a date. With A Man."

"No!" I breathed, wide-eyed. "You're going to deliver the plans!"

"For the Embassy wine cellar!" She nodded. "And tomorrow night, the vintners' agents are going to sneak in and *shake* every bottle."

"Well, *that's* a relief," I said in a normal voice. "Maybe George will stop serving that terrible claret for every meal."

Maggie chuckled. "You're fun, Siri. How glad I am I brought you. Do you really not mind being alone? You could come too, but I think you'd be bored. It's only Robert Fenton, who's an old friend on sabbatical, and we'll talk college."

"You'll have more fun without me. I'll wander around, find a movie or go to bed early. I could use some sleep." I didn't really want to meet yet another polite stranger, and I could see that Maggie was looking forward to a good academic gossip session. I went along later to zip her up, and by the time I dispatched her, she was delicately flushed, excited as a girl. She went primly down the stairs, like a good child controlling a skip on Sunday morning, and for the first time I wondered about Mr. Corwin—when he'd died, why she hadn't remarried. She never spoke of *family*, although Bess had said there were children, and once Maggie had mentioned a summer exploring national parks with her granddaughter, but she'd changed the subject so swiftly that I'd asked no questions. "Hadn't you better find out what *I* don't want to talk about?"

I was not exactly curious; I merely . . . wondered. From what she had said, I had the impression she'd lived alone in Cambridge for many years. She had a house; I'd no idea of its size, but a few students lived with her, one of whom was a well-known writer who must have graduated around 1950. I had no idea whether Mr. Corwin had been alive then or whether Maggie was widowed and needed rent money. It might have been one of those arrangements where students paid for board and lodging by domestic assistance— marketing, washing dishes, baby-sitting. Not my business, but it seemed a pity, a waste, for such a charming, vital woman to face retirement years alone. Maybe, after years of professoring, the last thing she wanted was anyone to talk to over a breakfast table. She never spoke of the future, either, beyond this summer in Greece and that one reference to writing a bit of grade-A trash. . . .

I went out about seven and found my way to the Piccolo, which was on the recommended list. It was small, but the amount of trade guaranteed the quality of the food. I had an Italian version of bouillabaisse that contained much more shellfish than the Marseilles variety, and tried to make sense out of the local evening paper without much success, except that there wasn't a cinema that sounded intriguing. I was back at the hotel by nine-thirty, but not quite tired enough for bed, so I opened the portable typewriter for a letter to Bess. Putting Maggie Corwin's explanation on paper only reinforced my doubts. I could not rid myself of the sense that there was something deeper and more serious than a jealous wife or that Gyorgy Jonas suspected it, didn't want me involved, yet had no way to disentangle me.

Only when I mentioned Villa Dresnatinko had Jonas become disturbed. He hadn't minded my being in Greece or visiting museums he suggested, so it must have been the tie-in with his family that upset him. Why? There might be some sort of major family fight brewing, based on what Maggie had said of Rosa, and Mr. Jonas wouldn't want me aware of it. That seemed a possibility. He wouldn't want anyone at the Villa to know we were acquainted—it might alter the status of guest-cottage tenants to unavoidable inclusion in dinner parties, whereby we couldn't fail to sense undercurrents. I knew instinctively he wouldn't like that for a number of reasons. If Maggie or I were the wrong sort, we could make a packet from the gossip columnists with a story of the Ionascu row. Conversely, if we weren't that sort, we'd be two strange gentlewomen involved in an embarrassing situation with his family.

Why hadn't he said right out that he owned the place? Did he think I wouldn't identify Jonas with Ionascu? Perhaps; I'd never called him anything but Jonas, and I didn't move in his social circles. For all he knew, I'd never find out. I wasn't offended that he might reason that way; but for Bess, I never would have known. You don't get to be a millionaire without calculated risks—maybe he thought we'd be gone before the explosion. I remembered he'd minutely questioned our dates and stopovers, even the hotels and the license number of the car! How subtly he'd

77

done it, too—completely by indirection. "If there's a difficulty at Split, try *these* hotels ... Lunch in Dubrovnik—ah, you do not go that way? Then in Titograd there is a pleasant place ... Be *sure* you remember the license number! It is very impressive to be able to rattle it off without consulting the registration in case of theft or accident."

And I had said, "Nobody will ever be able to flummox me on that one—it's my own initials! SQ twenty-seven—and the number is my age."

Now I realized. By the time we parted, Gyorgy Jonas had known our route as well as I did. And nobody would ever steal our car. That shocking-pink paint job drew every eye, wherever we went!

It was dimly beginning to make sense along these lines: a family row, Rosa tracing me not merely because of Zaro but because I'd been seen with Gyorgy and she anticipated the family row. Yes, that nearly solved it—except for that private address. Why had Gyorgy (I was calling him that in my mind now) thought I'd need to reach him day or night, wanted me to destroy the slip—because now I knew it hadn't been carrying out our gag. He'd meant every word of it, including Mahootma. So there was still *something*—something more than embarrassing, potentially dangerous, that might not happen but I had to have a pair of waterwings if it did.

Woman-like, my first reaction was flattery that Gyorgy Jonas liked me well enough to wish to protect me, but it still didn't explain what he wanted to protect me against.

For no particular reason but to kill time, I coded my letter to Bess; it might be just as well, in any case, because I had detailed every bit of reasoning with names, dates, and places—and it'd be my luck to have that particular letter get into the wrong hands. Then I looked at the typewriter and debated. There was no question that I must write Jonas, but what? I settled for unvarnished facts, lightly presented, and typed rapidly.

Communique to Chief Mahout: You have betrayed my trust. Since our last meeting, C.R.U.S.H. has (1) attempted illegal entry to my lair within twelve hours, (2) sent Agent Philipous requesting return of the paper you gave me, and (3) searched both my room and my auto luggage at Grenoble. Finally, I learn I am walking directly into your personal lion's den. But fear not! I will not recognize you until you recognize me—and maybe not then. Yours in disillusion, 006½

I thought that ought to do it. Everybody knew everything, and aside from Bess's story, nothing new had turned up since Grenoble. I went to bed and fell asleep over the newest bestseller.

Next day I mailed my letters, paid the hotel bill, and asked for the car to be ready in half an hour. Turning away, I bumped into a man standing behind me, waiting to pay his bill also. *"Perdone!"* I murmured, and he smiled politely, stepping aside so I could head for the restaurant. Maggie had a table, and Professor Fenton was with us—a plump, rosy little Santa Claus of a man with curly gray hair and twinkling hazel eyes. He was heading for Florence, where he hoped to be able to help in salvaging some of the water-damaged manuscripts, but from the way he was looking at Maggie, I had a hunch he was a sturgeon who'd need no urgin' to turn around and come to Greece with us. She never gave him a chance to go out on the limb with a definite suggestion, though. I've never seen such expert obtusity (if there is such a word). You'd have thought she couldn't spell her own name and I was her keeper.

The man I'd bumped at the hotel desk was at the next table, and although he wasn't looking our way, I felt certain he understood English from an involuntary twitch of his lips. Really, Maggie was being positively outrageous—and Dr. Fenton was lapping it up. Eventually I had to call a halt or we'd have been there all day. "They've brought down the luggage—shall I have it loaded while you're washing your hands?"

"Oh, what a good idea!" she exclaimed ingenuously. "You'll pay the bill, dear? And see we have enough petrol and everything?"

"Yes. I'll meet you at the car." I controlled my face while she tripped away, babbling sweetly to Dr. Fenton—but when I went out to the car and found that same hotel stranger leaning inquisitively to inspect our luggage tags, I was not amused. "You have some question, signor?"

He drew back hastily, banging his head on the edge of the trunk and rubbing it involuntarily. "No, no," he said confusedly. "I was merely interested in the—the make of the car. The color, you understand, is unusual."

That it was and had already collected a crowd divided between awe and guffaw. "Did you expect to find either the make or the paint shade listed in the luggage compartment, signor?"

"No, no, I was merely—merely interested in the amount of storage space, signorina. I meant no offense, I assure you . . . *scusi, perdone* . . ." He backed away, vanished while the bellboy stuffed the last bags into the trunk and slammed down the lid. Then Maggie emerged from the hotel with Dr. Fenton in attendance. She bade him a fond farewell, smiled at the populace, and blew a few kisses as I started forward.

When we'd turned the corner, I said austerely, "If I can't be Jane Eyre, you can't be an aged Dora Copperfield, either."

Maggie snorted. "That bad? I was trying for Becky Sharp."

"You'll never make it."

"No, it isn't my type," she sighed. "What did you think of Robert?"

"He's no Dobbin," I said impersonally. "More Cheeryble with a dash of Peter Pan. I expect he'd be fun across a breakfast table. Are you going to marry him?"

"You're right he's no Dobbin, but I hadn't thought of Peter Pan," she murmured, studying the map. "I think we're coming to the turn for Fiume—yes, there it is just ahead . . ."

But neither then nor later did the conversation return to Dr. Robert Fenton.

We'd planned to dawdle the two hundred-odd miles from Trieste to Split, looking at the countryside and exploring any intriguing side roads, but there's a funny *thing* about Communist countries, a sort of uneasy miasma in the air. The people smile and laugh. Some places—the ones not actually destroyed in the war—look prosperous and comfortable. There's food, rather simple and not much choice, but ample of what there is. Nobody appears maltreated, undernourished, ragged, or unhealthy; yet there's a *feeling*. . . .

You get it the instant you step beyond Checkpoint Charlie, of course—but it exists everywhere, more subtly borne in on you in Prague, Budapest, Warsaw. A reserve, a shuttered face at a casual remark, a speculative glance as though wondering if the person will later be suspect for talking with you.

It's sad—and damned uncomfortable. You wouldn't think freedom has a smell, but it does. By the time we'd reached Split, we'd encountered just enough reserve to make side-road exploration unattractive. "You know," Maggie said as we found our way toward the hotel, "I'm not liking this half so much as I'd expected. Would you be disappointed to cancel here and push on to Tiranë for tonight?"

"Not in the least," I said emphatically. "In fact, if you think you wouldn't be too tired, I'm for forgetting Tiranë, too, and going straight through to Greece. I don't know what we'll find for a hotel, but Igoumenitsa is fairly large—it's on the boat line from Patras to Brindisi. We could go over to Corfu tomorrow or amble toward Larissa. There's a famous cave at Ioannina, and we could consult the oracle at Dodona."

"You've been there?"

"Yes, but the oracle wasn't communicative. Up to you—what shall we do?"

"Corfu," she decided instantly. "It's supposed to be Prospero's island, although how Shakespeare heard of it . . . But we may as well see for ourselves. Can we really make Iggy-whatsis?"

"Igoumenitsa. I think so. I'll get new maps in Tiranë. We were headed for Kastoria, but that way is mountainous and I'd rather *not* after dark. It's only noon—if the roads hold up we should hit Tiranë by five or six . . . see how tired we feel, but with luck we should be over the border by eleven, and it's only a hiccup to Igoumenitsa as I remember."

"Then let's try."

Luck was with us all the way. We took turns driving, the roads were good, the weather was balmy. Mysteriously, now that we knew we were hastening away, we could look at the land, the occasional flashing glimpses of Adriatic, and appreciate. It was lovely—lush and stark by turns, with farmhouses tucked into the corners. Wild roses were flung across loose soil verges, an unidentifiable small yellow flower rioted beneath gray-green olive trees, whitewashed granite warned the driver of a sharp turn, and a froth of plum blossom danced in the breeze. "Ummm," said Maggie dreamily, "just look at all that slivovitz on the hoof!"

We made Tiranë by quarter to five, and there was no longer doubt of going on. "I'll concentrate on maps, you cancel the hotel and fill up with petrol." We relaxed for long enough for coffee and pastries. Maggie took one bite and said, "Shades of Betty Crocker, and I do mean shades. If the Communists want to claim a first on this cookie mix, they're welcome."

"It's the lard, although more likely it's congealed lamb fat. Better get used to it, Greece will be even worse. The olive oil oozes out of everything like an Arabian sump."

We had dinner near Berati, in a place mentioned dubiously by the auto-club representative, and he was right to be dubious, but we forged ahead chewing Tums. Around eleven P.M. we were checking into the Athena Hotel in Igoumenitsa, crawling up the stairs behind a sleepy bellboy to our rooms, and incapable of more than "Good night, see you in the morning."

"I just remembered," Maggie said. "I forgot to cancel the rooms at Split. Should we wire or something?"

"If they don't know we aren't coming by this time, they aren't suited to the hotel business. Go to bed!"

"D'you realize we have three full days to play with before we should get to Larissa?"

"Yes, that was the idea. We weren't much liking Commieland, why not come here? Already the air smells fresher, don't you think?"

"The coffee's better, too. Siri, you're a witch! What shall we do with the time?"

"Corfu first, stay overnight, and catch tomorrow's return boat," I said. "After that, it's up to you. We could stay on the Corfu boat to Patras, if you like, and drive around Peloponnesus to Corinth, Athens, up to Oinón. It might take an extra day—you'll want to stop for sightseeing. Or we can come back to Igoumenitsa, spend tomorrow night at Ioannina, and make Larissa as planned, where we pick up the coast highway."

Maggie finished her coffee absently. "I think," she said, "Corfu—back here, and Villa Dresnatinko on schedule. I'm sick of living out of one case and washing undies every night in the bathroom, aren't you? Let's establish home base and unpack. We can go to Corinth later."

It sounded good. That's what we did, and exactly a week after leaving Paris we rolled into the courtyard of the Villa Dresnatinko. It was as good as a home-coming, even if we'd never seen the place before. We were expected, eagerly awaited, welcomed with smiles and bobbing curtsies. Color was everywhere—in the roses and ivy festooning the pale pink stucco main house, in the massed flowering shrubs along drives and paths, in the majestic towering cedars of Lebanon and swaying aspens shading flower beds, and in the brilliant blouses over immaculate white trews and pleated skirts of the servants.

"It looks like something out of *The Student Prince*," Maggie murmured blankly.

"No steins," I muttered, while people opened car doors. "I think this one's *Blossom Time*."

By the time we'd crawled out to the crunchy white gravel and unkinked our legs, a majordomo had appeared. His costume was complete with a tasseled red cap, and if he could sing, Hollywood had the new Nelson Eddy—they'd have to bleach his hair, of course.

He spoke perfect English, though. "Doctor Corwin? I am Stefano. We are pleased to welcome you and your companion to Villa Dresnatinko. Madame Ionascu is on the terrace. If you will follow me?"

Maggie flashed one glance at me and went steadily forward while I gulped. After driving all day I was in no shape to meet a harpy who might accuse me of intrigue with a husband I'd never met, but I'd no choice but to follow, however slowly. We went through a latticed

85

arcade that was alternately shaded and golden in the late-afternoon sun, and turned a corner of the house. Forward again along a diagonal and another turn, across a flagged patio that seemed to stretch for miles beside a brilliant blue swimming pool until it focused on a feminine figure arranged upon a terrace lounge at the far end.

She was the apotheosis of indolent Oriental opulence, draped in gold-cloth harem pajamas, languidly tapping cigarette ashes into a tray on the mosaic table beside her, and smiling at a man who was working at a painter's easel near the edge of the pool . . . And she was not Rosa Philipous, unless Rosa had had a tint job. This was a lush, mature woman, heavy-hipped but with enough height to balance the Slavic squatness, with a square-jawed Tartar face beneath a wealth of ash-blond hair expertly arranged in a heavy rope threaded with flowers—a photograph out of *Vogue*.

She abandoned the cigarette, rose to her feet at sight of our little procession, and came forward, hand outstretched, to greet Maggie. The artist set aside his palette. His back was to me before he also got to his feet, but he didn't need to turn around. I knew that copper-brown hair, the close set of those ears, the flick of those slender, masterful fingers setting a brush into its jar. . . .

The artist was my ex-husband, Kai Penberthy.

VI

I had been hanging back, expecting to encounter Rosa Ionascu and in no haste for the meeting. Now I stopped dead, trying to pull together. Of all things I could never have anticipated, this was the ultimate, and my instinctive reaction was sheer fury. What in hell was Kai Penberthy doing here, had he known I was coming, was this some sort of rigged game for my discomfiture, and—oh, heavens!—was Sondra here too? Couldn't he think of any place but Greece for a honeymoon, dammit?

Maggie was shaking hands politely with Anya—it could only be Gyorgy's wife, unless there were still another brother—and my discomfiture had so sharpened my senses that I knew we were not welcome. Madame Ionascu was *correct,* no more. Clearly, we were her sister-in-law's guests for whom she felt no affinity. We would be served by the villa staff, Stefan would arrange our meal hours to suit us, the swimming pool was at our disposal—and it was all a terrible nuisance, though she didn't say so. Neither did she introduce her portrait painter, either because she classed him as a servant or to emphasize Maggie's exclusion from Dresnatinko family life. Kai was standing politely, on a line with Maggie; he hadn't seen me yet.

I could tell that Maggie was discomposed by the chilly reception, but she said only, "It's kind of you to let us come, Madame Ionascu. May I introduce my traveling companion, Miss Quain . . . and if Stefan will direct us to our cottage, we won't trespass further on your time."

I had the answer on Kai's foreknowledge—I was the last person *he* expected, either, and he swung around so violently that he nearly fell into the pool, while madame graciously inclined her head. "Miss Quain," she murmured, making no offer to shake hands.

I bowed and murmured conventionally on my side, ignoring Kai's stunned white face and blazing eyes. I wasn't sure Maggie had seen the byplay, and by the time she turned back to me, Kai was stiff-lipped with control. Madame Ionascu retreated to her former position, with the effect of washing her hands of us. Kai sat down again, and we followed Stefan around the far side of the pool to a path beyond the high metal fence and shrubbery. I could feel Maggie bristling with indignation beside me, but Stefan seemed oblivious to any lack. Perhaps Anya Ionascu always behaved like that.

Certainly Stefan could not have been more cordial, more respectful or welcoming as he led us through a sort of tidy miniature forest. There were glimpses of five buildings, half-hidden by trees as though set at random, yet cleverly placed to ensure privacy. Nor were they a uniform model. The one nearest the pool was no bigger than a luxurious motel cabin; its neighbor was a sprawling bungalow behind a vine-covered lattice. Farther on was a grand split-level, with its own small swimming pool and a two-position carport containing a wicked little white sports car.

The terrain was naturally rugged, a meandering ravine with the footpath running steadily upward along the top bank and a motor road enclosing all the houses in a one-way circuit that paralleled the path, then branched right and disappeared. The left branch led back to the main house.

It seemed a long way to the swimming pool, although not unpleasant beneath the shady trees. Just . . . a long way to go for a swim. Our cottage was the last of the group—white-washed, single-story simplicity set near the rear exit to a main road beyond the high stone wall. On top of Madame Ionascu's studied indifference, that figured—but Stefan proudly informed us that *he* had placed us here.

"Observe the ease for using the car! Madame Zaro says you will be driving a great deal, and I think you will not object to the longer distance from the main house in comparison with freedom to come or depart at any hour without fear of disturbing anyone."

Maggie flashed me an enigmatic glance. I knew she was still discomfited, uncertain whether to stay or go at once, wanting to talk it over with me, but she said, "That was very clever of you, Stefan. There are other guests?"

He shook his head, leading us into a charming salon. "Not at present, but shortly. A week or two for visitors at Villa Rosa, next to you (this is Villa Blondel) . . ." I could hear Stefan's voice while I wandered out to the terrace and caught my breath involuntarily. A pity if

89

we couldn't stay! We were the highest location, looking across the ravine road to a sparkling spread of sea with the craggy shoreline of Euboea curving away into the distance. A flash of pink below and to the right must be the Villa Rosa, with a tinge of lemon yellow just visible above and beyond. "The Villa Miranda is not a guest house," Stefan was saying. "It is the permanent home of Prince Boris, madame's son. He has his own staff, comes and goes as he chooses. There will be monsieur Foucald and his family as usual—he is from the Geneva office. I have not heard when they arrive, but they always occupy Villa Philemon. So at present, there is only the artist, Mr. Penberthy, but he is at the end nearest the house and will not disturb you, I am sure."

"Penberthy?" Maggie repeated. "Unusual name. How long has he been here?"

"A week, ten days." Stefan's voice was a shrug. "He accompanied madame when she returned from New York—a very pleasant young man."

Where's his wife? I wondered. If I knew Sondra, she wasn't being happy at getting the smallest pad on the estate. How long would they be here? Kai could be finished with a portrait in five days if he wanted. In my initial confusion I hadn't looked at the canvas, couldn't tell how far advanced he was. Much as I shrank from the necessity, I had no choice but to try to see Kai alone and ask his plans. For a few weeks we could easily avoid each other, especially after Maggie and I had tacitly been told not to bother the family. Surely he could keep Sondra quiet for so short a time. If they'd meant to stay all summer, I'd have to leave, although what excuse could I give Maggie?

90

"Siri?" Maggie came out to the terrace. "Stefan is supervising unpacking," she said enigmatically, leaning against the rail beside me. "Well?"

"Well what?"

"Do we stay or leave tomorrow, of course."

"Up to you, surely."

"And my bank account," she muttered dryly, "but you've got a say too. What d'you think?"

Damn, I'd forgotten Maggie was tight for money—and this terrace was a perfect spot to write "grade-A trash." I could tell she was simmering down, not wanting to leave such a lovely place, quite apart from the financial problem. Within the salon, Stefan was imperiously directing the musical-comedy servants in disposal of our bags; obviously whether or not Anya Ionascu wanted any part of us, the staff would fall over itself making us happy. Why need we encounter anyone else? If we wanted a swim, I bet we could get down to the sea—leaving only meals, and no doubt the family ate privately. Perhaps we were expected to eat in the kitchen?

Unconsciously, I chuckled. "What's funny?" Maggie asked, and snorted ruefully when I told her. "I'm sorry I got you into this, Siri. I should have known better than to accept in the first place. I never much liked Rosa, and I didn't know a thing about her in-laws, but she was so insistent, and I wanted to be persuaded. I never expected anything like this."

"I can't help feeling it's me. Perhaps I could stay in the village—I could still drive you about."

"No," she said. *"E pluribus unum, nous y sommes, nous y restons,* and anyway *I* think it's me. Maybe madame hates Rosa."

"Well, I'll bargain—we stay and see which way the cat jumps, providing that if it's me they don't want and you refuse to desert Micawber, you leave financing to me. No"—as she opened her mouth—"be sensible. You hadn't budgeted for this, but I always meant to be traveling. You can repay me from the grade-A trash, but don't cut off your nose to spite your face."

"But why should *you* . . . ?"

"I wish to be a patron of the arts," I stated. "Oh, don't be silly! You looked forward to this for years; chips fall where they may—*or I shall call Elspeth and George!*"

Maggie eyed me austerely. "No Radcliffe girl could sink so low," she observed. "Thank heavens you went to Mount Holyoke."

"I must say they do teach many useful subtleties not included in a purely classical curriculum," I returned blandly. She broke apart at that, and we were giggling helplessly when Stefan emerged with a sloe-eyed girl beside him. He surveyed our hilarity with a paternal smile.

"This is Danae, who is assigned to Villa Blondel." The girl sketched a demure curtsy, but by the looks of her, I thought she was well-named. All that would ever interest her was a shower of gold, whether or not Zeus was in it, and I wouldn't have hired her for my secretary, I can tell you. "She will prepare breakfast at whatever time you prefer. Her English is not good," Stefan apologized, "but if you leave a note in the kitchen, she will bring it to me." He snapped his fingers gently, without looking at Danae, and she disappeared at once. "If you have time, perhaps I might show you

92

the arrangements now—or I can return later, if you prefer."

"Now, I think, and we won't need to trouble you further."

"It is no trouble at all, Doctor Corwin," Stefan said emphatically. "Please remember that aside from Danae, I am at your service at any moment day or night." I sensed delicate stress in Stefan's words and looked up involuntarily. He might have addressed himself to Maggie, but his eyes were on me. So *that* was it! Gyorgy had suspected we'd meet unfriendliness at his home, my notes reached him too late for warning, but he'd thought for our comfort and telephoned Stefan to make us doubly welcome. How very kind of him.

Silently I followed, while Stefan led Maggie from room to room—here was the intercom for the main house, there was the telephone, which passed through the switchboard. The operator spoke English. The ramifications of opening the auto gate in the wall were demonstrated, the light switches, kitchenette supplies, location of liquor and postage stamps.

Unquestionably the Villa Blondel was a small jewel, complete in every detail. One felt that if so much as a lightbulb burned out, Stefan would commit suicide like Vatel. All during the briefing, we were being unpacked and arranged. One girl departed with two laundry bags, Danae was whisking crumpled dresses to the ironing board, while Stefan explained the air-conditioning system and meal hours, "but if this does not suit your schedule, you will instruct me accordingly. It may happen that you are delayed or, as today, tired from

93

driving," Stefan said smoothly. "In such event, any meal can be served here and at any hour. This"—he pointed to a handset mounted on the headboard of my bed—"rings my room directly—in case there is no answer from the staff intercom."

Again the delicate emphasis, although Stefan was completely impersonal as he showed me the call button. So that explained why, although the bedrooms were identical, I had been settled into the one with the better view—yet why on earth should Gyorgy Ionascu think I'd need physical protection? Well, he knew my ex-husband was here, and he didn't know Kai. Maybe he anticipated a Slavic attack of passion, attempted rape?

Sondra would see to that, I thought sardonically. Once she heard *I* was here, she'd put Kai on a leading string! Oh, damn! Why had he shown up before I was ready for him? I had a wild impulse to say, "Sorry, I can't stay. Pack my things and let me out."

Maggie's voice floated back from the salon. "If it's really not too much trouble, I think we would rather stay here for dinner. It's thoughtful of you to suggest it, Stefan."

No, I couldn't run away after convincing her to relax and enjoy, couldn't evade the issue even if it came too soon—but that was my own fault. I should have been adjusting mentally these past eight months, which was the whole point of the Aged P's ten thousand dollars.

The clock said five. I went to the salon and looked at Stefan. "Could we have *meze* at once, Stefan? A shaker of very dry martinis for Doctor Corwin, Scotch sour for me," I said steadily, not even asking if he understood American drinks. Of *course* Stefan did. . . .

"Dinner at ten, I think, to give Doctor Corwin a chance to rest. I'll send word about tomorrow when she's decided our schedule."

Maggie stared at me blankly, but Stefan merely bowed, "Very good, Miss Quain. On the terrace or in the salon?"

"The terrace in fifteen minutes," I stated crisply. "Dinner in the salon, and perhaps a tiny fire if the sea wind turns cold—which reminds me, is it possible to get down to the shore for bathing?"

It was the first time he was discomposed. He admitted one could bathe in the sea, but he advised—nay, urged—against it. "The coast is rocky, the water dangerous in many places. I would appreciate your allowing me to conduct you personally. One must know the coves intimately to avoid the rocks, and there is a blowhole. . . ."

I remembered Gyorgy had mentioned rocks and riptides. "We'll wait until you show us a safe spot," I promised. "If there isn't one, we can still paddle at the shore and enjoy the view."

He relaxed visibly. "Thank you, Miss Quain. If you permit, I will prepare the *mezethakia.*" He bowed himself away to the kitchenette, where Danae was still ironing.

"What is *mezethakia?*"

"Greek for 'Sun's over the yardarm.' Go wash your hands. I'll see you on the terrace."

"I shall pay you a compliment," Maggie announced reflectively after the first martini. "I *am* glad you went to Mount Holyoke. No Radcliffe girl could have

95

coped so easily with Stefan—he *almost* frightens *me!* For a moment I thought he might suggest a nursemaid to bathe us."

"It's the liquor talking. Have another and tell me more."

"I felt it my duty to express approval."

"How ominous! Haven't you ever noticed that when someone thinks it a duty, it's always unpleasant?"

She chuckled. "This time it's more me than you. I don't quite like dumping myself on your bank account, which is what it amounts to, Siri—but I know you're right that I shouldn't refuse to gather my roses for stiff-necked pride, and bluntly, I'm stretched to my financial limit. You see," she said expressionlessly, "I'm a recent widow. My husband died last fall after ten years in a mental hospital. My son was killed in Korea, leaving a wife and two babies. My daughter's happily married, but her husband works in a supermarket. He'll end in the executive offices, but at present he can only take care of Lois and the children. You see why I have no reserve?"

I did, indeed! She wouldn't want any sympathetic twaddle. "Well, you *have* had your problems, haven't you?" I said calmly. "The more reason to forget 'em for a while. After all, it's only money. I offered, you didn't ask. Relax and enjoy. Where shall we go tomorrow, or would you like a day of rest?"

"Let's rest," she said after a moment. "Study the maps, plan future trips, maybe drive around the neighborhood, spy out the land and write wish-you-were-heres."

"Not to Rosa," I said suddenly, "and don't tell *anyone* I ever met Mr. Ionascu."

96

"Why not?"

I gave her my reasoning, and she nodded. "It doesn't explain why Rosa went to your apartment and only your luggage was searched," Maggie said finally, "unless madame is after Gyorgy, too. Otherwise, if you're right, nothing easier than to stay to ourselves. I'd much rather eat here than have to make conversation."

"Yes, so would I."

"You've some other reason for silence, haven't you, Siri?" Maggie murmured. "You needn't tell me, but I haven't professored thirty years for nothing." She drained her glass and set it aside with a sigh of satisfaction. "That Stefan makes a mean martini. I wonder if he's married."

"Where would he find the time?"

"Not if the rest of the staff is like Danae," Maggie agreed. "That one's Trouble with a capital *T* if I ever saw it. How she'll hate wasting time on a couple of women! Well . . ." She got up. "I'm for a bath and snooze." She left me chuckling to myself. Decidedly, Maggie *had* learned a few things in thirty years. I wished I knew half as much . . . such as what to do about Kai.

I continued to lie on the terrace looking at the changing sea colors in the last rays of the sun behind me, while the world turned imperceptibly, carrying me forward into the blue-purple-black of night. The gathering darkness seemed somehow symbolic. Because it was no good, no good at all. It was going to have to be faced and thought about. I couldn't spend the rest of my life running away. I was *sick* at me for wasting old Marcus's reprieve money. Lucky I had run

97

into Kai while I still had four months left.

All right, start thinking. I picked up my glass and headed for the kitchenette, pushing aside cocktail ingredients in favor of a stiff highball. With my hand on the water tap, I suddenly realized: if Gyorgy had told Stefan to look after me, he'd also undoubtedly said Mr. Penberthy was my former husband. That might be a help, if Sondra made a nuisance of herself. Odd that Stefan hadn't mentioned Mrs. Penberthy, odd that she hadn't been at the pool. On second thought, I'd back Anya Ionascu against Sondra any day!

I took the drink to the bathroom, stripped while the tub filled, and paraphrased Ogden Nash. "I went *cum laude* from Holyoke to Madison Avenue,/ And I say to myself, 'you *must* have some brains, havenue?'"

It takes two to divorce, as well as two to tango. I had to accept some part of the marital failure. What part? Smugness? We were so absurdly happy at first—when and why had it changed?

About two years ago, I thought—when I'd aborted for the second time and Kai said, "Why go back to work, darling? Stay home and really get in shape. The doctor says only a year to wait."

"In a way, that's the more reason. If I stay home, what will I do with myself all day, aside from housework? We'd have to let Leora go, and we mightn't get anyone so good later when I'd need the help. Isn't it more sensible to plump the bank account in preparation?"

"If you'd had any sense you wouldn't have married an artist in the first place," he said cynically, "and if we add a nickel to the sinking fund, I'll eat it for breakfast. But have it your way. I can't blame you for rejecting

98

love in a garret, when you can easily earn cream and jam."

That was our first major disagreement. Not a fight, simply a basic difference of opinion—and perhaps if I hadn't been physically a bit under par, I wouldn't have insisted, because I did see Kai's point of view. I just didn't realize how deep it went. He was right, of course. We didn't save my salary. That was the year the owner of the New Mexico shack died and the estate had to sell instead of leasing. I gave it to Kai for Christmas.

Now I thought dryly, *That was some present! I gave him the made-to-order way to divorce me.* Did he still have the place? Sondra wouldn't like it—only a single-room hut miles from town. No pool, no country club. Nothing but cactus, sand, stars, distant mountains. We'd spent a month there every winter at first. Everything Kai painted at Truth or Consequences sold at once, despite my domestic incompetence. "Silly Siri, if you researched *la haute cuisine,* you'd be another Julia Child, but much as I adore the woman on TV, I'd rather have your TV dinners in my home."

I shivered slightly and added more hot water to the tub. What had Kai needed that I failed to give? Was it my *fault* I did well in business? If you have to work, you may as well put your back into it; why piddle about being a clerk with nothing but Five P.M. and Friday, Thank God, on your mind? Besides, the increased salary paid for proper frames, occasional client parties, guaranteed gallery expenses. Not that Kai needed them beyond the first few shows. There were always enough red stars after the private viewing.

No, not my ability to earn. Kai kept pace financially, we lived on his income always; what I made was for

99

extras, to establish him more quickly. Was it the lost babies? Not my fault, nothing really wrong with me— the first was probably third-period conception and anything would have dislodged it, let alone a jolting fall on a ski slope . . . and the second was because it was too soon after the first. The doctor had explained soothingly that he wasn't at all worried about me . . . but perhaps Kai *was,* because if I couldn't have a baby, the Penberthy line would be extinct.

He *said* everything sweet and comforting—he'd rather have me than a baby . . . let Robert Penberthy carry on the name . . . it's only a year. It was the crucial year, I saw that now. Had my childlessness gone deeper than I knew, until Kai felt trapped between his physical love of me and bondage to a barren woman? Penberthys don't divorce; it had taken him two years to bring himself to the conviction that a child was more important than marriage vows.

I couldn't latch on to that wholeheartedly, because in the interim he'd changed—or was the change simply an attempt to make the best of his marriage? Sondra wasn't the first, she was merely the most determined in a series that started with Mrs. Whittaker, who bought a Penberthy and asked the artist to tea.

I couldn't go because of my job; Kai went alone. "She's a game old biddy, fit as a fighting cock," he reported. "She wants to meet you—next Friday?"

That time I managed it. Thereafter, if I were caught at the office—and perhaps once a week I was, because I'd got my first exclusive clients that winter—Kai went to Mrs. Whittaker and killed time between his end of work and mine. That set the pattern—when the light went, Kai no longer walked over to the library to change our books, bought a new phonograph record, got postage stamps or some flowers. He closed up and went visiting until I could join him, whether at home or abroad.

He always let me know where he was, always called at quarter to five. Kai was welcome anywhere, had dozens of friends. Some were pretty women. He never concealed his admirations, but neither husbands nor lovers objected. It was an amusing part of Kai, the perennial young man of fancy. "Who is she this week, old boy?"

"I'm between flames temporarily, lend me one of yours?"

Should I have objected? Mostly it was a relief to know he was occupied when I was tied up unexpectedly. I didn't take his flirtations any more seriously than anyone else did; he always got over them in about six weeks until Sondra. Had he got over me in six weeks, only we were married and he couldn't flit lightly away?

I could hear Maggie's voice dimly in the salon, Stefan replying. Time to get dressed—and after all my thinking, I felt discouraged to have no definite result. The end product seemed to be only more questions than I'd had before. If it weren't for the personal involvement, this could be a fascinating problem of "either . . . or." Had I ever loved Kai—or been dazzled by his will-o'-the-wisp screwball personality? Had I outgrown him, or had we simply grown in different directions? Had I smugly accepted my preeminence because he always came home to Mummy for loving, or was he a clever, elegant tomcat who fooled everyone, until he was bored with a wife?

101

Had I been drifting through the disintegration, making the best of a bad marriage because I was a healthy, normal woman and so long as I had a legal bedfellow, I could be satisfied? It was a troublesome, vaguely nasty conclusion, but Kai was the only man I'd ever had. Perhaps I should find a lover and get Kai out of my system. That sounded even nastier. I slapped powder on my nose and went out to the salon. "Oh, *ouzo!* I'll have a glass too."

"Which way is the village, Stefan?"

"To the right, but it is not very satisfactory. If you will give me a note of what you want, the market wagon will bring it tomorrow morning."

"I only need a post office."

"The post bag goes to Athens morning and afternoon," Stefan said. "If you'll give me the letter . . ."

"Thank you, but it isn't ready." Maggie knitted placidly, but when I leaned to set my coffee cup on the table, I distinctly saw a sealed envelope between the hanks of yarn. To whom was she writing so secretly that Stefan must not see the address?

"Very good, madam. If you will leave outgoing mail on this shelf by the door? The estate wagon leaves at eight and again at two; the market wagon leaves at four-thirty in the morning, but anything you wish can be procured by any of them." Stefan took a final glance about, added one briquette to the tiny fire, removed used ashtrays and replaced with clean. "I have left an extra pot of coffee on the warmer. Is there anything else, Doctor Corwin?"

"No, thank you, Stefan."

"Then I will bid you good night. I trust you will sleep well."

When he'd gone I looked idly at Maggie's knitting needles. "What are you making?"

"A sweater."

"Why is it you can watch someone crochet or embroider, but knitting makes you peculiarly restless? I haven't the slightest need for anything knitted, but watching you, I'm hypnotized into thinking I ought to be busy too."

"Feminine atavism. Knitting comes after spinning in our heritage. You can think while you knit, helpful in a quandary. If you yearn to be busy"—she dug in the knitting bag, produced tan fingering yarn and a needle case—"you can start some socks for me. Man-sized."

"Plain, circular ribbed, or Argyle?"

"I haven't bobbins." She tossed everything into my lap blandly and returned to her work. By the practiced flash of her fingers, I thought Maggie must have knitted herself out of many quandaries. I had an impulse to confide my own . . . but that was precisely what she hadn't wanted—girlish confidences. I cast on, began the ribbing. One inch later I heard an approaching whistle, "Chiri-biri-bim."

The one thing I hadn't thought of, that Kai would calmly walk up to the front door and announce to Maggie that he was my former husband! Had he already told Anya Ionascu? I sat frozen, my fingers trembling on the needles, until Maggie suddenly folded her work together and stuffed it briskly into the bag. "Midnight! I'm for bed. Will you close up, Siri? See you in the morning." I stared at the door clicking shut—too

103

tactful to be true, but how could Maggie know? Bess would never have told her.

The whistle had stopped, but there was no knock at the door. Then it began again, apparently receding along the back road. I went out to the terrace, and Kai was sitting on an outcrop above and across from the villa, evidently prepared to wait until I got there. I felt my way carefully down the rear steps and across the road. "A bit farther to the left," said Kai's voice, "there's a path." I found it, stumbled against rocks, and finally emerged on the plateau. Kai stood up politely. "Well, we meet again. How are you?"

"Very good, thanks, and you?"

"Never better. What are you doing here? Tubby told me you were in Sweden. Fill me in?" The impersonality of his voice steadied me. I filled him in. "How long are you staying?"

"That depends somewhat on you."

"What have I got to do with it?" He sounded surprised.

"Well, Maggie was invited for the summer, but we can't very well be falling over each other all the time. I mean, it won't matter for a while. Madame Ionascu obviously doesn't want us around, but when Rosa gets here it'll probably be different. She'll invite Maggie, and even if she omitted me, Maggie wouldn't stand for it," I said. "So it does depend on how long you're staying, or it's bound to be damned awkward."

"Why?" He drew out cigarettes and lighter.

"What about Sondra?"

"Well, what about her?" In the tiny flame his face was genuinely blank.

"But—isn't she here?" I asked, exasperated by his

deliberate obtuseness. "Forgive me if I missed an installment, but you did tell me you found her company more desirable than mine eight months ago."

"Perhaps I did. That was eight months ago."

"You gave me to understand you meant to marry her."

"How could I? You've got the Penberthy rings."

"Dammit, stop acting like a character from Noel Coward!" I said furiously. "Yes, I've got the rings, and they'll go in trust for your son, if you ever have one. You can use your mother's ring for your next wife—if you ever have one, but you won't, will you? That's why it took you so long to get the divorce, isn't it? So you could walk away from Sondra. I suppose you told her I wouldn't cooperate, and went and hid in Truth or Consequences until she got tired of waiting. That was one time you slipped, laddie, picking an unmarried girl! You're much safer with the Madame Ionascus, they don't expect permanency, and they can afford to buy pictures, too."

"Don't be waspish," he said calmly. "Anya's the best commission I've ever had. I'll get others in the world that pays best, if she's pleased—and she'll be pleased. She's superbly paintable."

"And I'm not?"

"That wasn't what I said," he corrected me. "I said *I* couldn't paint you."

"All right, put it politely. What's the difference?"

"Like night from day," Kai said impatiently. "Didn't you ever listen to anything I told you about portraiture? If you yearn to be painted, go to Soyer. Get back to here and now. Do I gather you're pretending to be unmarried?"

105

"Where's the pretense? I *am* unmarried. I've papers to prove it—and while I think of it, what possessed you to object to my using my maiden name?" I demanded hotly.

"I had my reasons," he said, "and apparently you don't believe in obeying the law. I notice you're calling yourself Quain in private life as well as business now—or is this sojourn in Europe business?"

Didn't he know the Aged P was paying for it? No, probably not; Tubby wouldn't have said, and I doubted Marcus would have told his grandson privately. But Kai would know I hadn't enough personal money for a year in Europe. He ought to, I thought grimly, considering he'd had the benefit of my salary one way or another for these past years, between Leora and keeping the apartment in shape to impress potential customers.

If Marcus hadn't explained, I couldn't. "Yes, it's primarily business," I said after a moment. "Have you told Madame Ionascu?"

"No."

"How long will you be here?"

"As long as you are. I was invited for the summer too."

"All right," I sighed. "Give me a few days to get Maggie settled, and I'll leave."

"Why should you?" Kai asked, surprised.

"This is where I came in. If you can't see for yourself—or is this some sort of refined nerve warfare?" I countered bitterly. "*You* wanted out, if you recall—not me. Now it develops you're out of Sondra, too—flitting carefree as the honeybee from one flower to another, totally unembarrassed to encounter the

106

former ball and chain."

"As you say," he agreed imperturbably. "I don't say I wouldn't rather you hadn't turned up, but I can't see anything so *desperate* in the situation. Or"—his voice deepened—"does the sight of me still flutter your heart, create a tiny leap in the pulse for auld lang syne?"

I leaned transfixed against the rocks. How could Kai be so beastly, why was it only to me he could be unkind? Before I could find my voice, he said lazily, "Not like you to be caught off-balance, Serendipity, but all to the good for you to develop the proper Madison Avenue whatchamacallit far from the madding throng. Get used to the stiff upper lip and all like that there."

"I've been used to a stiff upper lip for several years," I told him, "and *don't call me Serendipity!* That's exactly what I'm talking about, dammit. You'll come out with something that'll give the whole show away and embarrass everyone."

Kai lit two cigarettes, handed me one, exhaled deeply. "What strange words you use!" he remarked, "What could possibly be embarrassing in the fact that we were once married for five years? You can't go back, you know, no matter what name you use. You'll never be a virgin again. You're a woman, who knows the feel of lips and arms, the touch of fingers on her body—and what's wrong with that? It was entirely legal, you used to enjoy it. At least, if you didn't, you certainly fooled *me.*"

For several minutes I'd been vaguely aware of a rhythmic subterranean growling that swelled and receded. Now, suddenly, as if on cue, the growl became a pounding rush that seemed to explode almost

107

beneath my feet. Involuntarily I screamed faintly. "What was that?"

"The blowhole," he said. "It's out on the headland, not really so close as it sounds—the coastal rocks produce a bad echo. It's fairly spectacular. I'll take you out to see it tomorrow."

"No!" The blowhole was spouting now with nerve-wracking regularity until my head felt ready to burst. I backed away from Kai. "How long does that thing go on? I can't *stand* it!"

"Lasts about fifteen or twenty minutes while the tide's turning. You'll get used to it."

"I don't want to get used to it," I said childishly. "I just want to get away from the whole damn mess. If I have to have *that* on top of you making difficulties, being deliberately perverse, uncooperative"—I caught back a sob—"never knowing what you'll say or do next, I'll . . . the whole trip will be wasted. How can I concentrate on anything, if you insist on upsetting the applecart? You wanted the divorce, you said it was to marry Sondra, you *did* say so, you know you did!" I raged at him wildly. "And if you've changed your mind, why take it out on me?"

"Strikes me what I should have taken out on you was the application of a hairbrush to your bottom," he said grimly, "and I've never changed my mind about anything in my life. With your flair for misunderstanding the simplest statements, I always wondered how you got anywhere in business, but maybe you paid more attention to what Atherton said, and the strain of interpreting me was too much." He pulled away from the rock and stood up. "All right, play it your way, Miss Quain; you will anyway. I'll stay out of your way and say nothing. I'm not sure I care to claim the relationship any longer. A pretty shrew you've become, my dear, but my taming days are over. You'd better let me help you down. The path is uneven."

Kai's hand on my elbow was firm but completely impersonal, awakening no response in me even when I stumbled and he caught my shoulders. I was only shocked by his ugly words, by the whole miserable scene. How could five years end in such nothingness?

"Here are the steps for Blondel," he said, dropping my elbow. "Good night, Miss Quain. Sleep well, and have no fears for troubadours beneath your window." In the faint starlight, Kai's face was impassive. He bowed, sauntered away along the road, turned a curve into darkness. Dimly I could hear his light whistle *Adeste Fidelis.* No more "Chiri-biri-bim." I sagged against the iron handrail, aware of tears flooding my cheeks—but for what did I weep? The sorrow of finality or the rage of total disillusion?

But finality was eight months back, reinforced by legal papers, and after the past two years, how could I have had any illusions? Was I angry with Kai for ruthlessly ripping away the last veils or with myself for mawkish feminine pathos, the delicate melancholy of *recherche du temps perdu?* Kai retained no memories, *he* could lock the door behind him, make callous references to physical intimacy. His pulse didn't flutter. He'd only be startled to meet me on the scene of his current absorption. I bet he did "rather wish I hadn't turned up right now!" It didn't prevent him from needling, making it appear he was graciously acceding to a silence he certainly wanted as much as, if not more than, I. By the look of her, Anya Ionascu wouldn't be happy to learn her handsome artistic pussycat's ex-wife was at hand!

And when I thought how *easily* I could have queered the whole thing with Gyorgy in Paris! I still could if I called the bluff, but it would only rebound on me in the end. Kai could always adapt instantly to any change in the wind. I'd never catch *him* off-balance with an ill-timed reminiscence or languishing glance. He'd turn about, make some outrageous romantic play for me, have everyone enjoying the gag at my expense, while I blushed and bit my tongue. I was always unable to make a public riposte. "Why not blow your stack whenever you feel like it, Sexy Siri? Such a pretty stack! . . ."

The salon was dark, only a few embers left in the grate. Even as I looked, one of them died. Very quietly. One moment it was faintly glowing, as if hoping for encouragement—the next, it was gray depression. Oh, *stop* the suburban housewife romanticism! I went to my room and across to close the window. The sea wind was chilly for undressing. On the outcrop we'd just left there was motion. I stood still, hidden by the draperies.

It was a man, peering cautiously around the rocks, making sure the coast was clear. He cast a quick glance at my window—he evidently didn't see me. Then soundless, lithe as a cat, he swung himself down to the road and trotted away toward the auto gates. Involuntarily, I pushed open the casement and leaned out for another look. It wasn't Stefan; yet as the man loped around the corner and was briefly caught in the beam of a road lantern, there was an odd familiarity.

Who was that? A servant not supposed to be off-duty? He was awfully anxious to be unobserved. Had

Kai and I been overheard? Between our angry words and the blowhole, half a dozen minotaurs could have trampled the shrubbery unnoticed—and the man might not understand English anyway. He'd know only that the artist had talked with Miss Quain, and if he wasn't supposed to be there, he'd keep his mouth shut. Ironic if all that unpleasantness were wasted because we'd happened to block the usual servants' escape route—although the more I thought of it, the more I felt that man was no servant. For one thing, he'd been wearing a business suit; all the staff wore uniform Greek costume. For a moment I was tempted to use Stefan's direct line, report a suspicious stranger—but the man knew his way in the dark; he'd swung down that path with perfect ease.

He must be someone on the staff. Unquestionably I hadn't seen them all. If he reported to Stefan, it'd be no news—and if it emerged that Kai and Miss Quain were acquainted, it'd be annoying but inevitable. Forget it.

VII

We lingered over breakfast on the terrace. Danae made up our rooms. All our laundry returned, all our clothes were pressed, and a small girl was neatly tightening buttons and hooks. She looked about twelve, and Danae was throwing her weight around. In Greek, but no mistaking the tone or the child's giggling amusement. "Is sister to train," Danae informed us sadly. "Not know mooch. Loonch here? You write, please?"

"Shall we—and prowl later?" Maggie scribbled on the pad, and Danae went off, sister in tow and still giggling. Maggie said, "I'll be in my room," and vanished. After a while I heard her typewriter clacking away furiously. If this was the start of a book, she seemed in no uncertainty of what to say.

By daylight the outcrop was only a small plateau between the studied wildness of underbrush and trees that nowhere interfered with a view. It must take an army of gardeners to maintain that artless rusticity. Was last night's man one of them, perhaps? On impulse I left terrace and typewriter behind me. The path was actually almost a series of rock steps, once you could see it, and the boulders formed impromptu seats. For some reason the surf was increasingly clear on the plateau, although one scarcely heard it in the villa. Today it was a chuckling companion as I rambled about. Logically there must be another path somewhere, and so there was. Furnished with a sturdy iron handrail, it curved down to the sea, with a stone lookout on the bluff. The path continued in a businesslike fashion, but this was halfway and quite far enough.

Leaning over the heavy stone parapet, I could see the water swirling about jagged rocks, and what looked like the edge of a boathouse. The cliff above was rugged as an Alp and evidently honeycombed with caves, into which the sea rushed and spilled out. Probably that explained the strong surf sound. The path wound tortuously up and down before emerging on the plateau, but the plateau was probably above these caves. I wondered where the blowhole was and whether there was another simpler way to reach the shore. Otherwise, I could understand Stefan's discouragement of sea bathing. I wasn't sure Maggie could safely make it. Sixty-five is sixty-five, after all, and I found the ascent rough going for twenty-seven.

I hit the outcrop exactly as the blowhole fired off. It was still alarming, even when I knew what it was. The ominous growling seemed to be directly beneath me, and the ground trembled in my imagination, although I knew it was solid granite. No wonder the ancient Greeks developed so many legends and mysteries. I was quite happy to trot down the farther path and across to Villa Blondel—and once more the threatening water sounds decreased to a pleasant crash in the distance.

*　　　*　　　*

We ate Stefan's concept of a light lunch in the shaded section of the terrace.

"What's this?" Maggie inquired.

"*Tarata*—Greek version of *gazpacho*. Like it?"

"Very much, but what *is* it?"

"Mostly yogurt, very digestible. They use it in everything."

"Good day, so far?" she asked.

"Yes. I explored a bit, but I see why Stefan insisted on taking us to the shore personally. I came back and wrote a letter to Bess. I thought, if you don't need me after lunch, I'd drive to the PO."

"I'll come with you."

"You needn't, it'll be hot as Tunket. I can mail it for you."

"No, thanks. I'll enjoy getting the lay of the land."

So it wasn't only Stefan who mustn't see whom she'd written? Intriguing! She really did mean to keep every bit of personality separate from our trip.

"I thought we might go to Athens tomorrow and present our various letters of introduction, get it out of the way." Maggie sampled the chef's salad with approval. "Amazing how good simple food tastes when it *is* simple. Can you cook?"

"No." I left it there. If Maggie could be politely terse, so could I. "Do you want to spend all day in Athens?"

"Better plan on it," she said. "I can do the pretty at the Embassy, if you'd like to line up your own work. If they don't ask me to lunch—but I have a horrid premonition they will, Elspeth knows 'em 'intimately'"—Maggie wrinkled her nose—"but if I'm lucky enough to avoid it, I'll poke about and meet you later."

"Whatever you like. If we list places you want to visit this evening, I can get maps and boat-departure times tomorrow." I poured another glass of iced tea. "What time d'you want to go to the post office?"

"Let's allow digestion time. . . ." She went off to her room, carrying the basket of figs with her, but I was unsurprised that she wasn't ready to leave until Danae had cleared away and departed. She came out then with a wad of postcards and a shade hat that was only a stiff straw circle with a crown of cotton strips tied under her chin. "Got it in Mexico, one of the most useful things I ever bought. If you think you can manage that gate mechanism, let's go."

I managed, we went. The car gas gauge pointed to FULL, the windshield sparkled, every inch of the shocking pink exterior had apparently just been Simonized, and the gleam from the bonnet in the strong sunlight was worse than full headlights. "If I slipped Stefan five bucks, do you think he'd let us get dirty?"

"No. He'd be mortally wounded, until you explained the driving hazard. Then he'd arrange to have it sprayed black, and it's a rented car."

"So it is. What possessed me?" Maggie put on dark glasses sadly.

"Elspeth, don't you remember? Cheer up, we'll never get lost in a car this color. Not even brigands would have us."

"Me, they'd never have. I'm not so sure about you."

"They wouldn't have me, either. I can't cook. Is *that* the village, for heaven's sake?"

It was an intersection of country roads, with a center well strategically placed so you didn't know which way

115

to go around it. There was a whitewashed stone building with a Greek flag hanging dispiritedly over the door in the sultry heat, and a few small peasant-type homes dotted about—all very neat and draped in enough roses to cover deficiencies. I came to a stop before the well, since there wasn't any other spot. The "main" road went left, meaning you might be able to find a place where two farm wagons could pass, but from the condition of the dust I didn't think it had been tried recently. The alternative was a narrow lane, and just now all parking space was occupied by several dozen sheep, ranging from spring lambs to somnolent ewes, with a large curly-horned ram standing in the middle and wearing a militant expression.

"I suppose that's the post office, but d'you think anyone ever collects the mail? Maybe we should take it to Athens tomorrow."

"Let's investigate and see if it's safe." Maggie hopped out.

It was safe. We were interrupting *siesta,* of course, but it would have finished in a little fifteen minutes anyway, and what is that compared to the joy of welcoming two such distinguished foreign ladies to Dispnopopoulos—or whatever the name was. Maggie called it Dipsy Doodle forever after, but no one minded.

The postman was also Lord High Everything Else, and despite the language barrier we were given the keys to the city, complete with a short speech. The post bag had been prepared and locked before *siesta,* but what fortune! Alexai has not yet arrived. Nothing to worry about, he is only an hour late, and it takes only a second to open bag again—if one can find key. Mama, where is key? Please to sit down, here in shade by grapevines, until key discovers itself. Ah, it is *here!* Someone has thought to put key on nail after using. *Boze moy,* the last place one would look, no? But how good to be organized!

All in Greek, of course, but write your own script. The dramatic gestures were all one needed. Maggie's face was a study when mama was hospitably pressing refreshments upon us. *Kafé, ouzo?* A few figs? Some early grapes? "You can eat the fruit, don't drink anything," I warned *sotto voce* after a glance at the encrusted glasses. "Dysentery!" Then I sat back and enjoyed. After the first bewilderment, Maggie got along fine, with a word or two here or there, pointing and smiling.

Eventually Alexai came steaming along in a Model T Ford that could advance no farther until I had removed our car—but he was in no hurry. First he must admire the brilliant color, second he must rest himself and communicate the gossip acquired on the route. It was time for us to depart tactfully. Everyone came out to wave goodbye. The postman directed the maneuver of turning the car, but fortunately I didn't take his authoritative shouts and gestures seriously, and we only scratched the bumper against the well coping instead of falling in.

"Could you make head or tail of that?" Maggie asked.

"Enough. Get used to it, you'll hit it again—but never forget the speaking may not be so good as the understanding! They won't trust themselves to use anything but Greek, but they often get the sense of what's said in English. D'you suppose Alexai will get to

117

Oinòn today?"

"Probably. I did gather he's been on this run for thirty years." She chuckled. "How glad I am I brought you, Siri. Can't you imagine Elspeth's face?"

We were examining maps in the salon when Stefan arrived. This, it appeared, was a good moment for him to show us the estate. He had brought another golf cart, which he proposed to leave at Blondel; we would find it more comfortable than using the car for short distances, and one tired unexpectedly when unused to such rocky terrain. The tour would take about an hour while the light was good—not if we were occupied, of course, and he was completely at our service whenever we wished, but otherwise . . .

"Why not?" said Maggie, poker-faced. "We can look at maps later."

The grounds seemed to stretch for miles behind the high cement walls but were actually no more than a strip irregularly curved about a big dimple in the coastline. The Villa Dresnatinko itself stood on a high promontory and was big as a hotel, with twenty-four guest bedrooms and two master suites (the guided tour included such information). The swimming pool was deserted, as Stefan whizzed us around to admire the view from the bluff. "Later I will show you the inside," he said casually. "Madame and Mr. Penberthy are gone to Athens for the evening." So that was why Stefan was at our service—but at least I needn't quiver for fear of running into Kai.

The swimming-pool side of the house gave no indication of its size or rambling charm. It must once have been no more than a pleasant country house, to which wings and upper floors had been added whenever they could be pasted on, irrespective of levels. On the other side of the house, the ground dropped off sharply, down to a tennis court and archery butts, flanked by a croquet field. Farther on was a midget golf course, fiendishly worked in among the beginnings of the final woods that contained dormitories for the staff and what looked like a supermarket parking lot. It was presumably for guest cars but was not considered worthy of inspection. Stefan turned us through the trees until we glimpsed the sea again. "This is the water road, not often used. It is steep but entirely safe. Please not to be alarmed."

Not merely steep as the first dip of a roller coaster, but full of rocks and grass tussocks that gravely disturbed Stefan. "Tchk, it has not been attended. Used or not, it must be kept in order," he muttered jerkily while we bounced downward. "Please to forgive discomfort. I should not have brought you this way if I had known road was not dragged, but it will be done at once. By morning it will be done, have no fear."

I thought I wouldn't like to be the culprit who *hadn't* dragged! It was a breath-taking ride in any case, even after the first plunge. The road had been fashioned principally from a natural ledge that followed the contour of the coast, and whatever blasting had been needed to form a congruent passage was so old that all scars were gone. A sturdy stone wall at the outer edge ensured against a sideslip but did not obscure the view of rippling water dotted with small boats, nor shut off an occasional dash of spume when the road dipped low.

"Hmmm," said Maggie. "What did they used to smuggle, Stefan—or do they still?"

He laughed heartily. "You are too quick, Doctor Corwin! Yes, it was for smugglers, and most profitable according to my grandmother, but not used in many years. In the wars it was a route to safety for sailors from bombed boats. There are steps in the rocks below, and in between we threw over chain ladders. There was no wall then. Monsieur Ionascu had it placed later when we were at peace."

We'd already heard that Monsieur Ionascu was Gyorgy; madame was his wife. Rosa and her husband were Monsieur and Madame Zaro; His Highness was Prince Boris Svishtov, madame's son by a former marriage—and madame was born Baroness Somebody but did not use her title. Damn right she didn't, I thought meanly. Better to adopt the humility of plain Madame Ionascu than insist on a second-rate title, particularly when a princely son would create the impression that his mama was also a princess!

The road went beneath the huge promontory of the main house, hence up and down, around hairpin curves and beneath beetling overhangs, until finally we came to the boathouse and the long flight of steps to the lookout I'd discovered this morning.

"The road goes no farther," Stefan said. "From here, the coast is increasingly rocky and impassible, extremely dangerous. It is possible to bathe in this cove, but"—he looked at us earnestly—"there are rocks nearly everywhere beneath the water. The tides are not high, but the current is strong."

Maggie eyed the ripples and eddies about the hidden

120

rocks. "You needn't worry, Stefan, I'm a coast woman, I know dangerous water when I see it. I doubt we'll have much time for swimming in any case. I suppose the buoys are a boat channel?"

"Yes, but I beg you, for your own safety, do not go alone. I will send an experienced man, whenever you like." He started the cart forward, and shortly we came back to the auto road nearly opposite the Villa Miranda. "You would like to see it? His Highness is in Geneva; he manages Monsieur Ionascu's shipping interests." Without waiting for an answer, Stefan whirled us through the gates and circled the house, waving jovially to a startled servant darting from a rear door. "That is Vulko, the caretaker." From what one could see, Miranda was the perfect bachelor hideaway, complete with discreet manservant. We went on to Villa Rosa, which was similar to Blondel but with an extra bedroom and without our view.

Finally we'd completed the tour—but not quite. "Stefan, where's the blowhole?"

"At the edge of the property, one takes the path across the road and goes left." Stefan debated, glancing at his watch. "It is rather a long, circuitous walk, too late to be attempted today. There's no driving road, but if you like, we could go tomorrow. I must warn you, it takes at least twenty minutes of climbing around the rocks and another twenty minutes to return when you are rested."

"No thank you, Stefan. We planned a day in Athens, and frankly it sounds too much for me, in any case."

We went back to our maps, ending with an immense list of places to see. . . . Finally we reduced them to combinations of one-day trips, two-day trips, and grand jaunts. It was fun but tiring. I think we'd both have liked to stay where we were, but Stefan had gently "suggested" dinner at the main house. I only hoped Kai and his patroness wouldn't return until we'd left. Still, it wasn't fair to expect quite so much hot and cold running maid service as we were already getting. We dressed and duly presented ourselves at Dresnatinko, where Stefan settled us comfortably on a rear patio overlooking the water.

He had just presented *mezethakia,* when the house door opened. For a moment I thought it was Gyorgy, but even before Stefan said, surprised, "Mr. Zaro!" I knew. Maggie had been right—the resemblance was startling. But this was a younger man. His face and figure were subtly less authoritative, his clothes faintly dandified, and there was a small scar on his left cheek just below the temple. Not unattractive—it gave him a certain panache. He was altogether more handsome than Gyorgy, but I'd prefer Gyorgy any day.

Zaro checked at the sight of us, and Stefan switched smoothly to Greek, of which we understood only our own names. Zaro said something that involved "Rosa" and came forward, smiling politely. "Doctor Corwin, we have met before?"

"At your wedding," she said. "This is my traveling companion, Miss Quain—Mr. Eleazar Ionascu, Siri."

He bowed gallantly, but the dark eyes were uneasy. He was disturbed to encounter us. "Rosa had told me, but I had the impression . . . that is, I did not realize you had already arrived. Rosa not here? Or does she come shortly? I, uh, thought she was in Paris, and there

122

is a matter of, uh, business for me, you understand. . . ." His voice trailed away.

"Of course," Maggie said sympathetically; "and we are not guests to be entertained, Mr. Ionascu. I think Rosa meant to be here in August, but not as a hostess. She merely offered the use of a cottage for the summer as a retirement present, knowing how much I wanted to explore the country. We got here yesterday, have spent today making plans. Tomorrow we mean to make arrangements in Athens, and after that we shall be away most of the time, sightseeing."

Zaro was so visibly cheered by the news that his wife wasn't expected that he begged permission to share our *mezethakia,* but when Stefan announced dinner, Zaro excused himself gracefully. "I must tear myself away from such pleasant distractions, it is why I have come—for concentration uninterrupted." He went away jauntily, and we could hear a swift interchange with Stefan in the hall while we settled at the table. Dimly we heard a motor starting, then dying away, and Stefan did not reappear. That figured. He could look after us, but a family member naturally came first.

We got back to Blondel about ten-thirty, to my relief not seeing Anya or Kai, and Maggie said, "I shall have a nightcap on the terrace, if you care to join me—but not to talk. I want to think."

"Story idea? All right, I'll fix drinks." I brought the glasses out to silent darkness—which was suddenly broken by a distant ripple of feminine laughter.

"There are lights in Villa Rosa," Maggie's voice said impersonally. "Perhaps, after all, it's a bit chilly out here, Siri."

"I'll light a fire." I took the glasses back to the salon, drew the draperies tight, and turned on the lamps. "Prop your feet up, it's good for thinking." I thrust a footstool under her ankles and set cigarettes, ashtray, lighter, drink on a table beside her. . . .

Another assemblage for me, add a briquette to the grate, continue the knitting . . . I don't know what Maggie was thinking, but I was amusedly shocked. Uninterrupted concentration on a matter of business? No wonder Zaro Ionascu was disconcerted at sight of us, the naughty dog! But of all places to choose—his own home!

Aside from the faint surprise at the unexpected arrival, Stefan had been entirely composed, needing no special instructions. This must be routine. It certainly reinforced Maggie's explanation of Rosa's descent on Bess's apartment! What about Anya, what about some innocent remark from us about a guest at Villa Rosa? Stefan would say we must have heard a servant laughing. Did Gyorgy know his brother used Villa Rosa for his *nid d'amour?* Oh, unquestionably—but men always stick together on extra-curricular activity. I didn't think American men would entirely approve of using home ground, but the Slavic view was probably different. For all I knew, Gyorgy might keep his mistress in Villa Philemon.

"Midnight, I am going to bed," Maggie announced. At the door to her room she looked at me over her shoulder. "You're a good girl, Siri."

Not so very, I thought. What would she say if she knew I was toying with the concept of Gyorgy Ionascu as a lover?

In the Villa Philemon, *next* to the current berth of

my ex-husband, who *might* be using it only to change clothes before sleeping in half a master suite at Dresnatinko? I set the fire screen with a chuckle. Now if we could combine Maggie with Stefan, we'd have a first-class French farce, except for Rosa. What should we do with Rosa? Oh, let her sleep with the chief of police, I decided gaily, and went to bed.

VIII

For nearly a week we followed our own schedule and kept our noses very clean, without so much as a glance at Villa Rosa. There was no sign of occupancy, but neither did we see Stefan. Danae served breakfast and dinner, and we were out for lunch and quite ready for bed before midnight. The car was filled with gas and sparkling clean each morning. The villa was immaculate each evening. Clothes were laundered, mended, cleaned, or pressed. Every box was refilled with cigarettes, and *all* the table lighters *worked!*

As Maggie had feared, she was caught at the Embassy the first day, while I consulted tourist bureaus and presented my own introductions. I came away in a positive tidal wave of enthusiasm and offers of help. I had never needed the aegis of Gyorgy Ionascu's name. I felt confirmed that he'd expected his wife to make us feel uncomfortable—but why not *say,* "My wife does not always welcome guests; if there is difficulty let me know"?

Walking along Patesia Road, I thought such bluntness would be impossible for him. For me, too. I hadn't been able to tell him about Kai over the cocktail

126

table, I'd written later. No matter what happens, there's an obscure loyalty to anyone you once married, slept with—or so it seemed to me. I wondered if I'd ever get over the automatic reflex of building him up by the casual word to the right prospect. Perhaps—in another five years.

Maggie wanted another day in Athens. "It won't be enough, but at least I'll scratch the surface. *Very* embarrassing to have to admit you haven't yet seen the Parthenon." She wanted a second day at Delphi, too. "We can go to Eleusis some other time," she said. "I'm not much for mysteries, I've always preferred boy meets girl." On Friday night, she said, "Would you like a day for research? I'm tired of looking at things. I think I'll stay here tomorrow and attack the typewriter."

When I came out of the library about three o'clock, there was a man loitering across the street. Although Greeks can hold up buildings by leaning against them as effectively as males of any other nationality, this wasn't that sort of neighborhood. I crawled into the Ghia and took another look. I might not have thought twice about him—he'd a right to stand where he liked to smoke a cigarette, after all—but he suddenly ducked his head and scurried around the corner. I stared after him with sudden uneasiness. Unless I was crazy with the heat, he was the same man who'd been so interested in our car at Trieste—and furthermore, he was the vaguely familiar figure I'd glimpsed leaving the plateau after my fight with Kai. I recognized that scuttling movement.

But who was he? An operative hired by Rosa to keep tabs on me? If he'd been eavesdropping, he knew I was connected to Kai rather than Zaro. *Zaro!* Good heavens, he'd turned up the next day! What more would Rosa need? Of all insane absurdities, for me to be tagged as the mistress of a man I never met until he arrived with the real mistress. How Maggie would laugh—or should I tell her? She might feel this the final straw, and just as she was starting the grade-A trash. I knew now that for all her lightness, she was pinning some hope for the future on that book . . . and these past days, she'd enjoyed every minute like a fairy tale come true.

No, I'd say nothing—although it was the joke of the year. All we needed for a game of Happy Families was for Rosa to arrive.

However, Rosa was not in the snazzy black Thunderbird that zoomed through the rear gate and nearly ran me down when I was crossing the back road an hour later. Maggie was still typing in her room, and I'd thought I'd walk down to the lookout point. When the car came tearing around the curve, I had just time to leap for the clearing path, where I landed in a painful sprawl against the rocks. I could hear squealing brakes and an ominous bump behind me, accompanied by a furious swearing. It was a foreign language, but there was no mistaking the import.

I turned around breathlessly, and at a glance this was His Highness, which only made me twice as angry. In swerving to avoid me, he'd whammed his right fender into the huge sentinel rock marking Blondel's terrace steps, and *Bully for the common people!* I thought viciously. I'd got a bruised knee, a torn stocking, and a bleeding scrape on my arm that was going to be painful as hell—and all that bothered him was a dent in his car?

I sat up on the path and said coldly, "I can't understand a word you say, but if you're swearing at me, don't! I'll swear right back. I don't know who the devil you are, but only an idiot would come around a blind curve at that speed."

For the first time, he looked at me. A fleeting glance. "I am Svishtov."

"Then you should know better than to drive Grand Prix on this road."

His eyebrows drew together in a scowl. "Perhaps I do," he said deliberately, "and who are you? What are you doing here at this hour? Slipping away from your duties to meet a lover, eh? Stefan shall hear of this, I promise you. Come on, what's your name?" impatiently. He got back into the car, fiddling with the starter key.

I stood up and brushed myself off. "My name is Sigrid Quain," I said, equally deliberate. "I am the traveling companion of Doctor Corwin, who is the summer guest of Madame Eleazar Ionascu. We are staying in Villa Blondel, I am taking a walk before dinner, and I doubt that Stefan will be in the least interested in your complaint."

That rocked him! "I—I beg your pardon," he stuttered, flushing brick-red. "I thought . . . Forgive me, but the light is not good, I should have seen by your clothes—but I thought you were . . ."

He'd got in a bind over that one! "One of the servants?" I said sweetly. "If that's the way you speak to

129

servants, I wonder anyone can be got for your staff." I turned my back and went up the rocky steps—regally, swiftly, suppressing a grunt when the bruised knee protested. I'd got up to the clearing while he was still stammering, "I say, wait a minute, you don't understand. . . ."

I wasn't waiting for anything. I could hear him reversing to draw back into the road, moving off slowly, while I leaned against the outcrop. When he'd gone, I clambered down again. I'd managed the insulting indifference, but I felt too shaky to continue.

Maggie was at the terrace doors. "I thought I heard something. . . ." Her eyes widened at sight of me. "Good heavens, Siri, what happened?"

"His Highness nearly ran over me. He thought I was a servant. You should have heard the cussing because he crumpled a fender on a serf!"

"Thiry lashes?"

"At least, plus the salt mines. So I cussed him back and came home. I wonder where is the first-aid kit."

"Are you really all right, Siri?"

"Aside from assorted bruises and general dishevelment, yes. Sorry you were interrupted."

"I was about through for the day, ready for a drink."

"I could use one too. Can you fix, or shall I?"

"I was making martinis before you were born!" she snorted. "What's yours?"

"Scotch on the rocks, please—and leave the bottle out. If I can't find any rubbing alcohol for this scrape, we may have to use liquor."

Stefan arrived at five-thirty and looked disconcerted

130

to find us already occupied with drinks. "You should have rung for Danae. Entirely simple for her to prepare *meze* an hour earlier, or when you wish."

"I know, but it was spur-of-the-moment—and we really can wait on ourselves, Stefan, much as we appreciate your pampering."

He shrugged off the blandishment with a modest smile. "Madame has instructed me to ask if you will give her the pleasure of your presence at dinner tonight. It will be *en famille*—His Highness has arrived, and madame wishes to make him known to you."

"Most gracious of her." Maggie glanced sideway at me. "What time, Stefan? We planned on early bed, to start early tomorrow."

"So she supposed, since you had commanded dinner for eight o'clock. She suggested you might join her at seven, allowing time for a drink."

"How kind of her," I broke in smoothly. "Maggie, why don't you? I'm sure madame will excuse me, I'm poor company tonight. I tripped on the path, skinned my arm," I told Stefan. "I'd like nothing better than to have a hot bath and a bowl of soup and crawl into bed . . . if Doctor Corwin is taken care of."

Maggie latched on to it at once, bless her, while Stefan was exclaiming in horror at my accident. Evident that Prince Boris had not reported me; I hadn't thought he would. I felt certain he'd got Mama to pull him out of a humiliating mistake. Well, let him sweat when Maggie showed up alone. It was she who was the guest. Most of all, let me avoid having to cope with Kai over a family dinner table.

I should have known it wouldn't be that easy. Stefan arrived at seven, bringing Danae and a dinner considered suitable for an invalid. He departed with Maggie, leaving Danae to fuss over me. Her eyes were bright with curiosity, shocked at the sight of the nasty scrape on my arm, but for once the language barrier was helpful—to me, if not to her. I knew she was dying for the details, but all she could manage was "Is how?"

"I tripped on the rock path." It meant nothing—she almost stamped her foot with impatience at her noncomprehension. I dug around in my mind and said experimentally, *"Petras . . . ?"* That she got. "Where?" I pantomimed slipping and falling, and pointed vaguely to the path. She nodded, but I could tell she felt pretty disillusioned to be serving anyone stupid enough to fall on that path.

When she'd gone, I found some music on the radio and settled down contentedly with Maggie's socks. Along about nine-thirty I went out to the kitchenette to reheat the coffee, and while I was hovering over it, there was a light knock on the door—followed immediately by its opening and a gay voice demanding, "May I come in?"

I poked my head out. It was Prince Boris, and on second meeting I didn't like his looks any better than I had the first time. Let alone his calmly walking into the villa without waiting for admission. "Why ask me?" I shrugged. "You *are* in, aren't you?"

He flushed slightly, but for some reason he was determined not to take offense. "Am I in disgrace again? But these doors are never locked, you know. We all walk in and out without thinking, I'm afraid. It's family, you see. Now please, dear Miss Quain, don't be angry?" He smiled ingratiatingly. "I came to see for myself how you are. Doctor Corwin (what a delightful

132

woman!) said only that you had scraped your arm on some rocks and didn't feel up to dining with us . . . but is it serious? Shouldn't you see a doctor? I shall never forgive myself!" he declared vehemently. "I know the road so well, you see, and my mind was occupied with other matters . . . I had no idea there were guests in Blondel . . . but it is no excuse. So I came to offer my sincere apologies, to be certain you were not injured."

"Not in the least," I assured him politely. "Aside from a torn stocking and a tiny bruise, I'm good as new. There's no need for apologies, Prince Boris; I should apologize to you for my rudeness. If I said anything impolite, I hope you'll forgive me. It was more than kind of you to take time to call, but quite unnecessary. Please don't interrupt your evening on my account, I'm sure your mother is looking forward to a talk with you." I smiled dismissingly, but he was not to be dislodged.

"On the contrary, she would be seriously angry with me if I did not first assure myself you were unharmed. Ought you to be out of bed?" he asked anxiously, coming forward and extending his hand for the coffee cup. "Please, allow me. . . ."

"Really, this is farcical," I said, impatiently. "There's nothing wrong with me, you've apologized sufficiently, and I am quite capable of carrying a cup. Thank you for your concern, and I won't detain you any longer, Prince Boris."

"But I like to be detained," he said smoothly, holding on to the cup and guiding me back to the couch. "Shall I confess? It was merely an excuse to see if my first impression was correct."

"Impression?" I stared at him.

"That you were a most charming, refreshing personality whom one would like to know better." Smiling, he tossed another briquette on the grate, straightened up, and inspected me. "Now I see that the first glance falls far short of reality," he announced.

I watched him refilling my brandy glass, getting one for himself, settling onto the fauteuil with perfect assurance, and I thought, *I can't say the same for you, kiddo!* If ever I had seen a nasty piece of work it was Prince Boris Svishtov, and now I knew what my mother's generation meant by lounge lizards. Personally I'd call him Too Much: black hair, *with* sideburns . . . olive skin, nicely tanned to set off the flashing white teeth when he smiled . . . black eyes, heavy-lidded à la Valentino . . . a star sapphire ring on small, well-manicured hands . . . an Oxford-accented light tenor voice, and total self-approval. From head to toe (an extent of about five feet nine), he gave the effect of patent leather, as well as no doubt that patent leather was the ultimate in desirability.

I was to be charmed, bowled over by the honor of capturing Prince Boris Svishtov's fancy. I wondered how long he thought it would take him, whether it would be more fun to play hard to get or capitulate at once. Most of all I wondered what he was after. Was it light dalliance to kill time on a boring visit? Did he contemplate seduction, or perhaps no more than ego-reinforcement? "They all fall for me, the poor little darlings!" Whatever the reason, I'd no choice but graceful acceptance of his gallantry, but on top of everything else, the pointed attentions of a distasteful little creep were above and beyond the call of duty. I began to have an almost superstitious sense that this

134

trip wasn't Meant, that Fate was giving me copious hints to get to hell out of it.

Boris was devoting himself to me cozily. *"Please,* I am Boris to all my friends, and we are going to be friends, are we not . . . Siri?" He gave me a languishing glance. "What a cunning nickname—and Doctor Corwin is so devoted to you. Ah, fortune smiles on the Svishtovs! Had to come here, braced for boredom, and what do I find? A gray-eyed nymph, an enchanting new playmate, right on my doorstep."

"Beneath your chariot wheels would be more accurate," I replied sweetly, "and I'm afraid I can't be much of a playmate. I'm hired help, you know—practically a servant, as you thought." His lips tightened, then relaxed. He was determined on suavity. Why?

"Surely you have some time off?"

"Of course. Whenever Doctor Corwin doesn't need me."

"But this is slavery!" he protested. "Do you seriously tell me you are at this woman's beck and call? Surely you cannot be so destitute, so untrained for wage-earning, as to submit to such tyranny!"

I picked up the knitting, mostly to keep from slapping him. "It isn't tyranny, and I'm far from destitute," I said casually. "Actually, I'm on a year's leave of absence from a highly paid job with a New York advertising firm."

"Then . . . why?" he asked, astonished.

"It suits us both." I shrugged. "It doesn't matter when I do my research. I like driving and Greece, I provide a bit of know-how in return for luxurious housing provided by Doctor Corwin's former pupil."

135

"Do you mean she pays you nothing, she gets all this service at Rosa's expense? Incredible! I cannot understand it at all."

"I cannot understand why you have to," I said gently. "It is not in the least your affair." I let it lie there, not looking at him, knowing he was controlling his temper; but it was useless. He wasn't going to fight. "How long shall you stay—is this a vacation?" I asked.

"A combination of business and much-needed rest." Boris tossed off his brandy and refilled the glass. "I don't know how long I shall stay. I hadn't meant to stay more than a few days." He eyed me obliquely, striking an effective pose before the fireplace. "And perhaps I still shall. Depending on what I find to amuse me."

"I can't believe you'll fail to dig up something," I said tranquilly, giving him the old one-two glance. "Dancing girls and nude swimming parties, I shouldn't wonder— with hookahs for the men and hashish for the girls. Princely splendor must be very enjoyable."

Boris tittered complacently. "It has its points, althought it's not very splendid these days. Afraid I'm only a prince in a small way," he returned, mock modest. "Don't even use the title much, and orgies are a thing of the past. My grandfather was rather renowned, I believe, but my father used whatever he hadn't spent." Boris shrugged lightly. "I am reduced to simple parties à deux."

"Well, they have their points too," I murmured absently, fishing about in Maggie's knitting bag for another hank of yarn. "Much cheaper to let the guests entertain each other."

"Exactly what I had in mind," said Boris, pushing forward the fauteuil and ensconcing himself for

136

kneesies. His were plump, mine were sore. I said, "Ouch!" involuntarily, and immediately he was all solicitude, insistent on calling a doctor, abasing himself dramatically. If not a doctor, perhaps a gentle application of cream or liniment?

"No, *thank* you."

"There must be *something* I can do."

"Why, yes—hold out your hands," I said briskly—and tossed the yarn over them. Boris was inclined to pout, but I let my fingers drift gently over his a couple of times until he began to think it a fascinating new game. I will say he was a quick thinker if you were on his narrow-gauge railway. It was necessary for me to light him a cigarette, give him occasional puffs. Also he got thirsty, needing tiny sips of brandy to restore him. That was the longest winding operation on record. I was *yearning* for Maggie's return. I worked over every conversational gambit, but all moves led back to Boris. Sports produced references to mouflon shooting on the family estates in Bulgaria, now (alas!) nationalized. Tourism led to the promise of a personal list of all the superb unspoiled restaurants where the name of Svishtov would procure instant attention ("Just mention my name in Sheboygan. . . .").

Games? Boris was a chess master, and he had reached the semifinals of international bridge competition, when a ski accident forced him to withdraw. Even the weather was Boris-oriented, with tales of dangerous snows in Switzerland and squalls on Lake Constance when only his sailing knowledge had prevented a fatality. I was beginning to run out of topics, fell back on the old reliable, "Tell me about your job. I understand you manage a shipping firm."

This is usually good for anything up to an hour of distilled boredom. It didn't work with Boris. For the first time, his face was wiped clean of the oily smile, the intimate glance. He seemed almost affronted—or was it suspicion?

"There is nothing to tell. As you say, it is a job," he said stiffly. "Why should you wish to hear about it?"

"I don't particularly. It's one of the questions one asks. Some of the answers are pretty dull, I can tell you." I could make nothing of his reaction, but if he didn't want to talk about his work, I certainly didn't.

As if aware of my surprise, Boris smiled sardonically. "As you say, jobs are dull, not worth discussing. If I ask you about your job, would you tell me?"

"I already have, and why would you ask, if you find jobs boring?"

"Ah, but yours sounds intriguing. This research— what is it you are doing, where and why?"

By now the answer was so pat that I'd nearly convinced myself I was on a special assignment. Without thinking, I rattled it off. "I'm working up a major report for use in a number of different advertising campaigns that will tie prehistoric legends to present-day products."

"That is really fascinating!" he exclaimed. "One had no idea American advertising firms would spend so much money and time for such an investigation. And to allow a whole year for it! Tell me, how long have you been in Europe, where have you gone, where do you plan to go next?" The questions were the sort anyone would ask, but I sensed undue attention to my replies. "So you have finished with Paris, and go to Scandinavia from here?"

"That's the present plan, but I might go to Spain instead," I said evasively. "Doesn't matter where I go, so long as I cover the field."

I could see his nod of satisfaction that this confirmed some private idea, a sort of "Aha, I thought so!" Once more Boris was all smiles, asking for a cigarette, a sip of brandy.

"It is a clever idea. I think you must be exceptional to be entrusted with such a project," he said admiringly, and abandoned the matter. "Tell me what you mean to see while you're here." That lasted some time. Boris had a few sensible suggestions, but I felt again that there was some underlying purpose, as though all my answers were adding up in his mind. Particularly when I said we meant to go to Rhodes. "Crete also, I suppose?"

"And other islands, but I'm afraid Doctor Corwin wants to see so many places that there may not be enough time. She'll have to stick to the typewriter occasionally to write her book."

"Ah, yes, the book. But while she writes, you will do your research, and it won't take all your time." He gave me a pleading spaniel glance. "You'll find a moment for me? Tennis, croquet? Water-skiing on the sea or a swim in my pool? It's much nicer than the big one. Come and see it tomorrow." He leaned forward coaxingly, just as the outer door opened.

Maggie had returned. She was not alone—behind her was Kai. They stopped briefly at sight of our cozy tête-à-tête, and Kai's face was thunderous. Then he turned to shut the door and Maggie came forward placidly. "Prince Boris, so this is where you were. Your mother had the impression you were coming back to

139

play bridge."

"I came to inquire about Siri's indisposition," he exclaimed in exaggerated despair. "Oh, I shall be in Mama's black book! I completely forgot bridge." He was gracefully on his feet as I twitched the final strands of yarn from his hands, hastening to hand Maggie to her chair. "You will forgive me?"

"Of course. Oh, Siri, I don't think you've met Kai Penberthy, who is painting Madame Ionascu's portrait. This is Miss Quain, my traveling companion, Mr. Penberthy. He was kind enough to bring me home. Won't you sit down, Kai? Have a drink, or something."

"May I have some 'something'? How d'you do, Miss Quain?" Kai approached lazily, but he was wearing his New England expression, and what the hell right had *he* to disapprove!

"Ah, you are of an adventurous turn of mind," Maggie remarked. "Well, I don't know what 'something' there is—a bowl of cereal? Or Siri could fix you a mashed-banana sandwich, if you prefer. I should like a brandy and soda." She looked wistfully at Boris. "Prince Boris, d'you mind? Only a man can make a proper drink."

"One of our greatest talents! Siri, what can I get you? Penberthy?" Boris snaked into the kitchenette for glasses and ice.

I said I'd have Scotch and water, and Kai's voice cut across the room plaintively, "I thought I was having a banana sandwich."

Boris was back with the makings, giving the effect of being host, laughing lightly, "Oh, come, my dear chap!

140

Be serious."

"I'm entirely serious. I was promised a mashed-banana sandwich prepared by Miss Quain."

"Now I come to think of it, I don't believe we have any bananas," Maggie mused dreamily, "nor any bread. Perhaps you should settle for the bowl of figs, if you really won't have a drink."

"Oh, I'll have Scotch—but for the record, you owe me one mashed-banana sandwich, Doctor Corwin."

Maggie raised her eyebrows. "From your painting, one would never suspect a teashop mentality, Mr. Penberthy. Prince Boris, if that is for me, pray don't drown it." She sampled the highball critically, nodded her head. "Ah, I knew I might rely upon you. Delicious."

Boris smirked modestly, extending my glass. "Siri—to your taste, I hope."

It wasn't, it was a shade too strong and not enough ice, but I sipped and flattered him with another one-two glance. He returned it like a grand slam in no trumps, and Kai suddenly preempted all the couch space beside me. "On the rocks for me, please." He eyed my knitting with gentle interest. "What are you making, Miss Quain?"

"Socks."

"A very pretty pattern."

"I'm glad you like it."

"I do. I always have, Miss Quain—or may I be numbered among the friends permitted to call you Siri?"

"Of course, of course! We are all friends at Dresnatinko, no need for formality, eh, Siri?" Boris jovially extended Kai's glass and positioned the ottoman beside my knee, where he lounged against the couch arm. His head was tilted for its best angle, looking up in smiling intimacy.

"Of course not, Boris." I could feel Kai stiffening, but I was too furious to care. How *dared* he mention the sock pattern, considering how many pairs I'd made for him by his own request!

"Kai," Maggie said reflectively. "Is it a nickname?"

"No, it's Persian, a legacy from an ancestor who married an exotic Oriental girl. My grandfather still has two incredibly small leather straps hung with ankle bells. We like to think she was a slave girl, but I'm afraid it was much more prosaic. She was probably the daughter of a merchant, and a wise economic venture. In those days, the Penberthys chose their wives very carefully."

The odious, insufferable gall of him—and I had to sit there and take it! I hung on to the needles, outwardly unruffled and inwardly raging, while Boris said, "Several Svishtovs in the seventeenth and eighteenth centuries married slave girls. They were not serfs, of course. Slavery was different in those days."

"How?" asked Maggie.

"Oh, after a war, one could often buy women of excellent family, you know. Well educated, gently bred"—he shrugged—"with a little training, they were entirely suited for marriage to their owners' relatives. I myself am descended from an Ottoman princess."

"A princess would naturally rate a head of family," Maggie agreed sweetly, "and I suppose any husband would be better than iron chains. One assumes

142

marriage automatically carried manumission?"

"Oh, certainly. Generally, they made excellent wives. Oh, yes, one could do worse than a slave girl."

"What a pity times have changed."

"Yes, indeed, Doctor Corwin. You can't hardly get them no more." Kai heaved a long sigh, and I was fed up.

"Are you the Kai Penberthy whose *Girl in Green* was in Germond's window?" I inquired, innocently admiring. "Superb composition." I launched into a fulsome description for Boris and Maggie—the choice of colors, the beauty of the model, the delicacy of brushwork. Boris was loudly impressed. No wonder Mama had selected Kai for her portrait. I burbled more flattery, until Kai was thoroughly unstrung and Maggie gave me a thoughtful look. Then I changed the subject to Corinth and let her carry the ball. To tell the truth, I was feeling sick inside. We knew so well how to destroy each other with verbal subtlety, Kai and I—but why must we? What had I ever done to draw such hatred?

Maggie said, "Midnight, bedtime for tourists. It's been lovely to see you, come again some time, but now—go home."

Boris stood up, laughing. "One hates to leave such charming company, but there is always tomorrow and tomorrow. Siri promises to swim with me if you do not need her, Doctor Corwin. Please—do not need her!"

"I make no promises, but I am liking my book, and Sunday is not good for sightseeing. Too many tourists," Maggie sniffed. "May we let you know in the morning?"

"Of course. Kai, do you have a cart, or shall I run you back?" Boris kissed Maggie's hand with a flourish, then turned to me with an intimate smile. "Siri, good night, *chérie,*" he murmured, pressing my hand tenderly and holding it rather too long after the kiss. I could have told him he was courting the whirlwind; one thing Kai does awfully well is kissing hands. He was leaning over Maggie, saying something that drew a chuckle. Then he was beside us. "Aren't you through *yet,* Boris? Move over, old man. My turn. . . ."

It was not too difficult, after all. Kai's fingers were coolly impersonal, his lips barely brushed my skin. "Good night. Siri. Sleep well. Coming, Boris?"

Maggie was knitting calmly when I'd closed the door and come back to the couch. "You had better have another drink," she remarked. "You must need it—and as long as you're up, I'll have another, too."

"How was dinner?"

"The food was delicious," she said noncommittally.

"No." Maggie counted stitches under her breath, cast off a few. "Siri, did you tell me the truth about this afternoon? You weren't knocked down by his car or something you thought would upset me?"

"No, it was exactly as I said. Why?" I asked, astonished.

"Because madame didn't want us; at least, she didn't want me alone. Boris made her ask us, and she was thoroughly annoyed when I made your excuses. They had a bit of a go-around in Bulgarian, or maybe it was Greek, but anybody could get the gist. He shut her up in one sentence, and whatever he said, Stefan was grim. Ater that, she was all over me—we must use the pool, play tennis, feel free to come and go. All the new

144

books and magazines are in the library or will be gotten for us.

"You can see why I began to wonder? Boris barely finished dinner before he recalled an 'errand,' and every time I tried to leave, madame insisted I stay until he returned for bridge." Maggie raised her eyebrows at me. "I hadn't any doubt he was here, Siri, but it added up to your being more seriously hurt than you said and Boris making sure you wouldn't sue."

I shook my head. "Nothing like that, but he's got something on his mind. He'd have you think he's bowled over by my physical attractions, the original irresistible force . . . and I'm not the girl nobody wants, but I'm no femme fatale, either. In fact"—I frowned thoughtfully—"if anything, I'd have said I was exactly the sort Boris would most dislike—a sentiment I heartily return."

"You are not impressed by titles and money?"

"No. I'm not too great for uniforms, either. The young ones are apt to be truck drivers in real life, and generals are too old," I said absently. "Anyway, I don't think Boris has much money. Mr. Ionascu may be loaded, but I bet he helps only those who help themselves. The one thing Boris said"—I chuckled—"he doesn't use his title because he's only a prince in a small way—and how right! Did you ever see such a thorough-paced little swipe?"

"He is a bit of a bounder," Maggie agreed. "What did you think of the other one?"

"Very pleasant," I said impersonally. "What are the plans for tomorrow?"

She was silent for a long while. I thought she was counting stitches, but finally she said, "Let's go over to

145

Kalkis. I'd like to see what Dresnatinko looks like from outside, if we can get down to the shore someplace, and you'll still get back in time for a swim."

"Not me—unless you come along for protection."

Maggie laughed. "I might, at that, just to watch the fun."

IX

I couldn't figure Maggie out that next week. She was writing steadily, but she seemed determined to thrust me into Boris's arms at every turn. Considering she knew I didn't like him, she was either singularly obtuse or playing a private concave suit. Perhaps she deliberately made use of him to occupy my time and prevent my growing bored with twiddling my fingers while she got on with her book. Perhaps she didn't grasp my true distaste—or maybe it was because she did—I remembered she hadn't wanted a girl who might leave her in the lurch for romance.

Whatever the reasoning, she had Boris under my feet every blessed day, beginning Monday, when a beribboned parcel containing a dozen pairs of gossamer-sheer stockings arrived at the end of breakfast, accompanied by a tender message from Boris. "A princely gesture," Maggie approved. "Are they the right size?"

"Of course. If I know him, he could probably get my correct size in bras." I was tidily repacking.

"What are you doing?"

"Sending them back, naturally. You don't suggest I

should accept them?"

"I don't see why not."

"Come off it, darling! The oldest wheeze in the world next to jeweled garters. 'I'm so happy you liked them . . . do let me help you put them on!'"

"Or maybe take 'em off—but I'm not so sure this time, Siri. If you accept, mightn't it convince him the incident is closed?"

"If I were *sure* of that . . ." I hesitated. "How d'you suppose he got 'em so quickly?"

Danae had been fluttering around with fresh coffee. "Athens," she said. "Svishtov drive fast, not coffee, nothing . . . go first. Is beautiful, no? Lucky Mees!" I looked up quickly, and despite her politeness, her eyes were decidedly sly, her smile practically establishing us as two of a kind, before she disappeared into the villa.

"Dammit, isn't it bad enough Rosa thinks I'm Zaro's mistress—and now Danae will inform the staff I'm Boris's!"

Maggie chuckled infectiously. "My dear Siri, I don't know when I've been more entertained! You may as well keep them; one can always use hosiery, after all, and I fear your reputation is ruined no matter what. If you send them back with snoots, it will only convince the staff that 'Mees' is waiting for diamonds. Your stock will soar, as having a proper value of yourself, but the suspense will be frightful. Service will be disrupted, and Stefan will be unhappy."

"We can't have that," I agreed, "but on the other hand, if I settle for stockings, isn't that likely to give them a poor opinion of American womanhood?"

She laughed helplessly. "Since knowing you, I have become sorry I taught at Radcliffe. Mount Holyoke must be much more fun." She simmered down. "What do you have to pay to keep them?"

"Lunch at some little *boîte* around Piraeus."

"Oh, why not, Siri? Least said, soonest mended. I wanted to work today, anyway. Go along with him, get it over with. You'll probably get a good lunch."

"I suppose you're right."

I'll admit he laid himself out to be charming. Unfortunately, we had different concepts of charm, but I did get a good lunch and a pleasant drive. Maybe it was because I told Maggie it was an okay day that she announced next morning, "I believe I'll work today, too. You can play tennis with Boris, he'll be here at ten." When I refused in favor of research in Athens, she said, "Let Boris take you, then. I'd rather like to have the car, in case I want a breather."

"I'll stay here, in that case."

"No, you're not to put off your own work, Siri. It would make me extremely nervous to think of you hanging about all day. Ten to one I'll be so engrossed I won't go anywhere. Boris will pick you up in a half hour."

The week limped along from day to day, and every day was Boring Boris. What he couldn't think of, she could. We lunched, very formally, at Miranda on Wednesday. Maggie then left us to swim *à deux,* while she returned to Blondel. On Thursday, she discovered a crucial need for typewriter paper—Boris would drive me to Athens to get it.

"Why can't the estate wagon bring it?"

"I'll need it sooner than that."

"All right, I'll take our car. Why do I need Boris?"

"His car is faster. You said yourself he was a superb driver . . . and you can have lunch somewhere along the way."

"If we take time for lunch, you may as well send for it by the wagon."

"The wagon doesn't return until nearly four," she said blandly. "I'll need it by three, so you'll have plenty of time."

By Friday I was fed to the teeth with Boris. He switched from the initial rushing intimacy to devoted respect, which was at least easier to stand. It was still a terrible strain—we had nothing to *talk* about, really. We didn't agree about anything under the sun, and how long can you discuss the good books you've read recently? He was a devout segregationist, not merely on color, and about the only time we had a meeting of minds (though for different reasons) was when he said neither Governor Maddox nor the Wallaces would be acceptable at a dinner party. I was still sick of him, and when Maggie blandly announced that Boris was taking me to yet another *recherché boîte* for lunch, I waited until she was typing and quietly called Stefan. Nothing was simpler than to go to Athens in the estate car and be brought back in the afternoon. . . .

It didn't get me anywhere. Maggie had accepted dinner at the main house for both of us, and there was a look in her eye that said no excuse would suffice. She went back to work, but I think she called Boris to say I was home, because he came bounding in with suspicious promptness five minutes later. There was plenty of time for a swim or tennis. He was faintly reproachful at my escape to Athens; why should I ride with servants when he was available?"

"I thought you had business to attend to?"

Boris smiled thoughtfully. "I have decided that you are my business, Siri. Come, where shall we go, what would you like to do?"

At random, I said, "I haven't seen the blowhole. Stefan said it was a long walk—perhaps there isn't time."

"A long walk, yes—but who walks?"

"Stefan said you couldn't get there any other way."

"Not within the grounds, but from outside. Unless," he added dubiously, "you are afraid of heights. You need shoes that will not slip on wet rocks."

"I have espadrilles."

"Perfect!" He was back with the sports car by the time I'd changed clothes, and we went out the rear gate and followed the Dresnatinko wall until it turned seaward from the road. We turned with it, along a frightful meandering trail that was no more than a goat track. "This is not our land, but its owners are family friends. They wouldn't like strangers trooping across the property constantly, but I am different," he explained. "In any case, you'd never find your way, even if Stefan had told you."

"I can see that," I agreed jerkily. The path turned and twisted, now squeezing between rocks and then zigzagging beneath trees. "Is this a path at all, or are you making it up as you go along?"

Boris laughed. "More or less, but we're nearly there." He stopped on a small grassy patch with a beautiful view of the shoreline stretching north. The Dresnatinko wall towered behind us, running across outcrops dropping sharply down in random grass

151

hummocks, like a medieval dry moat. This cove was entirely different from the Ionascus'—far fewer rocks, no minor promontories jutting out to endanger boats. There was even a bathing party in progress down in the most sheltered part. "The Goulenkis—I didn't know they were home. I must phone," Boris said, "You will like them, Siri. For the blowhole we go this way."

At the end of the wall there was a fan of heavy iron spikes thrusting out into space. It looked like a jumping-off spot, end of the world. The restless growling of the water was everywhere, completely drowning conversation. I thought we must be directly beside the cave, and even knowing the cause, I found the sounds frightening. Elemental, furious frustration in the surge and retreat to gather strength for the next assault.

I supposed we'd stop at the spikes and merely look, but Boris said, "Not for fat ladies, but you can make it, Siri." If you turned around and half-lay on the rocks, you could pull yourself under the bottom spike. Boris demonstrated. He had a little squeeze—his tummy wasn't as flat as mine. Then we went cautiously upward, hugging the wall and steadying ourselves on the rough stones. Here, there was almost no grass, and the rocks were worn glassy-smooth by centuries of the pounding water. Spume filled the air and filmed the granite. It was tricky walking even with rope-soled shoes. For once I could admire Boris. He moved ahead of me, sure-footed as a chamois, extending a hand to brace me from one foothold to another, and for all his faintly puffy appearance, he was amazingly strong.

We came out on a barren wasteland of damp, uneven rocks that seemed heaved into place at random by angry giants. It was crazy paving that had slipped, like a news photo of a major highway after an earthquake—everything there, but nothing fitting together. I saw why Stefan had warned of danger. The water had slowly polished the rocks until they tilted minutely toward the sea around the blowhole. There were six solid-iron stanchions embedded in the rock and looped together by heavy chains, to prevent anyone from getting too close to the tilt. Fatally easy to slide inexorably, helplessly over the edge!

As if aware of my inner shiver, Boris said, "Originally there were leather straps and wooden barricades, but they constantly rotted from the salt water. My stepfather had them replaced with this arrangement. It was very difficult, very expensive to set the posts, when everyone in the locality knows enough to avoid the blowhole. It's not likely a guest would wander this far, but Gyorgy is a very careful man."

"Better to be safe than sorry, I should think."

"Oh, yes. There's a smugglers' path down to the cave—I won't take you, Siri. It really is dangerous, but it's possible to get across at the mouth, and no doubt the natives often use it as a shortcut. I suppose, at night, particularly after a drinking party in the village, a servant trying to sneak back to Dresnatinko could slip." His tone of indifference was faintly contemptuous of such financial outlay for a peasant. "Come over this way, Siri. You get a panorama view of the estate. Hold on to the chains, but it's quite safe; we're exactly between tides."

Again, he went easily ahead, while I clung breathlessly to the chains, not looking at anything but my feet, until I literally bumped into him. He was braced

153

against the final post, one arm about a wild wind-swept tree stubbornly rooted on the very edge of the cliff, and beyond him was . . . nothing. Not so much as a single step. A wave of horror engulfed me. If he hadn't turned, been waiting for me, I could have pushed him . . . Just that tiny jiggle might have been enough. . . . I closed my eyes, sickly, and Boris threw his arm about me with a triumphant laugh.

"Don't be frightened, it's perfectly safe and the most superb view of any place at Dresnatinko. See, it is all spread before us, one can see for miles."

He held me against him, and I was aware once more of his unsuspected strength, but when I opened my eyes obediently, we seemed to be hanging by our toes in empty space. I didn't dare move; Boris might lose his grip on the tree—or the tree might tear loose. . . . I closed my eyes, unable to repress a moan of terror, and Boris laughed recklessly. "Why, what's the matter? You do not trust me to know my own land? You are afraid I shall drop you? Are you afraid to die?"

Terror was replaced by temper. "Not in the least," I said coolly. "I'm simply not one for the immaturity of chicken games. If you meant to frighten me, you did. Could we go back now?"

Instantly Boris was all contrition. "Siri, no! I never meant to frighten you, *duzhka*. I thought you saw, realized . . ." He hugged me gently, pulling himself back from the precipice . . . and it was true—the ends of the chains were like clasps on a dog leash, and Boris had wrapped the slack completely around his waist and back to the iron loop on the post.

"No, I didn't see." I was totally unstrung, leaning

154

against him limply, because maybe *he* was secure—he *would* be, I thought angrily—but what about me? I wasn't chained. I fumbled for a firm grip while Boris cuddled and apologized. Finally I could force myself to look at the Dresnatinko land, but I didn't release my own hold. I'm not sure he knew I had it, but he was flatteringly surprised at my recovery, the brave way I enjoyed the view. I was still thankful to get away, retreat along the chains to a rock well back from the blowhole. "Have a cigarette before we return. I am truly sorry for this, Siri. It was unpardonably thoughtless. Can you ever forgive me?"

"Why, it's not your fault. I simply hadn't watched you because I was minding my steps, and when I bumped into you . . ." I shivered. "I hadn't seen the chain, I thought I could have pushed you . . . ugh!"

"Now that is most hopeful," he remarked. "One had realized you did not return my sentiments, it did not happen so quickly to you as to me—but already you would be sorry to lose me." He smiled mockingly at my confusion and stood silently looking out to sea. "It's possible, when the tide is right, to get into the cave and explore. Would you enjoy that? I can show you the old smugglers' path, but please"—he turned to me gravely—"don't try to follow it. It's safe enough for anyone accustomed to rock walking, but far too difficult for you. In one or two spots there are slides, and there's no retaining wall."

"I won't attempt it, I promise you, but I'd like to see the cave—I think."

"I'll bring you one day." He flipped his cigarette onto the wet stones beyond the chains. "We'd better start back, if you feel up to it."

After the nerveracking experience of the blowhole, I was in no shape to contemplate Kai. Further, there was scant time to dress. I picked something at random, and only when Maggie said, "What a lovely color, Siri—like fresh raspberries," did I realize it was an old favorite of Kai's. I glanced about wildly, but we were already at the door and there was nothing I could manage to upset over myself as an excuse to change. This was definitely not My Day. With a sinking heart, I followed Maggie to the golf cart as though to the tumbril.

How right I was! That evening will live forever in my memory, like *Calais* to Mary, Queen of Scots. Even now, when the truth has emerged, it's hard to recall. At the time it was inexplicable—or rather, the undercurrents were readily interpretable but no one got the right translation.

There was Anya, seductively beautiful and delighted to meet Miss Quain again. "But it must be Siri and Anya for us, no? One had abandoned Boris as hopeless, and now he finds his happiness right at home!"

Did she really think her son had fallen in love at first sight? That was the way she was playing it, and no question that it was on Boris's instructions. Even Maggie looked a bit startled at my sudden elevation to the post of unofficial fiancée, and as for me, I have rarely been more uncomfortable in my life.

Then there was Kai, who took one look at my dress and put on his New England face, while Boris was hanging on to my hand after he'd kissed it and

156

admiring my impeccable taste. "One knows the American woman is celebrated for appearance, but too often it is merely the money for grooming and not, as here, true chic. The color! Kai, you will agree it is superb?"

"I do, I've always been fond of it."

"Then it's lucky Boris delayed me so I put on the first thing to hand," I said sweetly. "I wonder what you'll think of the dress I got in Paris last month—it's ice-blue." I knew I was hitting below the belt. Kai never dictated my clothes, but as a favor to him, cold crystal colors were ruled out. He said they detracted from my eyes.

"I long to see it," he said evenly. "You will need only diamonds to be an ice queen."

"The Svishtov parure! Kai, when you have finished with Mama, you must paint Siri. I insist! I commission you on the spot."

"I'm sure Kai prefers to choose his own subjects, Boris, and I'm not very paintable anyway."

"Kai can do it. When you see what he has made of me, you will know he could paint God himself." Anya's dark eyes turned to him intimately.

"You're prejudiced, Anya darling." Kai kissed her hand lightly.

There was Stefan, giving me a discreet smile of approval. That pleased me. I liked feeling I was upholding Gyorgy's good judgment in the eyes of his servants.

Most of all there was Boris—very *haute couture* in a steel-gray dinner suit, crimson cummberbund, and ruffled shirt with lace falls at throat and wrists. An immense ruby winked in the neck folds instead of a dinner tie. I couldn't imagine Kai in such a rig, except for a fancy dress party, but on Boris it was surprisingly impressive. For the first time he looked like a prince, with manners to match. The insufferable arrogance was still there, but less noticeable in a host giving courteous attention to his guests. He was quieter, as though the clothes gave him a different personality—or was this the real Boris, born to the purple and ill at ease in a workaday world?

Whatever the reason, he was easier to take, thank goodness—because I was going to have to take him. It developed we were driving to Athens for an Embassy party, and while that was going to be better than watching Kai hold hands verbally, optically, and *sotto voce* with Anya, I was still stuck with equal devotion from Boris. Maybe I could manage to lose him at the party, but meanwhile it was possible to be tactfully absorbed—although Kai seemed unconcerned, and at least he kept Anya in a happy frame of mind. I began to think all that had ever bothered her was the possible interruption of her solitude with Kai. I didn't think she gave a damn whom Boris married—I wasn't even too sure she even liked her son, although he obviously held the whip hand. At one moment I made some remark to Kai, and Boris called her to order in one sentence—silky-smooth and smiling. She apologized at once for inattention, but her glance to Boris was very nearly hatred, and Stefan's jaw tightened.

Maggie tried for a red herring. "Where did you and Boris go?"

"To the blowhole. Very . . . exciting, but only for mountain goats."

Boris smiled at her gravely. "She is too loyal. I must

158

confess my sins—I terrified her!" He laid his hand warmly over mine, his voice gently reflective, his eyes smiling at me. "We went to the end of the chains. She didn't see I was buckled to the post when she bumped into me." Boris kissed my palm softly. "She was afraid to move for fear I should fall to the rocks—but my beautiful darling forgave me, and I have sworn she shall never be frightened again."

Someone drew a sharp breath, but Boris was kissing my palm again. "Don't be dramatic," I said lightly. "You said yourself there wasn't the slightest danger, but I do think it may be a bit more rugged than Maggie will like." I withdrew my hand and buttered a bit of roll, casually. My eyes met Stefan's, and whether or not his had been the indrawn breath, there was no doubt he was deeply troubled. I thought I understood, if Gyorgy'd told him to look after me, Stefan was in a spot with Boris getting in the way. It seemed important to reassure him. When I was first out of the powder room later, I went out to the poolside where he was rearranging chairs. "It really was quite safe, Stefan."

"It would be," he replied, surprisingly. "His Highness knows every corner of the estate."

"What disturbs you?"

He straightened up slowly. "It is not my place to say, Miss Quain, but if I might suggest—perhaps you should stick to your original plans instead of so much time spent with His Highness."

"You don't suppose I welcome his . . . apparent devotion?"

Stefan eyed me sharply and nodded his head. "There will always be a car available if Doctor Corwin wishes to use her own," he said in a hurried undertone.

"Remember the direct line, for day or night!" He moved smoothly away, while I stood for a moment, wondering why Stefan had warned me away from Boris. Could he have thought me likely to take His Highness seriously?

Arms slid gently about me. "What are you dreaming of in the moonlight, *duzhka?*" Boris asked softly. "Shall we let the others go to this dull party and stay here for a midnight swim?"

"A bit too obvious," I murmured. "Besides, it's the first time a prince ever took me to the ball. I can't bear to waste such magnificence."

Boris laughed, rubbing his cheek against my temple. "Very well, Cinderella, there will be other nights," he whispered.

"Boris," Kai's voice said dryly, "the cars are waiting."

Anya was swathed in azure mink, Maggie was wrapped in a gold-brocade coat that was so old-fashioned it looked as though it *might* be next year's first word, and Stefan was waiting with the white-and-silver Indian evening shawl that is the only summer wrap I've ever owned. It developed that Maggie was to ride with Boris and myself, which produced a small interchange between the Svishtovs, but for once she stuck to her guns. All charming smiles, the steel hand in a velvet glove, and short of a full row Boris was worsted.

Stefan stood impassive, but I sensed his satisfaction with the arrangement. Boris wasn't through, though. He turned smiling to me and was suddenly struck by an idea. "The Svishtov diamonds! For such an evening, Siri must have them. Mama, you agree?"

160

Apparently, Kai was worth more than jewels! Anya's lips set briefly, but she wouldn't back down. "Of course! Only a minute to get them from the safe." She was turning, when Maggie rescued me.

"No!" she stated quietly. "I will not allow Siri to be placed in such a position. I am . . . surprised you would suggest it, Prince Boris." He stiffened angrily, but Maggie ignored him. Superbly! She had spoken, the matter was settled, and Boris hadn't a leg to stand on, or he'd be convicted of bad taste. In silence we went out and disposed ourselves in the cars. Maggie relented sufficiently to permit me to sit next Boris—but I noticed Anya was driving the second car, which figured. When Kai drives, he keeps both hands on the wheel; when he isn't driving, he has both hands free to keep on the driver.

Nor was I surprised that the second car was a full hour later than ours in reaching the Embassy.

By the time I saw Anya and Kai passing along the reception line I was too distracted to have any particular emotion, although a few wisps were coagulating nebulously in my mind. I'd counted on ditching Boris, who'd be caught by duty dances. He did only two—the Ambassador's wife, while I danced with His Excellency, and Maggie, while I danced with the First Secretary. After that, he simply "exchanged" dances, and I wound up with Boris for every intermission. I never got a chance really to talk to anyone, particularly not any of the Embassy attachés or aides. Boris was right there as the music ceased, his hand on my elbow while he bowed to his partner and smiled dismissingly to mine.

But—he was making no display of wooing. He was

an excellent dancer, doing his duty by a house guest. He laid his cheek against my hair and murmured intimately about the perfect blending of our steps—and between dances he introduced me to family friends, lapsed into Greek, and politely recalled himself to English "for Miss Quain's sake." He was correct to a hair's breadth. Not a soul at the ball would link our names to a future wedding ring. If I raised any question, he'd say *"Duzhka,* you are too new, too precious to be shared." But he knew I wouldn't. I was far too well bred to make a scene—if I'd any serious hopes of getting him—and far too smart to force his hand, only to wind up in the basket with a man I didn't like.

All I didn't know was whether Boris had yet realized I'd interpreted his delicate maneuver. Also I didn't know why.

Why was it imperative for Boris to convince Dresnatinko *and no one else* that he'd fallen for me? Was it some sort of squeeze play on Anya for going overboard with Kai? Was he afraid she'd kick over the traces, the financial anchor of Gyorgy—with consequent loss of Boris's job as well as Villa Miranda? I felt sure Boris wasn't acting out of loyalty to anyone but Boris, but I couldn't see how he expected to use me to bring Anya out of her infatuation.

"I have done everything expected of me, it is a very dull party," he murmured in my ear. "Shall we run away to a little nightclub for an hour, come back in time to say farewells and pick up Doctor Corwin? She seems entirely happy, and I want you to myself. Please?"

I was about to object, when Kai and Anya showed up

next us. "Exchange?"

"We were just going to leave—or will it be noticed if you don't dance with your mother?" I looked anxiously at Boris.

"Mama cares nothing for appearances, do you, Mama?"

He'd overreached himself. Anya smiled sweetly. "Nothing," she agreed. "It is a very good idea, Boris. We will come with you." From the involuntary tightening of his hand on mine, I thought Anya would be made to pay for her defiance, but I was too tired to care. "Siri, slip away with me? We will meet you at the side entrance, Boris?"

In the powder room she said casually, "You do not mind that Kai and I come with you, Siri?"

"Not in the least, Anya," I met her eye in the mirror. "I'm sure you'll understand when I say I find Boris a bit . . . impetuous?"

"Yes," she murmured. "I told him you would not like to be rushed."

"Perhaps you could tell him again."

"Yes." She dropped her lipstick into the pochette. "You would not like to be a princess, Siri?"

"No," I said baldly. "Do we get our wraps or sneak out as is?"

Boris was at the wheel of the Thunderbird. Kai and Anya slid cozily into the rear seat, I got in front, and we whizzed around a few corners until we reached an obvious nightclub, complete with uniformed doorman, street canopy, and neon lights.

It was a nightclub. What more need be said? There

163

wasn't a ringside table, but somehow everyone became pushed a few inches aside, and suddenly there *was* a ringside table for Prince Boris Svishtov. ("Just mention my name in Sheboygan. . . .") There was a postage stamp pretending to be a dance floor and a magnum of champagne cooling while we danced—which amounted to toddling a few steps right or left. There was a floor show, which Boris assured us we would enjoy even if we didn't understand a word.

"Boris only comes to see the girls," Anya remarked, "and one does not need words to understand them."

Actually, the chorus line was exceptionally pretty. They came out first in Greek native dress and got progressively more nude with each turn. Several seemed on good terms with Boris, who sat back like a Regency buck admiring pretty bits of fluff. Apparently it was the thing for patrons to get into the act. All over the room men were calling out the Greek equivalent of "Take it off!" The girls obliged, with giggles and suggestive winks. Everyone seemed to know everyone else, like a private club. When Boris made a loud remark, a male voice yelled something incomprehensible, "Eh, Svishtov?" which drew a general burst of laughter.

The stars were standard—the cheap act was a belly dancer, there was a girl singer (gypsy ballads) and a boy singer who also danced. The headliner was a Greek Sinatra, except he played guitar, and he either owned the club or was the permanent MC. Everyone knew him and heartily applauded his songs, but it was the girls they came to see. Each appearance in less and less clothing was greeted wildly. I had no doubt the comments were getting as bare as the girls, but there was a good-humored gaiety in the bawdiness that was irresistible.

The finale was a humdinger, although it certainly cost nothing for costumes. "That's the finest display of belly buttons I ever saw," Kai stated judicially and enough people understood English that he got a laugh all to himself. The girl singer was in gauzy harem pants, the belly dancer was down to a bikini of gold fringe, while the girls . . . wow! Each had a small baby-blue ruffle pasted around her nipple and a larger (but not too large!) heart-shaped baby-blue ruffle pasted at the crotch. That was all.

What hadn't been spent on costumes went into special effects of sets and lighting. Very well done, too. The audience was loudly enthusiastic, demanding encores from every star. Each girl got a chance to wiggle by herself, producing the ultimate in shouts of excitement—yet somehow you couldn't say it was dirty. There was a sort of innocent enjoyment in the display and a genuine pleasure for the girl who got the most applause. She wasn't Boris's choice, but every woman in the club picked her unanimously, including me, and Kai was positively shouting. Caught up in the moment, we'd forgotten the divorce, were babbling to each other excitedly, "Isn't she a beauty?" "Yes, you have to paint her, Kai—ask the manager!" "On the way out. . . . look at that curve in her arm, and those buttocks! She'll go to fat later, but right now . . ." "Yes, she's perfect; I do hope you can get her to model . . ."

At last the windup—lights dimmed, girls provided with zithers and arranged tastefully about the stage, while the headliner sang. Then the girls sang and processed about, while the lights changed from one soft color to another. It was very pretty. I thought it was some Greek ballad, until I felt Kai stiffen beside me.

Then I realized. It was no ballad. They were singing the "Ave Maria."

In the nude, with baby-blue breast ruffles and orchestral "arrangements," with stained-glass lighting and religious "effects." Boris and Anya were sipping champagne and smoking, blandly approving the spectacle. "Amscray?" Kai suggested quietly. Silently we rose and threaded between tables to the exit, hearing gentle applause behind us. In the foyer, he scribbled a note on a bar napkin, handed it to the maitre d'. "Svishtov?"

The man nodded, smiled, and went back to his observation post. Kai helped me into a cab and said, "American Embassy." We sat silent for a moment while the cab rolled forward. Kai lit cigarettes absently, handed me one. I said, "Maybe they don't do Hail Marys in the Greek Orthodox Church?"

"We don't do 'em in the Presbyterian Church either, but I still don't want to see a nightclub version," he said with finality. "By the way, I'm leaving Sunday."

"Leaving?" I felt stunned, almost panic-stricken. "But you can't!"

"Why not? The portrait's done. I thought you'd be happy to have me out of your way."

"But . . . what about the other commissions? I mean, Anya's obviously ready to help, Rosa's probably good for a portrait, I thought you meant to stay all summer. If it weren't for Maggie's damn book and this stupid Boris complicating things, I wouldn't be around at all. I'm sorry, Kai." I fought back tears. "Oh, I *wish* I'd never come! Every blessed thing's gone wrong,

166

nothing's worked as planned, and I don't know why. It seemed perfectly simple. Even when you were here"—I gulped—"I thought we might as well get used to running into each other. After all, it's bound to happen in New York, but all you do is nip at me until you make me be unpleasant back—and now you just walk out and *leave* me here."

"You've hooked Boris. Why d'you need me?"

"I *haven't* hooked Boris, and if I had, I'd throw him back!"

Kai was silent for a long moment while I found a hanky and surreptitiously removed the moisture collecting in my eyes. "You're scared," he said finally, and his voice was incredulous. "What are you afraid of, Siri? Don't tell me there's anything you can't handle, including Boris. And even if you can't, what d'you expect me to do about it? You won't admit we were ever married, which leaves me no status at all."

"Yes, of course. For a moment I forgot—sorry Kai. Where do you go from here?"

"Turkey, perhaps. There's a Svishtov summer place near Tekirdag on the Sea of Marmara, about a hundred miles from Istanbul."

"Sounds promising. You'll drive, of course? Will you go straight through or stop for sketches?" Fury kept my voice politely impersonal. He'd said *he* was leaving, lured me into making a fool of myself, when all the time it was simply a jaunt for greater privacy with Anya!

"Perhaps—or perhaps I'll go to Spain," he said indifferently. So he was already bored with Anya, ready to walk away? I had my mouth open to protest, to say, "Is she ready to be ditched, because if she isn't, she'll as deliberately ruin your career as make it." In the nick of time I remembered it was no longer my business. I closed my mouth. Firmly. "Siri, what's wrong?" For the first time Kai's voice was warm, concerned. "If you're in some sort of bind, ask me and I'll stay, hon."

I was tempted. And how I was tempted! I knew that even if he regretted it tomorrow, he'd see it through—but a piece of paper said he wasn't responsible for me any longer. Anyway I detest the sort of ex-wife who hangs on for things like "I can't seem to balance my checkbook" or "Would you terribly much mind stopping by to rewire my electric iron?"

"Nothing's up," I said. "No bind, no sweat, but thanks, sweetie." We were drawing up at the Embassy. "The best of luck, wherever you go. Don't worry about me, everything'll straighten out."

"What d'you mean?" Kai thrust money at the driver and caught my arm, turning me toward him. "What has to be straightened out?"

"Nothing. I mean it, don't worry about me."

"Will you for God's sake stop being cryptic!" he said impatiently, as the cab drew away. "How can I help being worried?"

"Well, stop it," I said, equally impatient from weariness. "You haven't worried about me in years, why start now?" I twitched away and went into the Embassy, where the party was beginning to break up. I could tell Maggie knew we'd ducked out, was relieved to see someone who'd get her the hell out of the place, but she asked no questions. There was no sign of Boris or Anya; we got the other car and drove back to Dresnatinko, talking very little. When Kai had dropped us at Blondel, I looked at Maggie and said,

168

"From now on, I should appreciate your allowing me to handle my own social life. I don't know what you had in mind, but I'm through being polite. If you get me into another rendezvous with any of these people, I'll pack up and leave."

"Yes. I don't know what I had in mind either," she sighed, "but it seemed a good idea at the time. Let's go to Corinth tomorrow." She looked at me apologetically. "I mean, we'll really go, Siri. I won't change my mind. Pack a bag, we'll get away early. . . ."

X

We went to Corinth. We spent a full week exploring the
Peloponnesos and came home only because we needed
clean clothes. There was a small pile of mail waiting for
Maggie but nothing much for me, which seemed odd. I
should have had a letter from Bess, telling me whatever
she'd turned up in Paris—but perhaps there was
nothing to tell, and she was always busy. After a placid
week of rambling about ruins, with no emotional
undercurrents, all the unnerving incidents of luggage
search and possible complications with Rosa seemed
unimportant. At long last the trip was turning out as I'd
expected. By now Kai must have left; we were staying
only overnight at Blondel before going to Thessalonike, and if Boris were still at Dresnatinko, I'd be in-
again-gone-again before he knew it. Surely he'd have
gone for good before I got back again.

It was after eleven when we'd unloaded the car. "I
must say it'll be good to sleep in our own beds again,"
Maggie remarked wearily. "D'you suppose there's
anything to eat, Siri? That dinner was a bad mistake."

"Native food is always loaded with olive oil. I should
have remembered to say 'tourist style,' although that

170

place was so small, they might not have known what I meant anyway. Why don't you undress and I'll inspect the pantry."

There wasn't much but soup packets and crackers—we hadn't been expected for another few days. I had my hand on the phone—Stefan ought to be told we'd returned, and Maggie really ought to have some proper food. She'd eaten almost none of the dinner . . . and there was a knock on the outer door. I could hear Maggie, "Stefan! How did you know we were here?"

"There is a signal whenever the gate is used at night. Everyone else is away, it could only be your car," Stefan explained. "I hope you enjoyed your trip, Doctor Corwin."

"Very much indeed." By the sound, Stefan was already busy in the kitchenette. I wondered why I'd ever thought anything or anyone got past him! Sure enough, when I emerged in my housecoat, Maggie sat before the fire contentedly sipping a martini. Small tables waited beside our seats. Stefan hovered over a chafing dish, and a delicious smell of fresh coffee filled the air. We were such old friends by now that Stefan permitted himself to gossip while we consumed Yorkshire buck and green salad.

"His Highness was most distressed and surprised by your unexpected departure," Stefan said noncommittally. "He was very anxious to follow in order to accompany you, but I was unable to say where you might have gone."

"How fortunate," said Maggie. "What else is new, Stefan?"

Stefan's lips twitched slightly. "Nothing precisely *new* Doctor Corwin. Merely life as usual." We had, it appeared, missed numerous social events—a swimming party at the Goulenkis, a formal dinner to unveil Mr. Penberthy's portrait of madame ("It was highly praised!"). Monsieur Foucald had arrived in advance of his usual vacation for special conferences with His Highness. The smugglers' road had been cleaned, it would now be safe if we wanted to repeat the drive by ourselves.

The big event had been a games afternoon hosted by His Highness the previous Sunday, at which Mr. Penberthy had triumphed in every department—tennis, croquet, miniature golf, and archery. Kai had apparently licked everyone in the house, plus making high score at bridge after dinner and doing nicely when (Stefan coughed discreetly) late guests arrived at Villa Miranda for midnight supper, and uh, poker.

"Strip, of course, followed by a breakfast swim party?" Maggie commented blandly. "It sounds exactly the sort of orgy I am happy to have missed."

Stefan's lips twitched. "I fear your sleep might have been disturbed," he agreed, "although the following day was unusually quiet."

"Sleeping it off, were they? Where are they now? You said everyone was away."

"Gone to Tekirdag—that is a summer place in Turkey," Stefan explained. "Monsieur Foucald went with His Highness, they left this morning. I don't know when they plan to return."

I could have said, "Not until Mr. Penberthy has exhausted the artistic possibilities," but the major point was that Dresnatinko was temporarily deserted. In fact, Stefan delicately indicated as much and was most persuasively insistent that we should take a breathing spell before our next trip. I knew Maggie was itching to get back to her book. "Why not?" I asked. "I can write up my notes and be fresh to start whenever you hit a good stopping point."

Privately I felt sure that neither Kai nor Anya would be coming back any time soon, and if Boris showed up we'd leave at once. For two days all was peace and quiet. Maggie worked and said it was going well. I went over my notes and discovered they really were shaping into something, which led to a long outline for Wells, Atherton. In between, we swam in the Dresnatinko pool and drove down the smugglers road. Danae produced breakfast and lunch, her small sister washed dishes and made beds amid giggles. All our clothes were laundered, cleaned, pressed, mended, and neatly hung on scented padded hangers.

On the third day I took myself around the miniature golf course with not too bad a score and tried the archery butts. I was awfully out of practice, even puffing slightly, but it came back to me, and finally I was getting inside the middle ring, working up to a bull's-eye. My closest shot was still quivering when a second arrow landed neatly beside it. I swung around, throbbing with fright, but it was only Zaro Ionascu standing behind me and smiling cockily. He came forward, hand outstretched. "Miss Quain, I see you are a veritable Artemis! How do you do? Good to see you again."

"And you, Mr. Ionascu—but compared to me, you are a veritable Apollo."

He laughed and shook his head modestly. "No, a lucky shot, that's all. Are you tired, or shall we make a match?"

"With pleasure, but I'm not up to you."

"Well, let us see, I suspect you are better than you think."

For half an hour we worked out, ending with a complete sweep for him. A servant materialized to put away bows and retrieve arrows, while we went back to the house. I wondered whether his *petite amie* was once more in Villa Rosa, but apparently not. This visit was for some other reason, and he was decidedly unhappy to find no one at home. In fact, he had expected to see Gyorgy.

"I missed him in Paris, and I had the impression he was here, but"—he shrugged resignedly—"one never knows where Gyorgy is. Annoying to have my trip for nothing. I shall wait a few days on the chance." He smiled at me politely. "Shall we have another competition tomorrow, Miss Quain?"

"With pleasure, if you can stand it and if Doctor Corwin doesn't need me."

With Zaro's arrival, I had plenty of mild amusement, inspired (surprisingly) by Stefan. Apparently, Mr. Zaro was considered safe company for Miss Quain. I found him very likeable, and so did Maggie. He could always beat me at the butts, but I could usually beat him at tennis, and Maggie trounced us both at croquet. "You don't mind delaying Thessalonike, do you?" she asked.

"Not at all. Better for you to make hay while the sun shines."

The days drifted by very pleasantly. Mine is the white skin that doesn't tan easily, but Danae oiled me from head to toe every day, and gradually I turned a light toast color. Zaro was black in two sessions at the pool, not that he was underfoot every second like Boris. Sometimes he was there, sometimes he wasn't—or he'd excuse himself to work in the study. Apparently he was handling his business by telephone, and he had no objection to talking about it.

Zaro was Gyorgy's partner, in charge of real estate and small business operations. Boris took care of shipping interests and export-import. He was not a partner, and while Zaro didn't say so, he obviously had no high opinion of Boris. It was equally obvious that he was very attached to Gyorgy, who was the mastermind for the Ionascu tribe. And it was a tribe! There were elderly aunts and uncles, dozens of cousins, three sisters with numerous progeny, as well as all sorts of relatives by marriage—and all of them, even in-laws of in-laws, were part of the Ionascu empire. Either they had jobs or they were sleeping partners and titular heads of this and that, but the mainspring was Gyorgy.

I was sincerely thrilled and admiring, which pleased Zaro immensely. "I hope very much you will meet my brother. You will enjoy knowing each other, I feel sure."

Well, I was hoping Gyorgy would turn up too—one reason I was in no hurry to leave for Thessalonike. When there were faint but unmistakable sounds of an arrival the next day while we were all enjoying *mezethakia* by the pool, I had a definite leap in the pulse. Zaro set aside his glass and got up eagerly, half-sighing with relief—but the figure tripping toward us was feminine. Unquestionably, Rosa had arrived.

Maggie flashed a warning glance at me and got up swiftly. "Rosa, my dear, how pleasant to see you. I hadn't hoped for you before August." I was on my feet, poised to run for my life, while she went forward for an affectionate embrace—but it appeared Rosa was not after me. She was all smiles and cordiality, enchanted to meet Miss Quain, all but kissing me for taking such good care of our beloved Maggie. I sensed a tiny wariness in her dark eyes while she was holding my hand and softly patting my cheek. She must be wondering whether I knew of her visit to the apartment, but I gave nothing away.

She wasn't interested in me, anyhow. She dropped my hand and fluttered toward her husband, cooing endearments. Her rapture was not returned. Zaro's face was black angry. When she was about to precipitate herself on his chest, he stepped back behind the chair. "What are you doing here?" he demanded.

Rosa made a graceful recovery, but her eyes were frightened. "Oh, it was hot and tiresome in Paris."

"Paris? You said you were going to Montreux."

"Yes, but that was even more boring, darling, and they said you were here—as well as dear Maggie—"

"'They'?" he interrupted. "Who is 'they'?"

Rosa shrugged. "Someone in your office."

"Who did you speak to? Not Rouget?"

"Well, no, she was out, or is she on vacation?" Rosa said, pacifically. "But the operator said you'd called from Dresnatinko and were probably still here. She hadn't heard to the contrary, so I thought I'd join you. Surprise!"

"Quite," Zaro agreed grimly. "How long do you mean to stay?"

"As long as you like, dearest. If only you'd told me you could get away! There I sat, killing time in that dreary Montreux, when I might have been here with

176

you," Rosa mourned dramatically.

She's talking too much, I thought; yet I had a reluctant sympathy for her. Whatever the situation between them, even if (based on Maggie's original summation) Rosa had finally overreached herself with possessiveness, I thought she hadn't expected quite such implacability. Not that Zaro said anything, but his very restraint before his wife's guests was indicative of a major battle to come.

Stefan had emerged with replenishments for us and a glass for Rosa. Perforce we sat down to finish our drinks in a pretence of normality. Zaro said nothing. Rosa was unnerved and covering with animated queries about Maggie's trip. Maggie carried the ball with an occasional assist from me. Rosa proposed half a dozen sights Maggie must on no account miss, we would all go together, how delightful! "You have not seen Sounion? And there is a charming drive from Kalkis to Karystos, you must not miss this. Why do we not go tomorrow, Zaro?"

Maggie cut in swiftly, "We had planned on leaving for Thessalonike. Perhaps when we return, if you are still here, Rosa." She finished her drink and glanced at me. "Siri, are you ready?"

Rosa was in favor of our staying to dine, but Maggie was firm. We rose, shook hands, expressed gratitude, and retreated in good order, abandoning Rosa to her fate. "Whew!" said Maggie when we got back to Blondel. "We were supposed to be eating with Zaro. You'd better tell Stefan."

"It won't be necessary," I told her. "If you think he doesn't know trouble when he sees it . . . Wow! What d'you suppose is going on?"

"Fence mending," Maggie said tersely, walking into our villa. "Good evening, Danae. I think we would like dinner in an hour." She eyed me expressionlessly. "Shall we have another drink on the terrace or take a walk?"

"Why not both? There's a lookout spot halfway down the cliff. Change your shoes, and when we get back we'll want a drink."

She puffed a bit and needed a steady hand here and there, but she declared the effort was worthwhile. "I've been thinking," she announced when she'd got her breath, "and I'm afraid Rosa changes things, Siri. After all, she did arrange the whole trip for me. I don't particularly like the girl, and we seem to be squarely in the middle of private Ionascu problems, but I believe we'd better wait another day. Stay quietly to ourselves, see what develops. It may blow over"—she sounded dubious—"in which case, I ought to be here for the reconciliation. Can you amuse yourself?"

"Of course, and I think you're right to be at hand, but something says this one is going to blow not over but up."

Maggie sighed. "Yes, I got that impression too. I wonder what in hell she's done, silly bitch—something major this time."

"Oh, definitely. He's absolutely got the whip hand, you can see that. Why aren't there any children? It's usually the first thing that sort of woman does to make the noose binding."

"Yes, I'd have thought Rosa would reproduce at once—and if she'd got a boy, that'd be the end of it," Maggie agreed. "Maybe she's got an infantile uterus or

178

something. I don't know her all that well. Let's go back. . . ."

There was neither sight nor sound of Zaro and Rosa next day. Maggie pounded her typewriter; I sunned on the terrace and wrote a batch of "wish you were heres" and took them to the local post office for lack of anything to do. I came back to restrained turmoil. "Thank heaven you're here!" Maggie said distractedly. "I'm sorry, Siri, but so is everyone else, including Boris, and we're expected for a swim party with poolside buffet—but it's only tonight. We'll leave for Thessalonike first thing tomorrow."

"Don't worry, it's easy enough when there's a crowd. Anya's back too?"

"I don't know who's here. Rosa called to invite us, but when Danae brought back the laundry, she said His Highness had returned. I'm sorry, Siri," she said again.

"Oh, it may be rather fun. Aren't you dying to see if Rosa's pulled it off?"

"Yes, but I don't think she has," Maggie said, unexpectedly. "I think we're wanted to run interference and give her a breathing spell. Anyway, we're going to be late."

The poolside was thronged when we arrived, likewise the pool. Rosa, clad in a leopard-spotted bikini, was febrile in her greetings. She was still talking too much, so the problem was not solved. Zaro was, if anything, more top dog than yesterday, although he waved to us heartily from the other end of the pool. There were endless introductions. At last I met the Goulenkis, who were as placid as the ripe olives they resembled, and a dozen other neighbors, family friends. Our Man in Athens was waving from the middle of the pool. His wife was stretched on a chaise longue in the far corner.

Beside her was Kai, attentively leaning to light a cigarette, and beside me with a shout of delight was Boris. "Siri, *duzhenka!*" He swept me into a bear hug, turning me discreetly away from the interested gaze of other guests and murmuring reproachfully between nibbly kisses on my cheek. "How could you do this to me? To vanish overnight, to leave no word of your schedule? Don't you know I'd have come to be with you, no matter how dull the trip?"

"Yes," I said ingenuously. "That's why I didn't leave word." Then I pushed him into the pool.

I had to go with him, of course—he had me firmly locked against him—but my wraparound was washable. I wasn't so sure of his slacks. He wasn't either, and when we came up spluttering, by the look on his face I thought it best to make tracks for the nearest exit steps. Boris came after me, surprisingly fast considering his wet clothes. A ring of guests crowded to the pool edge, shouting encouragements in six languages. I'd got the buttons loose on my dress, but I knew I'd never beat him to the steps—not when his prestige was at stake. He was already grasping for the hem of my skirt, while I thrashed ahead frantically . . . and clear above the excited laughter, Kai's voice rolled across the pool, "Ten to one the girl gets away from him!"

"Done, for a thousand drachmas!" someone yelled, and the place went wild. All I heard was Kai's bet. At ten to one it was three thousand bucks, but he'd only said, "The girl *gets away*." I let the dress slip from my shoulders as Boris grasped the fabric. I swerved aside and did a racing turn against the pool wall, and before Boris could disentangle himself from the floating wet cloth, I'd streaked across to the opposite steps and pulled myself up to the patio tiles.

Then the place really went wild. Someone thrust a drink into my hand, people cheered, and Kai's eyes were sparkling wickedly. "Serendipitous Siri," he said softly, handing me a cigarette, "how shall we split the profits?"

"Buy me an emerald nose ring," I said, pushing past him to go down the pool steps and extend both drink and cigarette to Boris. His face was ugly with humiliation . . . no point to a public scene. I knew exactly what he'd say, I said it first. "Forgive, dear, darling Boris? I'm a mean, tricky little witch, but princes can afford to be generous, no?" I gave him my best smile, and reluctantly he decided to play, although I knew he'd be thinking of some way to get even.

For the duration of the party I let him handle our romance as he pleased, and I must admit he did it well. The impression created was of a private running gag between us, a joke we both understood meant nothing, an act we were putting on to amuse the bystanders. He was going a bit farther than at the Embassy ball but still leaving room for doubt of serious intentions.

Eventually the party rearranged itself. Some people left, a few others dropped in for a drink before going on to other parties. Older people got dressed and settled for bridge after dinner, younger people ate in bathing suits and lay about the floodlit pool. It was all very informal, great good fun. Someone suggested tennis, someone else suggested golf, there was a general move toward the games field, and Zaro said, "Siri, shall we challenge a team for archery?"

I swung about to say yes, and across the pool, Rosa was on a chaise longue with Boris leaning forward. She turned her head, looking up at him—and there was an almost audible click in my mind. I knew that smile. It's the one Sagan used for a novel title—it's the one any married woman can instantly interpret, the one that says, "Mmmmm, *good!* Let's do it again!"

Rosa and Boris were lovers.

"Siri?" Zaro recalled me.

"Yes, I'd love it. . . ." I got up slowly, my eyes still on the couple opposite, deducing, evaluating. Not a new *affaire* . . . something so long and well-established that Rosa could accept Boris's flirtation with me in perfect confidence, something so long that there was need for a red herring. Did Zaro know? Was that the cause of his cold fury when she arrived? No—or he wouldn't be jovially hailing Boris to join us now. Zaro had no suspicion, it was something else between him and Rosa. Had she come to see him—or perhaps really to see Boris? She'd been in Montreux, a scant distance from Geneva, where Boris would normally have been at business, but instead he'd been at Dresnatinko, and Rosa had followed, not knowing Zaro was here. Did Boris want out, was that the fence she was mending?

No . . . by his satisfied expression when he turned to wave at Zaro, and by Rosa's happy animation, there was no slightest shade of misunderstanding between them. In fact, they were two against the world. Then why was it important for Rosa to hang on to Zaro?— and it obviously was. She was being honey-sweet, doing everything possible to convince Zaro she adored him, and Maggie was right. It wasn't working, aside from making Zaro nervous.

He was off his game at first, and I wasn't any better, because Boris had dragged Kai along for his teammate, which automatically outclassed me at once. Kai is a dead shot at anything—the only person who occasionally beats him is the Aged P. Whatever training old Marcus skipped was provided by the U.S. Navy, and aside from Kai's cups and medals, I have the most revolting collection of Coney Island prizes in existence.

So the instant Kai fluffed a couple of bull's-eyes that reduced their score, I knew it was deliberate. He and Boris were going to win, but *kind* of Kai to make it less of a clobber. Not quite so kind to say the instant we finished, "How about Americans against Greeks? Come on, Siri."

"I am not Greek," Boris said stiffly.

"All right," Kai returned affably. "Americans against barbarians, if you insist on accuracy."

"Shall we make a small wager?" Boris asked silkily.

"Why not? I'll bet you my winnings at the pool, when Siri got away from you. Good enough?"

"*I* will bet on Siri," Zaro announced before Boris could say anything. "Never mind if I bet against myself! A thousand drachmas I've taught her enough this past week to place all her shots within the center ring."

"Done!" Boris said promptly, picking up his bow and stalking off to stand beside Zaro, while I went shakily toward Kai.

183

"Dammit, now you've done it," I muttered.

"Yes, haven't I?" Kai agreed cheerfully. "Very neat, that touch about the barbarians, wasn't it?"

"He'll never forgive you, and he's perfectly capable of putting an arrow 'accidentally' through your painting hand."

"Why, what a low opinion you have of your intended." Kai took the arrows from a servant panting up from the butts, chose one, and nocked it carefully.

"He's *not* my intended!" I raged, nocking my own arrow while the servant went on to Boris and Zaro. "If you can't tell a prop when you see one . . . !"

"Why should you need a prop?" Kai sounded amazed. "Not trying to make me regret what I've lost, are you?"

"Oh, come off it," I said impatiently. "You were never jealous of me in your life, nor needed to be—and what the hell are you doing here? I thought you were through with Dresnatinko and Anya, off to pastures new."

"So I was, but then I decided to come back—and already you've made money for me."

"Which you're going to lose, like a fool. What possessed you? You know I'm not in this league."

"You're better than you think, particularly when you're mad. Are you mad, Sulfurous Siri?"

"Mad enough to call the whole thing off, if you're going to stand there sniping at me."

"That's mad enough. Now think whom you most dislike in the world—Mao Tse-tung, Boris, the Russian Ambassador to the U.N., Adam Clayton Powell . . . me . . . and that's us on the target. Spit in our collective eyes, eh?" He turned, drew back his arm casually, and

184

the arrow was quivering dead center. Simultaneously, two other arrows hit their targets, Zaro's a bit wide and Boris's just tipping the bull's-eye. "Come on, babe—for King Kong and Uncle Sam," Kai remarked quietly.

I needed all the time allowed for my shot, but I got it within the center ring. "You can do better, hon. You're still pulling to the right." Kai readied for his second shot. "For Saint George and the dragon!"

Involuntarily I chuckled. Kai always dedicated his arrows; so did his grandfather, and they always outdid each other in absurdities. "For Sara Crewe, little lost princess," I said dramatically, and landed on the left rim, but still inside. I'd completely forgotten Boris and Zaro, I was caught by auld lang syne, thinking of ridiculous dedications. "For Tobermory . . . for Fafnir . . . for Zarathustra. . . ." Kai matched me, and we grew helpless with laughter but still scored. In the end they came out a quarter point ahead, no more! But all my shots were inside, so Kai's money went to Boris and passed directly to Zaro—who insisted upon presenting it to me. "You are my best pupil," he declared, kissing my hand gallantly. "No, no, you must take it. A woman is always entitled to the spoils, and I should not know what to buy for you. You must get something for yourself."

"An emerald nose ring," Kai suggested, smoothly turning away. "Anya—you want me for bridge, forgive?"

Boris had won. No matter how slim the margin, the winning was all. The rest of the evening was pleasant smiles, hugs, intimate murmurs, until we ended at

Miranda for midnight supper and swim. I knew Maggie would put aside her book to get me out of Dresnatinko, and I lacked one road map. I didn't say when we were going, but I asked Zaro if Dresnatinko would have the map.

"Yes, but Boris will have it also, in the study." He led me into the villa and along the hall, but the door was locked. Zaro clucked with mild annoyance, fumbled in various pockets, and found a key. "Boris is inclined to lock up during a party," he chuckled. "Occasionally the wrong young lady manages to pass out in his bedroom." The door swung back, and Zaro reached to turn on a lamp that disclosed a small paneled room lined with shelves. "The maps are here." He walked across, pulled out a shelf file, and rapidly thumbed through it. "These are what you want, and here"—he picked a couple of books—"are guide books on what to see. Boris won't mind lending them."

He took everything to an untidy desk, turned on another lamp, and was about to go through them with me, when there was a shout from outside. "Zaro? Where the devil is he? Zaro, we need you to judge a diving contest."

Zaro raised his eyebrows. "You will excuse me? I think I'd better go, or they'll all pile in here and make hash of Boris's papers."

"Of course—go along. I shan't be a minute." I bent over the maps . . . and glimpsed a typed sheet. Zaro had disarranged the covering papers. I could see a corner, the name "Siri . . ." Delicately I raised the overlay, and it was a letter from Bess. It was dated two weeks back, it was short and in code. It was the letter I should have found when we returned from Corinth,

186

when I'd wondered at hearing nothing.

What was it doing here? Despite a quiver of uneasiness, I smiled grimly to myself. If Gizmo had had trouble with Squarawb, it was bound to defeat Svishtov. But why should Boris want to supervise my correspondence? The pool party was in full swing . . . chance I could decipher before I was missed? I looked at the date of Bess's letter, at the desk calendar— Wednesday. She'd made it plain code, no embellishments.

In ten minutes I had it. His Excellency admitted nothing but was deeply disturbed to discover Maggie's location. I remembered that Elspeth had complained she couldn't get anything out of Maggie, couldn't find the name in the alumni list. At the time I had thought it was self-preservation from any more of Elspeth's interfering ideas for helping Maggie enjoy her trip. If George had known, evidently he would have moved heaven and earth to stop us from coming here—and I heartily wished he had known!

But now we were here—and something serious must be afoot. "H. E. advises an immediate boat trip and hopes you will return direct to Paris thereafter. He says late summer in Greece is likely to be uncomfortably hot. Draw on him for funds, if needed."

Carefully I let the letter lie where it was, turned off the desk light, and was examining the tour guide across the room when Boris came in. If I'd had any doubt of trouble, it was ended with his narrowed eyes and vicious bark, "What are you doing here!"

"Zaro said you had some books on Thessalonike," I faltered ingenuously. "Do you mind lending?"

"How did you get in?" He was standing suspicious

and bristling, his eyes sliding to the desk.

"The door was open," I lied automatically. "Boris, I'm sorry . . . Zaro showed me, but then he had to go back to the pool. I didn't think you'd mind. Oh, I've done everything wrong today," I wailed, "and now you're angry with me again."

Had I pulled it off? Yes, and no. He calmed down, stuffed the book into my hand, and firmly led me to the door. He assured me everything he had was mine, but please (rueful shrug) not unless he was there to find it for me. "Business papers," he sighed, "and I am lost without a secretary. I have my own filing system— unorthodox but it works providing no one touches anything." He was looking at the desk again, but his eyes were fixed on a lower drawer.

"I didn't touch a thing," I assured him earnestly. "I was only with the maps, and Zaro got them out for me. Boris, if you need a secretary, let me help, to show you forgive me?" I knew it was dangerously close to the wind, but it reinforced innocence. He refused, of course, "Siri, *duzhka*—like you to offer, but you are not to be grubbing about when we can be playing in the sun together. No, I won't hear of it! You are not a clerk, *chérie.*" And so on. The door was unobtrusively relocked behind us. We returned to the pool, and I wondered what was in that desk drawer.

Zaro brought me back to Blondel just as Stefan returned with Maggie. We said good nights, Zaro departed, but Stefan quietly escorted us into the villa on the pretext of arranging our breakfast schedule. He didn't ask if we wanted nightcaps, the drinks simply appeared. Maggie kicked off her shoes with a sigh. "Thank you, Stefan. About breakfast—what time would you suggest?"

"Seven o'clock," he replied. "I have taken the liberty of arranging a special trip for you. That is, if you will like to take it, but if it does not please you, it can be canceled." There was something in his voice that made me look at him, and there was no doubt he was conveying something to me.

"Occasionally it is possible for a few guests to join a private boat for Delos. One sails from Marathon about nine in the morning, reaches the island in time for lunch and a view of the antiquities. There is dinner aboard and a moonlight sail home." Stefan's eyes held mine meaningly. "It is a rather . . . special affair, not the ordinary tourist trip. The guests are carefully chosen, one meets unusual travelers of a better class, deeper interest." He shrugged. "In short, when I learned one of these was scheduled for tomorrow, I felt it something you should not miss. If I was presumptuous, please forgive me."

"Not at all, it was most kind of you to think of us," Maggie said, "but we had rather meant to start on our northern trip—"

"We've delayed so long," I put in swiftly, "couldn't we wait another day, Maggie? I—from the way Stefan describes it . . . and we did want to see something of the islands. This seems an exceptional opportunity."

"Does it mean so much? Of course we'll go, in that case," Maggie said kindly. "Give Miss Quain the directions, Stefan, and thank you very much."

"Not at all, Doctor Corwin." Stefan whipped out a piece of paper. "I have written everything down, Miss Quain, but you will have no difficulty. It is only to find the wharf for the *Ariadne,* and if you are delayed, do not worry; she will not sail without you."

No, I thought; *of course she won't.* I had no doubt Gyorgy Ionascu would be on that boat. . . .

XI

I fell asleep full of peace and awoke to yet another problem. Kai had decided to accompany us. Wherever we were going. He had arrived complete with overnight bag simultaneous with breakfast, and before I could get into my clothes, he'd charmed Maggie into innocently explaining the change of plans and inviting him along.

"But will there be room enough?" I asked helplessly. "You know Stefan said it was a special deal not open for everyone. Perhaps there won't be any extra space."

Stefan did look a bit taken aback; then he nodded his head. "It is a good idea. I think Doctor Corwin will be glad of Mr. Penberthy's assistance. The island is rather rocky in some places."

It was a beautiful soft summer day, perfect for sailing. Insensibly, our spirits soared once we were away from Dresnatinko. Kai seemed to have left the snipery behind and was altogether at his best—gay, carefree, natural. He and Maggie got on like childhood friends. I could almost have thought this a day at Marblehead with the Aged P. I felt a bit reckless. *Let* Maggie suspect I'd known Kai before. If she commented, I'd tell her; she wouldn't feel, now, that she had to leave on my account.

Meanwhile it was going to be a good day on a boat with happy companions and Gyorgy to look forward to. I was filled with excitement at seeing him again; yet I didn't know why. An ugly, middle-aged, married Rumanian millionaire whom I'd met only twice—in contrast with the rapscallion charm of my former husband sitting in front of me? Was it delayed adolescence, a teenage crush, or some sort of father substitute? I knew I was going to tell Gyorgy every puzzling thing that had happened; I knew I was turning to him instinctively, confident as a child. *"Now* everything'll be all right, Gyorgy'll tell me what to do."

Had I ever felt that way about Kai? Dimly, I thought perhaps once I had, and Kai had done his best but—face it—he was an artist. Often he couldn't see why there was any difficulty, and when he did, his advice was unrealistic. If it turned out badly, Kai took it as a big joke and told it all over town. "Wait till you hear! How stupid can I be?" He wouldn't understand my sense of danger at Dresnatinko. Anyway, it wasn't his affair. I hadn't even told Maggie anything disturbing after we arrived. I was sorry I'd said anything at all, if it was going to boil down to some messy sex entanglement in Gyorgy's family, but at least I'd get rid of it. Let him handle it, as head of the tribe.

Kai found the wharf, and someone came forward to help us out and take away the car to park. We stood for a moment, eyeing the *Ariadne* with excitement. No doubt she was a beauty—much more than a simple sailing boat. She was as long as the wharf, with three masts. Her paint gleamed white, the furled sails looked

192

blue. The deck was crowded with people in yachting clothes, interspersed with white uniformed crew, and everybody was smiling. "Wow, she's a ruddy tern," Kai said reverently.

"A what?"

I've never known as much as Kai about sailing, but it was Maggie who said unexpectedly, "A three-masted schooner. . . . Let's go aboard."

A small dark man in a dazzling white captain's uniform came forward. "Doctor Corwin, allow me to introduce myself—Captain Andropoulos. It is a pleasure to welcome you." He shook our hands, then led us about and introduced us to various other passengers. As Stefan had said, this was no run-of-the-mill tourist jaunt. We were guests, invited to a private party. Did Gyorgy Ionascu own the *Ariadne?* Apparently not. She belonged to the captain's father, who now left the work to his sons but who still personally accompanied each trip. See, that is the old man . . . over there, in the corner beside the woman in red. Oh, yes, one has always heard of the *Ariadne,* but it is not a matter of buying tickets. One pays in Athens beforehand, but Andropoulos selects his guests.

"It is necessary to be recommended, and there is no settled schedule. It is his personal boat, you see; he goes when and where he chooses. The money is not much, only for the crew. We had hoped last year"—Maggie's informant shrugged sadly—"but there was no recommendation. This year, the Venezuelan Ambassador—his cousin has married into my husband's family, so all is arranged. Through whom do you come, Doctor Corwin?"

Maggie glanced at me. "The American Embassy,"

she said.

Kai was already fraternizing with Captain Andropoulos, we were casting off, slipping forward into the mainstream—and there was no sign of Gyorgy. My heart sank. Had I completely misunderstood Stefan, and this whole trip was only something he'd thought would please by its exclusivity? I fought down tears of disappointment and went to the rail among the other guests, who were exclaiming, "Oh, we're off! Isn't it lovely! What's that over there?"

"Siri! Siri, the *sails!*" Kai's voice rolled over the babble. I swung instinctively to look up . . . and unless I was crazy, Gyorgy Ionascu was in the rigging of the center mast. Then the sails broke, cascading down and out to catch the breeze. They were all shades of blue, bellying proudly so that the *Adriadne* almost seemed to leap forward. The crew was climbing down, grinning like monkeys at the ohs and ahs of the guests. Gyorgy (if it was he) had disappeared, but it was a relief to hope he was aboard—or was it?

The mere fact that he was incognito among the crew implied that any meeting between us was not to be known . . . a conclusion that created a definite *frisson* on my spine. Why was he unable to mingle with the crowd, recognize me with polite surprise—"Miss Quain, didn't we meet at the Granets'?"

I did what I'd be expected to do, made friends here and there, rambled about exploring casually. Maggie was already the center of a delighted group to whom her charm bridged all language barriers. Kai was hovering over Andropoulos at the wheel. I went below to the powder room, poked my nose into various cabins, dawdled about, but there seemed to be *people*

194

everywhere. Had I been deluded, that sailor wasn't Gyorgy—I'd only thought so because I'd been so certain of seeing him? I went on deck again and took a good look. Where could I go that a common seaman might be able to talk to me without creating surprise? That is, if there really were a common seaman anxious to address me. . . .

Aft, behind the wheel. Aside from Kai, no guests were being welcomed there. I went up to the afterbridge. "Having fun, sweetie?"

Kai threw his arm about me joyously, "Marvelous! Isn't she a honey? Andropoulos says I can take her for a bit when we hit open water. Guess what—he knows Robbie Tilden, remember him?"

"The one who waltzes?"

"That's Robbie!" Kai chuckled. "On sea or on land, he waltzes!"

I stood for a few minutes, admiring the view and chatting politely. There were sailors moving back and forth . . . one of them went past us to the stern, where he fussed about with some lines. "May I go aft for a minute? You know how I love watching the wake."

"What? Oh, sure, hon. Captain, where d'you get your sails?"

I made my way aft and a voice said quietly, "Mahootma. Don't look around, please."

"I thought it was you. You can't think how glad I am to see you. What next?" I gazed steadily at the curling foam behind us.

"When we land, there will be a jeep behind the buildings to the left of the wharf. Get into it as unobtrusively as possible."

"Yes. I'll have to tell Maggie—Doctor Corwin—or

she'll worry, but she knows I know you."

"Yes, but no one else, including"—the voice sounded amused—"your handsome husband."

"He isn't, any longer," I protested, but there was no answer except a faint laugh, and when I looked around I was alone. I went forward past Kai and Andropoulos until I came to Maggie. "I'm going to the Ladies'—come with me?"

"I don't mind if I do," she said instantly, and once we were locked in, "Who was that *sale type* you were foregathering with at the stern?"

"That *sale type* is Gyorgy Ionascu," I said tersely, "and we are conferring. Privately. When I find out what we're conferring about, I'll tell you. Meanwhile you are responsible for diverting Kai's attention at landing time, until I vanish."

Maggie's eyebrows rose. "Then what do I tell him?"

"I've gone to do some research, which is why we took the trip, and it's so good he came along to amuse you." I looked at her anxiously. "Sorry, Maggie, but I really must talk to Gyorgy."

Maggie narrowed her eyes. "Something more has happened. I had a hunch there was a reason for today. All right, Siri, I'll take care of Penberthy—but I'll expect a full explanation later, and if I don't like what I hear, we're leaving tomorrow. That's flat."

"I don't think it's anything like that. I think it's some sort of private family mess, and as soon as I pass it on, Mr. Ionascu will take care of it."

"If it were anything simple, there wouldn't be all this cloak and dagger."

*   *   *

I got away easily enough, after all. Kai was absorbed in the mechanics of furling the sails, and I slid across the gangplank while his back was turned and walked along with a group until I found a place to duck between the buildings. The jeep was there, but as I hopped in, I glimpsed that scuttling motion—someone observing. I was frankly scared to death. Should I pretend I'd noticed nothing, or was Gyorgy in danger? Should I try to warn him? I was still shaking when he calmly got behind the wheel. "What's the matter?"

"There was someone," I whispered urgently, "watching. . . ."

Gyorgy laughed. "Marko," he said, starting the engine. "He is Stefan's brother, and after you got away from him in Trieste, he is afraid to take his eye off you."

"You mean he's on our side?" I asked confusedly. "At least, I guess that's not the way to put it, exactly, but I wish Stefan had told me. I kept seeing someone watching me, you know. It was a bit unnerving."

"Poor Marko! He takes his instructions so literally," Gyorgy chuckled, "but I had no one else to send at that moment."

"Why should you send anyone?"

"Because you did put it correctly—there are two sides, and you have innocently got in the middle. If I had had any idea before you left Paris, I would have found some way to stop you," he said soberly, "but it did not occur to me you could be involved—and later was too late. If only you had not changed your route! When I had your letter from Trieste, it should have been possible to intercept you in Tiranë. Instead, Marko confesses he has lost you at Split.

"My dear Miss Quain—but I am thinking of you

197

now as Siri, I hope you do not object, but"—he laughed
helplessly—"you can have *no* idea of the difficulties
you created by going straight through! Embassies have
been hunting for you, Greek Immigration had to be
asked where you presented your passports, His
Excellency in Paris was insisting on alerting Interpol
. . . and at the same time, everything must be kept top-
secret because we have only begun to collect facts, have
no idea how far the affair extends."

"Gosh, I'm sorry. Bess said the Ambassador was in a
flap when he found where we'd gone, but wouldn't
admit anything . . . and at first I thought Maggie was a
secret agent," I laughed, "and all the time she was
thinking perhaps *I* was."

"How much have you told her?" he asked quickly.

"Nothing, recently. I didn't want to unsettle her
while she's writing her book—and of course I thought
it was only awkward, not serious, but I gather it is?"

"Very," he said emphatically. "You are going to tell
me everything, Siri, and you will return to Dresnatinko
only long enough to pack your bags tonight. Stefan will
take you to his family farmhouse up the coast, and the
Ariadne will pick you up tomorrow night for an
indefinite cruise in the islands. Marko will go with you.
I cannot spare Stefan."

I was more and more uneasy by his decisive tone.
"Shouldn't we just go back to Paris, or even home?
Maggie will accept any official story, even if it means
losing the trip—but couldn't she come back later?"

"I hope she will, I like the look of her," he said, "but
at present, there must be no major alteration in what
are known to be her plans. Nothing to cause
uncertainty. Do you understand?"

"Yes. They'll go to ground and recheck all fences."

He laughed. "A truly succinct American way to put it—but you're right, although this particular business is past the point of no return. That much we know—they can't retreat. But for just that reason, they won't hesitate to shoot first and ask questions later. Everything must appear normal, and the devil of it is, we haven't enough facts, we don't know how much time there is or where to look."

"I just thought, 'If I were a horse, where would I go? And then I went and looked, and there I was,'" I murmured.

"What?"

"Oh, the old gag about the little boy finding a lost horse the whole village was searching for," I said absently. "I suppose you can't tell me exactly what's involved—aside from Boris, which means ships, which explains Foucald, but I don't see where Rosa fits unless Zaro's involved, and *that,*" I said vigorously, "I don't believe for a moment!" We jerked to a stop above a small deserted cove. "Oh, is this where we're going? How lovely!"

"Isn't it?" Gyorgy's voice was tinged with amusement. "No, I can't tell you what's involved—but I begin to think I shall not have to." He fished in the rear and brought out a picnic basket. "We will have lunch, and you will tell me why you include Rosa, if you please."

"Because she's . . ." I stopped, appalled.

"She's . . .?" Gyorgy prompted, holding my arm insistently. "Never mind tact, Siri—this is no time for it. What is Rosa?"

"I *think* she's Boris's mistress," I whispered uncomfortably, "but please—I've no right to say so, it's only

199

an impression."

His hand gripped me painfully, his eyes blazing while I trembled for my unguarded tongue. Of all things to say to a Slavic temperament, to impugn his sister-in-law's morals on no evidence at all! Slowly, his face closed in speculation. "My God—if you are right . . . !" he muttered, releasing my arm and fingering his chin with a tiny smile. "It would explain . . . but who could have guessed? You are right, Zaro is not involved—and if he'd had the least smell of this . . ." Gyorgy threw back his head, guffawing. "Oh, Siri, no matter what happens, if you are right, Zaro will be in your debt forever! So will we all." He pushed me briskly from the jeep. "Come, I can scarcely wait!"

I was thankful he'd taken it this way, but with the hint of a new angle, I could scarcely wait to hear. We picked our way down a rocky path, and Gyorgy set down the picnic basket and neatly spread a thin blanket to sit on. "Here we are!"

I looked at the metal compartment of ice cubes and bottles, the section with sandwich packets neatly fitted among plastic containers, the fruit tucked into corners. "Stefan?"

Gyorgy's eyes twinkled. "The ice was replenished on the boat."

I sipped a perfect Scotch sour and looked dreamily at the waves lapping the coarse sand. "Is it nice to be rich?"

"Yes, at moments like these," he said reflectively, "but otherwise it is often more trouble than it is worth."

"I expect rich people simply have rich problems."

Gyorgy's shoulders quivered with silent laughter. "My dear Siri, you have the most devastating clarity of mind!" He refilled our glasses, gave me a cigarette, and settled down comfortably. "Begin at the beginning, please, and tell me where we shall look for our horses."

"Tekirdag," I said, "and the lower drawer of the desk in Boris's study—except it'll be empty now. Oh, dear, I wish I'd known."

Gyorgy slopped half his glass convulsively. "Tekirdag?" he echoed in a strangled voice. "No, never mind now—begin. . . ."

"Well, apparently we were seen at the Ritz," I said obediently, "and they wanted that slip of paper you gave me with your address."

"Did they get it?" he asked tensely, and sighed with relief when I shook my head. "Go on."

It took the best part of an hour, because he wanted every detail, every word, and particularly my personal impressions until I simply reported, mincing no words. If he could take Rosa's link with Boris, he could take Kai's dalliance with Anya and Zaro's *petite amie* at Villa Rosa. I couldn't tell what he thought, although it was making some sort of pattern. He didn't miss a trick, either. Repeatedly he asked, "You said earlier . . . Why do you think now . . . ?"

"It looks different once you link Rosa to Boris," I explained. "We'd never heard of him, you see. Maggie's explanation was possible—a detective had confused you with Zaro. On their side, they had only an unidentified girl to whom you gave a paper, and before they could get to me, I was gone. Bess rattled Rosa into giving her right name. That was a bad slip, but at that point she didn't know I was traveling with Maggie.

"I suppose she alerted Boris to send over from Geneva to Grenoble, but all the man knew was Quain.

If he reported I was with Doctor Corwin, it would mean nothing to Boris—until someone said Doctor Corwin was at Dresnatinko. It might even have been Stefan," I said, "if Boris phoned and asked who was around. Then everything fitted *their* suspicions, but *I* was still wide of the mark. I couldn't imagine why he was making such a dead set at me, forcing Anya to be sweet, and underfoot all the time."

"I thought it was because I didn't swoon with delight. Now I see he was keeping tabs on me as a possible agent of yours. He was very agitated when we skipped to Corinth; yesterday he kept getting the conversation back to our trip—making sure we really went, I suppose. Two days ago Rosa showed up. That was when I thought we'd been wrong in the beginning, but it still didn't register with me that it was because it *was* you and not Zaro, you see?"

"Actually, until this minute there was an alternate explanation for everything," I finished. "Zaro miffed with Rosa, Boris making a play for me—I thought it was a cover for their affair."

Gyorgy nodded. "Yes, as you say, now it looks different."

"Why did you give me the address?" I asked. "What did you expect to happen?"

"Nothing like this," he said emphatically. "I'd only just stumbled on it, I'd no idea of the magnitude. No, I realized you must be Rosa's guests, and if Anya were here, you might be made uncomfortable. She detests Rosa. So do we all, but I didn't want you embarrassed. In the event of unpleasantness, I would have informed Anya that you were my guests, that's all. I must tell you I trembled later! If Boris got that address"—he

202

shrugged—"all the shreds of evidence we've painfully accumulated would be destroyed."

"I see. Well, I burned it, but I put it in Bess's address book," I said troubled, "and Maggie knew that was the 'paper.' Neither will mention it. I told Bess it was E for Emergency, and when it turned out Anya was here, I asked Maggie not to say I'd ever met you." I laughed suddenly. "She asked me, very seriously, if I were having an *affaire* with you, I remember now."

Gyorgy eyed me obliquely. "If I were ten years younger I should certainly try to change your answer," he remarked, "and then there would be a duel. That husband of yours is a dangerous man, my dear. One wonders how you ever got away from him."

"Other way around," I said clearly, examining the lunch box while my cheeks cooled. "He wanted the divorce. I thought he meant to marry that model, but it seems to have fallen through. Shall we have something to eat?"

"By all means." He glanced at his watch. "There is plenty of time. Go back to Rosa's arrival, please."

"Maggie said she was 'fence mending,' and she didn't think it was going to work, but she thought—because Rosa invited her—she ought to stay another day, for politeness." Again I went over yesterday's party. I thought Gyorgy was trying to identify possible confederates, but there was only Foucald, whom I'd scarcely noticed.

"One doesn't," Gyorgy observed. "It's his most valuable characteristic."

Again I described Rosa and Boris at the pool.

"Never mind that, it is conjecture, Siri. This may be vital, not merely to Zaro but to the world." When I sat

203

stupefied, he smiled. "I will tell you a little. There are always those who defy embargos on strategic materials. Recently it has emerged that some of my ships are concerned in this. I am . . . tarred with my own brush." He shrugged. "I've been known to be very close to the wind, so it was a while before anyone said, 'But *this* does not sound like Gyorgy.' Nor is it. I will, I have, destroyed competitors, but I've never failed to cooperate with governments. Most of all, the United Nations. Finally some clever chap pointed this out, a casual question was dropped in my ear, and now my honor is at stake. Can you believe a robber baron has honor?"

"Oh definitely. You mean Boris is shipping things to Rhodesia, and you'd rather he didn't use your ships. Maggie said it was going to be cloak and dagger. What a pity I can't tell her!"

"You're . . . a bit frightening," he murmured. "I never said. . . ."

"I'm sorry," I said in a small voice. "Perhaps it's Mainland China or Hanoi, but you did say United Nations, and it's exactly the sort of thing Boris would do. I shouldn't think he'd ever thought of anything in his life but the glory of being Prince Svishtov, and when you consider," I added indignantly, "that the Balkans are simply crawling with titles, you wonder how they can possibly take themselves seriously."

Gyorgy choked on his sandwich. "My dear Siri, what a scalpel you carry! Oh, don't apologize, you're right. Anya brought him up that way, it's why she married me—to give him money to be a prince. He's never forgiven me for making him work for it."

"Then why is she afraid of him to the point of hatred?"

"I didn't know she was." He was startled. "Why do you say so?"

"I don't know," I said slowly, "but it's more than doting motherhood. I don't think she even likes him, but when he says frog, she jumps. Hasn't Stefan told you?"

"He says Boris is abominably rude to his mother, that's all. This is most unexpected."

"I may be wrong," I said uncomfortably. "It might have been momentary annoyance. I'm sure, if she thought for a second he was serious about me, she'd break it up at once."

"Yes," he said absently. "She was once hopeful of getting Margaret of England for him."

"You're kidding!"

"Not in the least. The best was never good enough for Boris, but perhaps it has changed. Have a sandwich and let me think." I found thin-slivered lamb tasting delicately of orange and ginger, and we ate silently. "You see," he said suddenly, "one *immediately* assumes Boris, naturally, but he hasn't the money. He never has had, not even by gambling, and this sort of thing is entirely cash. Obviously. Where did he get it, if he is the principal? Anya, of course—but there is not the slightest irregularity in her accounts. We thought of pawned or duplicated jewels—everything is there, and there are no substitutions. It might still have been the beginning—her jewels in escrow to cover a first cargo and the profits sufficient to finance the second, and so on . . . but now you imply Boris has some hold over his mother."

Gyorgy leaned his head back against the rock thoughtfully. "If so, he would never have gone to her

205

for any such assistance. It would cancel his hold, whatever it is. I know Anya." He smiled faintly. "Boris might get a few hundred, even a thousand, on the pretext of gambling debts—but here we are dealing with fifty or a hundred thousand, and no matter what his excuse, no matter if she were willing to give it, Anya would have verified. You see?"

"Could he have forced her to help him?" I asked hesitantly.

"Never," Gyorgy said positively. "Whatever this secret hold, it could never be so illegal as what Boris is doing. I don't say she might not have agreed to help, but only to be free of him—yet you say she is still obedient. That is very important, because the alternative is someone higher up, and this does not fit his personality. If he's concerned, he is the boss. I am convinced of this. There is the minor chance he merely accepted presents for knowing nothing. I think it unlikely. Even if it were legally in the clear, Boris would not take bribes from underlings. Still, it was all we had, we've worked on those lines—but Rosa would explain everything."

"I didn't know she had any money."

"Her marriage settlement," he said tersely. "Half a million dollars, and the stock exchange is her hobby. She cannot touch the principal, but she's always done well with her income. She's amazingly shrewd at picking up tips. I don't doubt by now that she's got a Swiss account, as well as Boris."

"That fits," I murmured. "If she's money mad, she wouldn't ask questions, and as long as her lover produced results, he'd be the kingpin. I wonder where they got the idea. From a captain, I shouldn't wonder;

Boris wouldn't speak to anything less. Have you got a few old-timers who'd be wistful over the good old days of skullduggery?"

"I give up," he said, helplessly. "Of *course* the captains of the boats involved are part of my original crews. I'd even swear it was Sulieman Reza who suggested it. The first shipments were only picking up extra change for private pockets—a cargo loaded and delivered quickly during a week when the ship was, on our official records, lying at anchor, waiting the official return load. So long as it was food, clothing, household goods"—he shrugged—"it was merely illicit use of my ship to make ten or twenty thousand dollars that wouldn't appear on any balance sheet. A present to the harbor official, a cut for the ship's officers . . . you see?"

"Innocent bilking of the Ionascu company, which could well afford it," I nodded.

"Yes, but then it became embargo materials. The crews were reassigned so constantly that they can't swear to anything, and the officers are afraid for their lives." His jaw tightened. "They killed Reza before he reached me—and Foucald's secretary, poor woman. Supposedly an accident, but it was too opportune—for them." He sighed. "Well . . . finished with yesterday?"

"Zaro let me into Miranda's study for guide books. He was called away. I was under the desk light, and there was a letter to me from Bess, half-hidden. Fortunately in Squarawb, but I don't know if that's good or bad," I said anxiously.

"This is code? He's an expert cryptographer." Gyorgy frowned.

"He'll never break this—even Gizmo sweated."

I explained, while Gyorgy muttered, "Good heavens!" incredulously.

"It's only a sort of private shorthand for us. Anyway, if Boris had broken it, he'd have replaced the letter and chanced I wouldn't notice the delay."

"Probably. Did he know you saw it?"

"Doubtful. I hadn't moved anything. He was much more worried about that bottom drawer and about finding me there in the first place. I didn't say Zaro had a key. . . ."

"Good! The estate has a master system. Stefan, Zaro, and I can open any lock, but Boris is unaware of this." Gyorgy smiled grimly. "At one time he had new locks fitted throughout. As it happened, the locksmith is a relative of Stefan's. The new locks were made to accord with the master system"—he shrugged—"and now everybody is happy." He grinned at my snort of laughter. "I must think. Would you like to swim? The beach is quite safe."

The water was delicious. After a while, Gyorgy plunged in beside me. He was a magnificent, strong swimmer, a born water baby—but so is Kai. It was fun, but too reminiscent of Marblehead. "We must dry off and make ready to return. Let us see if the final drinks are drinkable?"

"I've been thinking," I said while he poked about for the melting ice cubes, "and I'm not leaving, Gyorgy. No matter how you arrange, it's the very thing to unease them. Boris was frightfully upset over Corinth—this time he'll really check if it's getting to the countdown. I don't say I'm any sleuth," I went on frankly, "but I'm more apt to catch a word or look than Stefan."

"Your safety is more important. My dear, he

208

wouldn't hesitate to immobilize me permanently. Why d'you think I'm staying out of sight, living at the Paris office and moving about too quickly to be traced? At least two people are already dead for their association with me. There may be others who tried to reach me without my knowledge," he said soberly. "We don't know who is involved nor how much time we have. Inquiries can't be made in the usual way. You see why I fear for you, Siri?"

"Yes." I suppressed a shiver. "But he always knew I'd met you. Aside from the code letter and finding me in the study, what's he got? I agree he'll watch me like a hawk—but he's evidently already been doing that, and so far it checks out. Maggie *is* writing a book, I *am* doing research, we *are* taking trips. . . ." I worked it out slowly. "I think we've got the drop on him, and exactly as I said—words, looks, impressions.

"*That* isn't what he expects, Gyorgy," I said earnestly. "He'll watch for something like searching, or taking photographs. I won't be doing anything of that sort, and there are Stefan and Marko, Maggie to protect me. Even Kai, if it came to a ruckus," I added thoughtfully. "And Zaro—does he know?"

Gyorgy shook his head and suddenly chuckled. "He is the fly in the ointment! Between us, Zaro's mistress is *enceinte*. He is determined on divorce, not merely to legalize the child but to be rid of Rosa. This is a long-established liaison, all poor Zaro has had to console him for some years."

"So that's why Rosa turned up!"

"Not ostensibly. I'm sure she always knew of Louise, but according to Stefan, it was a matter of unpaid bills about which Zaro had asked awkward questions.

209

They should not have come to his attention, and led him to ask what she'd done with her money." He chortled malevolently. "Imagine her dismay when Zaro informed her he'd pay up in return for an immediate divorce!"

"Wow!" I said reverently. "If every penny is tied up in this venture and you quash it, she'll really be behind the eight ball."

"An excellent location."

"You know," I mused, "I wonder if Boris knows this. I have a hunch he wouldn't like hearing how her fecklessness is apt to gum the works. Could you persuade Zaro to say nothing until it's finished? If Boris hears 'divorce,' he'll get the story out of her, and you never know. He might be able to cancel out. At the very least, he'll have time to repair his fences too."

Gyorgy smiled. "I had also thought of this." He picked up my hand, put a light kiss in the palm, and folded my fingers over. "Perhaps you should have been a lady spy after all! Yes, we must not allow Boris to suspect anything of this development. If only we had the account numbers or any lead to the whereabouts of our horses—how many of my ships, how many people in the ring, where and what is being loaded? Tekirdag is a good possibility for the headquarters but not a suitable port for the action."

"Let me try to find out? Please, Gyorgy?"

It took all my salesmanship, but finally, reluctantly, he agreed. "I shall not go back on the *Ariadne* with you. Marko will take my place." He drew the jeep behind the wharf buildings and helped me out. "Siri—be very careful, my dear. Take *no* chance, and leave at once if

210

you discover anything. Stefan will handle it."

"I promise. Oh, Gyorgy, it was a perfect day—I hate for it to be over."

"Only five o'clock—it's far from over."

"For me it is," I said honestly. "Please—you will take care of yourself, too?"

"I will, I always have. Don't worry about me, Siri. I've been in far tighter spots than this in my day." He grinned at me wickedly, and suddenly his ugly monkey face became sad. "It is a pity," he murmured. "We could love each other, you and I, but it is too late for me and too soon for you." Gently he turned my face up and brushed my lips with his. "God bless!"

I walked through the alley to the pier, and Kai was at the top of the gangplank. He straightened up and ran down to meet me. "Where have you been!" he demanded roughly.

"Across island. Didn't Maggie tell you that's why we came?"

"Who was that man? You've been gone all day with him." Kai's eyes were hard.

"Of course. He's the guide who arranged the trip."

His jaw set angrily. "Do you always kiss your guides goodbye?"

"Always—and what's it to you?" I pushed past him ruthlessly and went aboard. Maggie was surrounded as always, unofficial queen bee of the cruise, but her eyes were questioning. "It was very satisfactory," I told her. "Did you have fun?"

"Yes, it was delightful."

Kai was less easy to deflect. He attached himself to me like a limpet, and every time there was a break in the

211

conversation, he got back to my trip—where had I gone exactly, did I get any lunch, what was I doing, and *who was that guide?* I gave monosyllable answers until I was exhausted, but he was like a dog who *knows* there's a rabbit in that hole and if he digs a bit farther, he'll get it. In vain I changed the subject, in vain I tried boring him with the legends I'd (supposedly) acquired today. Kai merely listened until I ran down—and asked if this was a guide I always used. Maggie helped out when she could, and I sensed deep amusement in her divagations, but she couldn't get him off the trail either. Her amusement changed quickly when Kai narrowed his eyes. "That guide—I've seen him before. Is he from Dresnatinko?"

Maggie flashed a glance at me. We both knew it was Gyorgy's resemblance to Zaro. In a second Kai was bound to get it; he mustn't be let! "The man's a local guide Stefan found for Siri, a perfectly respectable man. I," said Maggie superbly, "know all about him. Why are you so concerned? Really, Kai, you sound like a jealous suitor."

That shut him up. He recoiled as from a slap, and shortly afterward he went off to prowl about the ship, ending with the captain at the wheel. It was respite, but only temporary. Kai's artist eye would correlate the instant he saw Zaro.

No doubt it would have, but Zaro had taken the night plane for Paris, although we didn't know it until the following day. That was a small break. I had enough to explain to Maggie when we got back to

Blondel near midnight. The door had no sooner closed than she said, "Well?"

I had a story ready. "Anya hates Rosa, ergo Rosa's guests. Boris is up to financial hanky-panky, afraid Gyorgy's got wind of it and planted me here to check up. Zaro wants a divorce to marry his pregnant mistress," I said succinctly. "That's all."

"No, it isn't," she stated. "Why should Rosa try to get that paper?"

"Gyorgy thought because she was in Paris, and when Boris's agent latched on to me, he thought Rosa might have more chance to find out what instructions I had."

Maggie nodded impassively. "What are your instructions now?"

"None," I said in surprise. "I told you I never had any real connection with Gyorgy, it was all a mistake. I'm just glad it's cleared up."

"Is it? Why the secret meeting?"

"So he can work on Boris without involving me."

I knew Maggie wasn't convinced, but after a nightcap she decided to accept my version. "Do we go to Thessalonike tomorrow or not?"

"Wait and see how we feel? Today was fairly tiring as preparation for a motor trip."

But in the morning, we had Dresnatinko to ourselves once more. Stefan reported casually that His Highness and monsieur Foucald had returned to Geneva, Mr. Zaro was in Paris, and madame had taken Mr. Penberthy back to Tekirdag. Only Madame Zaro remained—and no doubt Dr. Corwin would be happy

213

to work undisturbed.

"Yes. I wonder," Maggie remarked cryptically, "if we shall ever get to Thessalonike."

"Whenever we want. It will still be there," I said absently. With Dresnatinko deserted, I thought I'd see what I could get out of Rosa without Boris at hand to prevent a slip.

XII

Maggie was at the typewriter; so was I, for I'd had a long communiqué from Wells, Atherton, who were crowing with excitement over my outline. They'd returned innumerable instructions, thought it half-sold already, and enclosed a check for $5000 expense money. A postscript from Mr. Atherton said, "Definite V-P when you get back, Siri, but take all the time you need."

I had to bottle my elation—there was no one to tell. No one would really care anyway, except Gyorgy. What a pity I hadn't known yesterday. One good thing—the reality of my assignment should help to unsettle Boris. I sat on the terrace rereading the close-typed sheets, with Gyorgy still in mind.

Despite the gravity of the situation, there'd been an odd sense of intimacy that was not sexual but renewal of friendship, as though we'd known each other for years. Even the final kiss had been no more than tender. I remembered his last words with a small thrill. "You and I could love each other." I could understand May-December marriages now, but what had he meant that it was too late for him and too soon for me? It could only be that even if he divorced Anya, I wasn't trained for such a position. I didn't know languages, how to choose jewels or couturiere clothes, the who's who of international society. It was too soon for me to be the correct companion for Gyorgy Ionascu.

I didn't feel particularly crushed. Gyorgy attracted me, not his life. I was tempted to send him a copy of both outline and response. That would make a fat bundle—better wait until he'd have time. I couldn't resist writing, though. "Mahootma! Salutations and chortles of frabjus joy! Research outline accepted with high praise and instructions to continue, plus money to effect same. I'm promised a V-P! This makes a perfect red herring of crimson cod proportions. C.R.U.S.H. has flitted leaving only Agent P in the roost. In, around, and about, yesterday was a lovely day. Yours, 006½." I didn't dare say anything specific, there must be some trusted aide in Paris who opened letters and relayed by phone. Embarrassing for Gyorgy to receive *affectionate* messages. . . .

All the same, it was meant as a love letter. I drove into Athens, posted the letter, and arranged to cash the check. Then I went to a restricted library with my Paris introduction and forgot Dresnatinko completely. Here was a gold mine; the only difficulty was my lack of Greek. So many of the best source books had never been translated, but when the librarian understood what I wanted, he was immensely practical.

"There will be many duplications; if you have one version, it will suffice, no? Bring a list of what you have, and I know of a young student—his English is good enough, and he needs the money. You will go through together, say what you do not already have, and he will

216

make a rough translation."

"All I need is a synthesis. Will you arrange it? I can afford to pay suitably, Mr. Kordos. How clever of you to think of this!"

"Not particularly," he said dryly. "It is my nephew, and his mother would give him to you for nothing, in order to have him out of the house with those Beatle records."

"Do you have them *here,* too?"

He nodded. "My nephew is also learning the guitar, and this is very difficult in hot weather. He will be here tomorrow at ten."

When I got back to Blondel, I made up my list, and it was surprising how much I'd already accumulated. Five o'clock when I finished, I decided on a swim. I stuck my head in Maggie's door. "Want to come?"

"Not today," she said abstractedly, rolling a fresh sheet of paper into the machine. "See you later."

So I was splashing around by myself when Rosa came out. She looked astounded for a moment. "Hello! What are you doing here? We thought you went to Thessalonike yesterday."

"No, it was only a day trip, but we got back very late, and Maggie's immersed in her book again."

"Stefan must have misunderstood," she murmured. "I certainly thought he said you'd started north early in the morning." I could understand her surprise. I'd already come to accept Stefan's words as tantamount to biblical truth. Why had he lied? Why had Kai said nothing? If he'd thought I was meeting a lover, he'd have shut his mouth and looked New England.

I clambered out of the pool and patted dry enough not to spot Rosa's summer dress. She looked decidedly

217

wan but seemed friendly enough. "Everyone is away, did you know? I am deserted," she said lightly. "How glad I am to see you, Siri. It is very dull to talk to oneself, after all. Do sit down, and let us have a drink. I've really had no chance to know you."

"Nothing to know," I said, equally light. "Shall I ring the bell?"

"Oh, please . . ." She settled in a lounge and motioned me to one adjoining. We lit cigarettes, and Stefan appeared. He was bearing a drink tray and followed by two servants with a rolling cart of *friandises*. It was enough for any army. "Are you expecting guests?" I asked. "I'm not properly dressed."

"No, no, it is simply that I do not care for the usual *meze*." Rosa leaned forward, inspecting the canapés, chose one. "Have one of these, Siri—delicious!"

If we made a dent in this, we'd never want any dinner. I took the drink and the plate of hot goodies selected by Stefan, thinking how sad to need the reassurance of conspicuous waste. What would become of all this delicious, delicate, expensive food? Rosa picked and chose, sighed with enjoyment, but she did not actually eat a great deal. I thought it was more pleasure in contemplating the lavishness—and she'd better take a good look while she could. If Zaro divorced her, if Gyorgy kiboshed Boris's scheme, Rosa wasn't going to see this again.

I settled to the softening-up process. Ease her mind about Paris and Grenoble first. I managed to give the impression that Miss Rawson was merely a fellow-alum who worked at our Embassy and had kindly put me up for a few nights before I left with Maggie. I had to chance Boris couldn't identify the writer of the

218

suppressed letter, even if he'd told Rosa of it. I hadn't
seen the envelope, but Bess habitually used plain ones
for personal letters, and I had a hunch she hadn't put a
return address, so all he had was a code message from
Paris signed B.

Rosa was visibly relieved when I said I'd liked Miss
Rawson but didn't expect to see her again. Then she
wanted to hear about the trip. I said the only mishap
was a Gypsy trying to steal our luggage at Grenoble.
After that, she listened with every appearance of
interest while I (meanly) gave her a naive burble about
everything we'd seen and how *much* her wonderful
invitation was meaning to darling Maggie. Ugh! I am
not one for the casual endearments, but Rosa lapped it
up.

"I'm so glad! Such a tiny thing, Siri—but I've always
wanted her to visit, and this was the perfect moment.
Dear Maggie, she's very special to me, Siri." Rosa
sighed affectionately and told me all about her life in
Cambridge. "She was my second mother! And now
she's writing a book—*here,"* she purred complacently.
"I do feel proud to have even this small share in it."

I wondered if she thought Maggie would dedicate it
to her. I finished the drink and stood up. "I'm sure she's
deeply grateful for the chance. I'd better get back to see
if she needs me."

"Oh—must you go?" Rosa's face was suddenly
pinched, not wanting to be left alone. "But you're
coming back for dinner?"

"No, I think not. Maggie rather likes to relax after a
day of writing, not have to get dressed." Rosa's eyes
were so forlorn that I said impulsively, "Why not come
back with me, instead? Then you can have a good chat

219

and Maggie can lounge in comfort. Tell Stefan to send your dinner along with ours." After all, Rosa had originally invited us here, and if I'd had on my mind what she must have on hers, I wouldn't have relished being alone in Dresnatinko. All those empty, empty rooms . . .

Her acceptance was almost feverish with relief. Unwillingly I felt sorry for her; her world was crashing about her, and I was going to assist without a qualm, but I was still sorry. I'll set traps for vermin—I can't bear to watch them struggle.

I'm not sure Maggie was best pleased to be forced to cope with Rosa at the end of a long day, but she bore with it. It took some bearing. I quickly regretted my sympathy. Rosa was *obnoxious*. Not quite so bad as Boris—she knew no American college graduate was a peasant, even if earning a living. But she lost no opportunity of referring to the glories of her life. She dragged in references to yachting parties, exclusive boar hunts in the château country, the Royal Enclosure at Ascot, until Maggie cut her down to size.

"Well, I'm glad everything's turned out so well for you, Rosa. We've both come a long way from those slum days in Cambridge when you had to wash dishes for your supper, haven't we? And when are you going to have a baby? I expected a crown prince by now. What's the matter with you—or is it your husband?"

I wouldn't have believed Maggie could wield a knife so delicately! It did the trick, though, Rosa went to pieces inside. She abandoned the recital of her social prominence and made an effort to placate. I tossed my

220

commission into the conversational pot, and this led to a major breakthrough, although I didn't suspect it at the time.

Maggie was sincerely interested and proud of me. Rosa followed the lead, exclaiming with admiration. When I explained my arrangements for translation, she protested, "But I could do this for you, Siri. Why pay? Nonsense, I would enjoy it."

"I don't doubt you'd be infinitely superior to what I'll get," I remarked, "but I've already contracted, and I can't back out. Mr. Kordos says I could have the boy for nothing, just to get him out of the house. The mother is going mad because he not only listens to Beatles all day, but is trying to learn the guitar."

"Oh, the poor woman!" Maggie agreed sympathetically. "No, you mustn't change the plan, but why not take Rosa with you? Let her dig around for anything you may have missed—and how about private libraries? Rosa, whom do you know who might have something rare?"

Rosa knew dozens of people. Enthusiastically, she embraced the project. I'll admit she was efficient. She had me get pad and pencil, make a list. She'd telephone tomorrow—and why not examine here first? "It's *all* legends!" she exclaimed. "Why not Turkish or Slav? Boris has a book in his study, I remember it well. Vulko will find it for us."

I sat up so sharply that Maggie glanced at me. "Could Vulko really get it for us? Boris would not mind?"

It was like taking candy from a child. "Of course not," Rosa scoffed. "Come—why not go over now?"

"You don't mind being deserted for a few minutes?"

Maggie looked at me impassively. "Take all the time you need," she said. "Fix me a drink before you go and come back for a nightcap."

It was that simple.

Rosa ran the cart over to Miranda. There was no sign of Vulko, but she was undisturbed. "When Boris is away, Vulko gets drunk." The study was locked, but Rosa had a key. Hmmmmm.

When the door swung open, I saw what I'd expected—a completely tidy room. The desk top was bare of papers, and whatever had been in the bottom drawer was gone. While Rosa was searching the shelves, I tried surreptitiously, and the desk was unlocked. I had time to peek—only the usual separations for upright files. There were even a few folders in the compartments. I'd got it shut before something struck me, and perhaps it wouldn't have registered with anyone less used to desks.

That drawer was shorter than the others. There must be a hidden section behind it. I couldn't investigate. Rosa turned around with several books in her hand. "I found another," she said happily. "An old fairy-tale book. It may have nothing but nursery stories, but sometimes they were based on folk legends."

I took the books while she turned off lights and locked the door. They were all completely incomprehensible in a variety of peculiar languages, and the fairy-tale book must be a relic of Boris's nursery days. It was battered and dog-eared, the pages childishly scrawled over. Who would have thought Prince Boris Svishtov capable of such sentimentality! I wondered cynically if the man could ever have been a nice little boy who loved his mummy and daddy. I thought more probably he'd always been the sort who enjoyed pulling wings off flies.

Still, the book was a springboard. Driving back to Blondel, I said, "How sweet of Boris to keep this old book!" Rosa was so glad to have something to keep her mind off her troubles that she was less on guard than she should have been.

"Boris has a very gentle side. He can be very tender and affectionate, underneath the frustration life has brought him. He is not at all understood by the Ionascus, they have never appreciated his fineness of intellect and temperament," she said critically. "To them, all must be business, business, business, like tradesmen. They have no opinion of poor Boris, no understanding of his difference from them. All must work, irrespective of unsuitability, and it is decreed Boris shall be exiled to Geneva as though he were a bourgeois clerk."

"What a pity! I felt he was desperately unhappy, but of course he is too gallant to speak of it."

She rose like a trout to the fly. "That is exactly the right word! Imagine the humiliation for one of his breeding, but of course it is *because* of that. Boris must toil in an office every day to satisfy their concept of equality. He cannot even take an occasional long weekend to be with people of his own class for a breath of refreshment without a lecture." She shook her head indignantly. "And it would be so easy, so much more suitable, for him to be placed on some of their directors' boards."

"I wonder Anya doesn't intervene."

"Oh, Anya!" Rosa sniffed. "She has no standing either. You do not understand, Siri. It is only the sacred Ionascus who may have the superior positions. The empire is entirely private, I assure you. Old *Tante* Emilia, who is ninety and totally senile, can be chairman of a board with a comfortable income because she is a blood relative. Boris cannot. Nor I. We are not Ionascus, our judgment cannot be trusted."

"I can see this would be frightfully frustrating for Boris."

"Oh, it is," she assured me, braking the cart before Blondel. "But very soon now, Boris will prove himself. He will force them to acknowledge his right to be accepted as equal to any Ionascu, you will see." In the moonlight filtering through the trees, Rosa's face wore a sly smile. She was a cat anticipating a meal of canary. "He'll be rid of them, and live as he should."

I took her back to Dresnatinko about one o'clock. We'd gone through one of the books, Rosa reading, me making notes, and Maggie knitting silently. On the surface, a most companionable trio, but I wondered if Rosa knew how much she'd revealed. She had no reason to suspect she'd reinforced my wild guess of the relationship between herself and Boris. Neither did she know that I was aware of Zaro's request for a divorce. I couldn't say I'd accomplished much that evening, aside from establishing a beachhead. Rosa was going to be with me a good deal of the time. With luck I'd pry something more useful out of her.

She'd left the books behind, untidily piled on the couch. I started to pick them up, and the fairy-tale

224

book slipped to the floor. Boris had certainly been a destructive little monster. He'd managed to deface the first two-thirds of the book with aimless pencil or ink scribbles before his nanny must have caught him and put a stop to it. Apparently he'd just been learning to write, because here and there I found printed Cyrillic letters. On the back cover were a series of laborous numbers, interspersed with more symbols, looking rather like a Slavic child's sampler. I studied it with interest. This was one we hadn't thought of trying on Gizmo, although he was probably better programmed for Cyrillic than Middle English. I supposed this was Bulgarian rather than Russian, but weren't the basic alphabets the same? I put the book on a side table with the others and went to bed.

Now the pattern was different. We were three women alone together, Rosa eating dinner at Blondel each evening and filling the time before bed by working over the day's notes with me. If Maggie thought our chumminess peculiar, she said nothing, but occasionally her eyes were speculative. I'd no doubt she knew I was after something. Unfortunately I couldn't feel I was getting it.

After that first evening, Rosa was not to be drawn farther concerning the family. She was as good as her word and had got entree to several private houses, but by our reception, I suspected she'd bullied the owners with the Ionascu name. Twice we were merely escorted to a side room by a servant and presented with a selection of books to examine. The family was noticeably "not at home."

I couldn't wonder at it, either. Rosa did not improve on acquaintance. In fact, she and Boris were a perfect match. How comfortable they must be, despising everyone together. A good deal of the time I couldn't stand her, although I tried to be charitable. There was no doubt she was under increasing nerve strain with every day. She admitted she'd heard nothing from Zaro, "which is not surprising, he thinks of nothing but his beloved business." I thought she'd also heard nothing from Boris. Not likely he'd chance phoning her through the switchboard, and not possible for Madame Zaro to be near Miranda's direct wire without a watertight excuse. The very fact that no one had ever suspected in five years showed the extreme care they took to avoid anything that might be added up to a question. Sometimes I wondered if Boris had ever told her the real business for which he was using her money. Not that she'd have the least objection. This girl wouldn't care who died, so long as it wasn't she.

At week's end I felt discouraged. I had plenty of invaluable material for my job, but otherwise there was only the desk, which I'd thought worth a wire to Paris—SUGGEST INSPECT SPACE BEHIND DRAWER. I'd a few clues for Zaro. The mention of Montreux produced That Smile, and several times Rosa spoke of Chamonix with a certain affection. I wrote Gyorgy, "Zaro should investigate Montreux and Chamonix," but it wasn't helpful to the main business.

I'd heard nothing from Gyorgy, I'd hardly seen Stefan. Marko was apparently taking his place. The first time he appeared, his face was tentative until I winked at him. No one came to Dresnatinko, and Rosa never went anywhere except with me, which was curious. Did she have no friends hereabouts, was she waiting for word from Boris, or licking her wounds in seclusion? Why was she hanging around here, when she made no secret of her dislike for the place? Had Zaro ordered her to remain, while he paid her bills and got his divorce?

Maggie came out best. She worked away steadily and one night announced she'd have the first draft in two days. "I hesitate to mention it, but after that— Thessalonike?"

"Shhh," I cautioned. "Don't let the Fates hear you!"

She laughed, but I was right. The next day everyone was back. I found Anya beside the pool, looking sulky, while Kai was making preliminary sketches of Rosa. "We got back late last night," Anya said. "I thought you were at Thessalonike, but Rosa says you've been here all the time."

"Maggie's finished the first draft. Did Rosa tell you she's been helping me with my own work?"

"Yes. You should have told me, Siri. *I* could have arranged all that and more," Anya said, loudly enough to reach Rosa. "You must show me what you have, and I'll get the rest. The King will be most interested, exactly the sort of thing he likes, and the royal libraries are very complete. I will telephone the palace this afternoon."

Oooh, was she needling! I could feel Rosa squirming inside, but aside from a taut jaw, she ignored the whole thing. Anya wasn't through. She was all honey, peaches and whipped cream, low-voiced appearance of intimate friendliness with me—a definite implication that she took precedence over Rosa in my affections and that I had merely endured Madame Zaro in the

227

absence of Madame Ionascu. I could tell by an occasional twitch of Kai's lips he was getting it, although he concentrated on his sketches. Rosa must have commissioned him to do her portrait, and there was no doubt of Anya's fury. At Rosa, not Kai. I thought it was because upstart Rosa had had the effrontery to select the same portraitist as her sister-in-law. When Anya took me up to her suite for a private viewing of Kai's portrait of her, she let it out. "Of course it is superb. You see that Rosa is so gracious as to approve my choice? Kai has done so well with me that she has no fears he will do even better with her."

"Well, as to that, I'm not so sure," I murmured. "He hasn't got the same material to work with, Anya, and he doesn't flatter." I caught myself in time. "He isn't well known in Europe, I believe, but he'd had New York showings, and I think museums have begun to buy. Of course, *this* will make his reputation here. I hope you mean to lend?"

"Why—I hadn't thought about it."

"Please do," I urged. "No matter what he does for Rosa, it'll be his portrait of Madame Ionascu that will establish him . . . and you, for being clever enough to recognize his ability. It's still hard for American painters to gain acceptance. He's immensely fortunate to have you for a patroness."

I was entirely sincere. The portrait was outstanding—he'd got much more than a beautiful, mature woman. There was an impression . . . of sadness, of gallantry in the face of defeat, of the remnants of hope flickering but not yet dead. It was completely true; I realized it was the synthesis of everything I'd felt about Anya. Kai had got it all. Would others understand as easily? What would Gyorgy think of it? Did Anya know her soul was revealed in those dabs of color?

"I have been painted many times before, but this," she said reflectively, "this is me." So she did know. "I must think about lending," she remarked after a moment. "I had meant—but you are right it would establish Kai, and I have no right to be selfish at the expense of his future. I am glad you pointed this out to me, Siri." She smiled speculatively. "One wonders what he will make of Rosa."

"I expect he'll get whatever there is, but of course, it won't be finished in time for the annual Germond exhibition," I said indifferently, "and she may not want it shown anyway."

Anya eyed me sharply, but I was still contemplating the portrait. I don't know why I bothered, Kai was no concern of mine—except that after so many months of not seeing his work, I was literally thrilled by his talent. Not that I'd ever doubted it, but either it had flowered magnificently in the hiatus or I hadn't comprehended his development in a day-in, day-out life. I thought that even if I hadn't known the artist, I'd have egged Anya into exhibiting. I knew she was going to. She'd got the point: If *this* were lent to Germond, Rosa would forever be second, rated a copycat instead of able to imply that Anya had for once found someone worthwhile among the stray cats and dogs she was forever trying to build into a salon. I knew Anya was purring inwardly at a major score over Rosa, but she was still uncertain.

"When is the exhibition? Would they want something not for sale?"

"I don't know the date, but it's not for selling alone. I

think it's supposed to be the best representative new work. I expect Kai could tell you."

She nodded. "I'd like to do it, but . . ." She frowned, considering. "You see," she explained simply, "my husband has not yet seen it. I couldn't offer it without his approval."

"Couldn't you write to him?"

Anya's face was suddenly bleak as she swung away to find cigarettes. "I don't know where he is. I often don't." She shrugged humorously, in control again. "You have no idea of the demands a man's career makes on his wife, Siri! He telephones occasionally from wherever he is—he's very international, you know—but"—her voice trembled slightly—"I have not heard recently, and I haven't seen Gyorgy in six months. I'd hoped . . . that is, he is fondest of Dresnatinko, and if he *can* snatch a breathing spell, he comes here. So I thought . . . I had been in Africa, it was something I had not done before, and then in New York where I met Kai . . . Dresnatinko is so pleasant in summer that I hoped . . . But apparently I was wrong." She stubbed out the cigarette half-smoked, turned to the long windows leading to a balcony. "Have you seen my lovely view, Siri?"

I grasped wildly for tact. "I don't wonder you like Dresnatinko, and at least Boris is often here."

"Yes," she said tonelessly, "I always have Boris." She leaned against the window jamb, her eyes on the outlines of Euboea beyond the sparkling blue water, and I was suddenly FURIOUS with absolutely everyone, including myself. How dumb, stupid, immature, ignorant can you *be?* I'd been so sure I knew the score, half-fancying myself into some sort of relationship with Gyorgy, discounting his wife as another (but superior) Rosa who'd only married for a mink-lined berth. And now . . .

Did Gyorgy know that Anya adored him? Had she any suspicion that her son was causing Gyorgy's non-appearance, might even murder him if he threatened Boris's little plot? How had Gyorgy's marriage gone haywire? He must once have loved her. Even twenty years ago, he could never have needed a widowed Bulgarian countess purely for social window dressing. Unhesitatingly, I said to myself, "Boris." I stared blindly at Anya's "lovely view." How many days, weeks, months had she sat here, waiting?"

"It's beautiful. I always wondered what it looked like from here. I've driven along the old smugglers' road several times."

"Now you know," she remarked sardonically, "and it is not only smugglers who use that path. If ever there was a lovers' lane, that is it, I assure you. The servants, and their friends and relatives, and the whole village—the coming and going, to-ing and fro-ing, cooing and groaning! You have no idea! I sit up here, and because it is dark they think I do not know, but," she said somberly, "but even in the dark, I know." She turned away. "Shall we go down?"

Boris walked in shortly after lunch, and he wasn't happy to see any of us, although he made a show of delight as he kissed my cheek. He sat down beside me, fondling my hand possessively, but his mind was elsewhere, working overtime. Dresnatinko should have been unoccupied—that was necessary to his

231

plans. Now he was hastily revising. I wondered why he hadn't known who was here. Surely Vulko or any of the servants could have told him, but Boris hadn't even expected to see Rosa. "I thought you were in Paris with Zaro."

"He insisted I stay here, he's always so considerate. You know Paris summer heat!" She shuddered dramatically, but her eyes were wary.

"Have you been here all alone then? What a bore! You should have gone to Tekirdag with Mama." He turned to Anya. "But why are you here? I told you to stay as long as you pleased at Tekirdag." There was a steely note in his voice. He had told her, why had she disobeyed?

Anya shrugged. "It was hot, and that air-conditioning system was a bad mistake, Boris. It broke down twice in one week, and yesterday, when we learned Doctor Corwin and Siri were here for company . . . and Rosa, of course"—her voice was a polite insult— "we decided to drive back. And Kai is going to paint Rosa's portrait."

Boris raised his eyebrows. "I commissioned him to do Siri. Rosa, why do you come first?"

"Because Madame Eleazar Ionascu is a much bigger feather for an artist's cap than a mere Sigrid Quain," I inserted swiftly. "Who ever heard of me? Besides, Kai didn't accept your commission."

"But I shall," Kai said imperturbably. "I feel sure Sigrid Quain is destined for future prominence and will be as big a feather as the other ladies of Dresnatinko. Boris, it's a deal."

"Good! How soon can you start? Rosa"—persuasively—"you will not mind to step aside, you can be

232

painted at any time, after all—if not here, then in Paris—but we must catch Siri while we can." He kissed my hand affectionately. "One fears she may fly away from us at any moment, particularly if Doctor Corwin ever finishes this book."

"She swears it'll be done in two days," I said desperately, "and that's not time enough. Besides, I can't let you—I mean, I don't want to be painted, Boris."

"Oh, but you must!" Rosa exclaimed earnestly. "Boris is right. Kai shall do you first, Siri, and then we'll see where he shall do me."

"But—"

"No 'buts.'" Boris smiled intimately. "I insist, *duzhka*. Kai, when can you begin?"

"Now," said Kai impersonally. "Just turn your head toward Boris for a minute, Siri." The pencil was moving swiftly over his sketch block while I was raging inside. Hateful, *hateful!* I couldn't be painted as his wife, I was an acceptable commission from anyone at all. . . . Well, he'd be neatly caught this time. Boris would never pay for that portrait. No matter how good it was, he'd be "disappointed," it wouldn't have captured the "real Siri." He'd get out of it somehow, because it was only a clever means of immobilizing two of the unwanted occupants of Dresnatinko.

I sat smiling ruefully at Boris, murmuring, "You *know* I can't accept this, Boris. It's far too expensive a present, even for a prince with quixotic generosity."

"Is it quixotic to want a portrait of the one woman I shall love for the rest of my life?" he said softly. "You have not believed me, have you, Siri? I have hardly believed myself these past weeks, I confess it." Boris's lips twisted sardonically, his eyes fixed on mine. "I have done it all wrong, haven't I? And now that I know my heart, how shall I reach yours? I have been stupid, thoughtless, arrogant, *blind* . . . it seemed so incredible." He smiled sadly. "I convict myself—but you will let me try for you, Siri? There is so much I must say, not in the midst of people. Will you give me the chance—tonight after dinner, can we be alone together?"

"Siri, turn the other way, will you? I want the right profile." Kai's voice cut through Boris's hypnotic murmurings, but when I reversed obediently, Boris was still holding my hand and continuing the snow job.

Anya had disappeared, Rosa was sitting beside Kai. By the way she wasn't looking at us, I thought she recognized Boris playing a game. She didn't much like it, though. Her eyes were distinctly cold when she glanced at me once. Was she wondering if perhaps I was the one who'd beat her time? Did she expect Boris to marry her eventually, when it could be managed without too much scandal?

I wasn't about to meet him alone at night anywhere any time, but if this was the way he'd worked on Rosa, I could see she must have gone down like a sitting duck. His verbal lovemaking was dangerous, though. No doubt that he was on the *qui vive,* alert for anything more that might upset his plans. If I repulsed too firmly, if I capitulated too easily, Boris would wonder. *If I were a horse, where would I go?* I'd be a typical clean-cut American girl, open, honest, troubled by the possibility of causing pain to a man who loved me. . . .

I played it that way, allowing myself to be convinced that Boris deserved a chance to state his case, even though it would be hopeless, because I didn't belong—

didn't want to belong—to his world. Still, I was willing to be friends.

"Friends! What I want from you is far more than your childish concept of the relations between men and women," he muttered vehemently. "As for not belonging, that is nonsense. You would enhance any position, merely as yourself."

"Please, Boris—I wish you'd stop, you're making me very uncomfortable. What will Kai and Rosa think?"

"That I have lost my heart, I'm pleading for my life, and they will be right."

"Siri, straight forward now, please," Kai said. Obediently, I swiveled, but Boris was still talking—and now I realized the full extent of the act. He was holding my hand, but with my head turned aside, I hadn't seen the casual disposal of his body—at ease in a lounge chair, merely chit-chatting.

"They say . . . what do they say . . . let them say," he was murmuring, looking indifferently across the pool, as though discussing the weather. "They will change the tune later."

"I wouldn't depend on it," I returned sweetly, looking directly ahead. "Nearly everyone is a mental Johnny One-note—and if you think getting into my bed is worth all this display of romance, you flatter me."

"Siri!" His hand gripped mine painfully, then relaxed. "I deserved that," he sighed, reaching for cigarettes on the side table, "but I beg you to believe I am only a man, my darling, not a libertine."

"Oh, I'll believe you, sweetie. I remember you said you hadn't the money for orgies."

"I haven't the money for a wife," he said somberly,

"but there is a harmony about Siri Svishtov . . . Princess Siri Svishtov . . . that undermines my judgment."

Kai glanced up from his sketch right then, and something of my shock must have shown, but he closed the pad and said, "That's all for today. Let's have a swim."

"What a good idea!" I wrenched free of Boris and stood up, stripping off the poolside wraparound and diving into the blessed coolness of the water before he could protest. He'd have to go change, those weren't matelot pants. I'd have a breathing spell at least, and how I needed it! I swam vigorously the length of the pool, turned, and pounded halfway back; then I turned over and floated . . . thinking.

It was going to be *now*—within a few days. The coup was ready to go, but where? Not Tekirdag, or Boris wouldn't have wanted Anya to stay there. Yet Dresnatinko was no better, was it? Why on earth had he come here? Why was he dangling the prospect of marriage before me? Did he really think I was that stupid? I decided coldly that he probably did, that it was a gambit that had worked on Rosa and innumerable other females in the past. I still had nothing definite, but I thought I'd wire Gyorgy anyway. . . .

We swam, we frolicked, we batted the pool ball about, and finally we dried off on pool pads. Anya came through the French windows. "Siri, I have arranged for you—the Palace at eleven o'clock the morning after tomorrow. His Majesty is away, but the archivist will give you anything you want." She sank complacently into a lounge.

"Oh, Anya, how can I thank you!"

"For nothing," she said lightly, as Boris turned over lazily beside me.

"What is this about?"

"My research assignment, don't you remember my telling you?" The perfect chance to emphasize innocence. "I made a preliminary report, they've expanded the original concept, and I'm promised a vice-presidency when I get home."

"And I have been assisting." Rosa wasn't going to let Anya triumph completely. "Siri cannot read these languages, you know, and she was going to pay a translator, but instead I have done it."

Let Rosa have some credit. "Twice as well as any hired hand," I praised. "She grasped what I wanted and saved any amount of time in duplications."

"We've been to . . ." Rosa ran through the list. "And all through the libraries here. I'm not sure Siri will find much that's new by now, even at the palace, unless there's a readable copy of your fairy-tale book, Boris."

"Fairy-tale . . . ?" Boris's voice was bewildered, but his hand twitched. Just once. Infinitesimally.

Rosa was so bent on proving she'd done more for me than Anya that she was heedless of implications. Of course, Boris knew he'd locked his study. I'd bet Vulko didn't have a key, but Rosa had—and she oughtn't to allow anyone to know it. She'd got all the way up to our running down to Miranda for the book on Tekirdag before she realized she'd put her foot in it. Her eyes were stricken, but it was too late. Was I going to mention that key? Hurriedly she glossed over the details while I said nothing. When she mentioned the fairy-tale book again, Boris murmured, "I didn't know

I had anything like that. Where could I have got it? Was it any use?"

"Not much," I said. "If it wasn't yours, it must have come out of someone's nursery with a child of destructive tendencies. The pages were so scrawled that Rosa gave up." I smiled at him. "We thought it must have some special significance for you, and Rosa put it back very carefully, but if you don't like to admit such sentimental affection, we won't tease."

"Oh, I'm neatly caught!" he laughed. "It must be one of the books from Svishtov. You remember, Mama?"

"Yes," Anya said drily. "I remember you insisted on using valuable packing space to bring half the contents of your playroom when the Huns and Bolsheviki were breathing down our necks and we scarcely had time to get out of the country. What became of that revolting stuffed elephant?"

"Etelka . . . must I confess? She is still with me, she lives in comfortable retirement in a storeroom at Miranda." Boris smiled at me. "I suppose you found the evidence of my depravity on every page?"

Why did he mention the book again? "I didn't look at it at all," I said, surprised. "Rosa said it was a mess, and if she couldn't read it, I certainly couldn't. She just put it back."

"As a matter of fact," said Anya, "you were rather a sweet little boy, Boris."

"A pity I turned out so badly, eh, Mama?"

She looked at him expressionlessly. "Well, you have certainly turned out," she remarked after a moment, "and I suppose you are what life made of you. We all are." She got up and turned to the salon. "I must make some calls."

It was Rosa who suggested bridge. "I don't play for money," I said at once.

"Only one drachma per hundred," she insisted persuasively.

That was still thirty bucks for a thousand points. I shook my head, but Boris said, "Nonsense, I pay your losses, Siri. Come on Siri."

I rather expected Kai to back me up—he had always used to say bridge was too good a game to spoil with stakes—but he was already fanning the cards for the draw. And as luck would have it, I ended up with Rosa. She was an avid gambler; her hands raking in tricks resembled predatory blood-tipped claws. Boris appeared more casual, but he was equally sharp. The cards ran more or less evenly for both sides. Presumably Boris and Rosa knew each other's play; what they didn't know was a similar knowledge between Kai and me. I rapidly realized he was deliberately keeping the score balanced. We were never more than a few hundred points apart—until Boris rashly doubled a small slam, which Rosa redoubled and which I couldn't avoid making. Vulnerable, doubled and redoubled, with an overtrick. For a few hands after that I discarded thirteenth cards or made poor leads, until they had a 500-point rubber and we were more or less back to normal.

Boris was dealing. Kai's hand rested on the table, tapping ash into the tray. Rosa leaned forward idly, fingering his silver bracelet. "My Kind Protector," she deciphered, turning it around. "How unusual! What does it mean, Kai—or shouldn't I ask?"

"Oh, it's not that private," he said lightly. "It doesn't really mean anything, just a play on my initials."

"A play?" she echoed, uncomprehending. "What d'you mean?"

"My full name is Marcus Kai Penberthy—M.K.P. . . . My Kind Protector," he said. "It's just one of the things people do—like using their street address or phone number for a safe-deposit password or criminals picking an alias with their own initials." He shrugged, drawing away his hand to pick up the cards. "It's a sort of unconscious fetish for people to use numbers or names with a personal significance. I read somewhere that the police depend on it."

I might have got it then, but Boris leaned forward to inspect in his turn. "Locked in place," he remarked. "My dear Kai, one had no idea you were in thrall. Who is she?"

"My personal Circe."

"And she locks you in a chastity belt!" Boris snickered. "I know a little locksmith—"

"Love laughs at them," Kai said. "Your bid, Svishtov."

I kept my eyes on my cards, hoping my face revealed nothing, playing automatically—but unable to forget the day we'd got those bracelets. Mine said *"Semper amo quis perturbant,"* for Sigrid Anna Quain Penberthy. The Aged P said it was bad Latin but probably true that "always I love what disturbs." We'd got them in Greenwich Village on our first wedding anniversary, sentimentally, ritually locking them into

240

place. And it was true Kai hadn't his key, but why hadn't he done what I did—gone to a local jeweler and had the cuff cut off his wrist?

Rosa bid me into another slam at that point, and I was so unnerved that I made it, which put us too far ahead. There wasn't time for another rubber to balance up. Anya swept out of the house. "The Goulenkis want us for a water party. Kai, you will like to ski? Boris?"

"By all means." Boris threw in his hand and stood up briskly. "We settle later? Shall I bring skis for you, Siri? And shall we take our boats? They have more power than Goulenkis'." He glanced around. "Six o'clock at the boathouse?"

I might have realized again when I was dressing, except that there wasn't a great deal of time. I knew something was tugging at the back door of my mind, something connected with that fairy-tale book. Trotting about, tucking cigarettes and makeup into the tote bag, I tried to think back. Boris had been disturbed, but not because I'd been in his study. He knew (and I'd verified) there wasn't anything left. Was it Rosa's indiscreet use of the key, annoyance at being caught in sentimental weakness, or something deeper?

Opening the junk box, digging for cork beach jewelry, the ruined halves of my silver cuff were dredged up. I pushed them aside angrily, but they deflected me. Why hadn't I thrown them away? Why had Kai kept his?

I went across to Maggie's room and said, "Aren't you ever going to be finished? We're all going water-skiing at the Goulenkis', why don't you knock off and come

241

with us?"

"Later, perhaps. I can drive myself over, or do you want the car?"

"No, we're going by boat."

But there was only Boris waiting for me, the back of the powerboat stacked with skis. "Am I first? Where is everyone?"

"Mama decided she did not feel like a boat ride after all. She has gone by car, taking Kai and Rosa with her." Boris stepped lithely from boat to pier, holding out his hand to help me. I didn't take it.

"You arranged this, didn't you?"

"Yes," he said quietly. "Please, Siri?"

"Thanks, but no thanks, Boris. I don't want to be made love to, really."

"Then I won't," he promised, "but at least give me a chance to mend my ways. Whether or not you believe me, it is very important to me. Come—the tide's exactly right for you to see the blowhole, and we'll still reach the Goulenkis' before the others."

I didn't want to be alone with him, but it wouldn't be more than fifteen minutes or so. I stepped into the boat, and first we went up the coast the other way to show me the old smugglers' landing, with a huge iron ring where they had tied up and worn rock steps leading up to the Dresnatinko road. Then we whizzed back past the boathouse cove and cautiously idled at the cave opening. It was a fantastic place, with jagged rocks in the swirling water and great sloping ledges on the walls. Boris tied up and helped me out.

"You can't take the boat in because of the rocks, but it's quite safe and easy to walk along the ledges."

So it was. The constant action of the water had worn

runnels in the ledges so they slanted toward the cavern wall, and there were plenty of hand holds. The blowhole was about three feet wide at the top of a smooth chute of rock. You could step across to the other cavern wall and continue back to the narrow entrance. The old smugglers' road was actually a rock bridge above and separate from the cavern. "You mean people walk over that?" I asked incredulously. It looked about two feet wide, hanging in space above the water growling around the vicious rocks. A single misstep and you'd be a very dead duck.

"Yes," Boris chuckled, "and when they're drunk, too."

We sat on two boulders in the sun, smoked a cigarette, and looked at the sea. It was very pleasant, very peaceful, and Boris didn't try any sort of intimacy. He talked instead of sailing trips when he was a boy and told a naughty escapade of frightening Anya most dreadfully by failing to return from Euboea because he'd made friends with some native boys who were camping out for a picnic supper. "Poor Gyorgy had to get out the power launch and come after me at midnight . . . and there I was, eating roast goat, drinking *retsina,* singing with a bunch of farm kids." Boris laughed reminiscently. "But he didn't say a word. He didn't have to, Mama said them all. I never did that again, I can tell you."

He looked at our boat suddenly. "Tchk, I think I forgot the tow lines—or did I put them in the store box?" He swung down and rooted about impatiently. "Damn, I *have* forgotten them," he said finally. "Siri, have another cigarette while I run back to the boathouse." He reached his lighter up to me. "I won't be a minute." He cast off, pushed the boat carefully away from the rocks into the open water, spun the motor, and was gone with a wave of the hand.

It was about ten minutes or the space of my cigarette before I wondered when he was coming back.

It was another ten or fifteen minutes before I discovered I couldn't get out of the blowhole cavern . . . and the tide was coming in.

XIII

I hadn't minimized danger from Boris, I simply hadn't expected it so soon. Gyorgy had said they took no chances; yet what could Boris think I knew to endanger him? I sat on the rock again, lit another cigarette, and told myself I was imagining. Something had delayed Boris, he'd be along in plenty of time with humble apologies.

If he didn't return?

I threw away the cigarette and made another careful exploration. If I got into the water, I'd be caught by the eddies and either dashed against the rocks or sucked down in the undertow. The smugglers' bridge was two feet above my reach. I sought something to stand on, but there were only loose boulders. One of them slid away under my testing foot and splashed ominously into the water. I retreated to my original seat until the shakes ceased.

Logically I must have some knowledge I hadn't identified unless the coup was so close that the mere belief of my employment by Gyorgy was enough. . . . If by any remote chance he'd broken Squarawb, it should tend to prove I was an innocent bystander. I went carefully over the afternoon, and quite suddenly I had the whole thing.

In that fairy-tale book was everything Gyorgy needed. Those apparently aimless childish scribbles were actually maps, whether land or sea was immaterial. They'd all be of places unknown to me. I'm not sure I'd recognize a map of the United States under similar circumstances, especially if I didn't expect to see it—and these were probably drawn upside-down or kitty-cornered for further confusion.

The numbers and letters on the back cover . . . they were some sort of code, of course, and the confirmation was the two groups of numbers set randomly in the middle—1010HRH2 and 2121RP12. . . . They were the license numbers for Boris and Rosa. They must be the Swiss account numbers. I gritted my teeth in sheer rage for my stupidity. I had so nearly known—but I'd been unstrung by the silver cuff, because it meant something to me emotionally. Kai had given me the clue, talking of the way people habitually use personal names or numbers for private matters. When I was dressing I'd had the uneasy feeling that I'd missed something. I had even *seen* that number on Boris's car when I passed Miranda on the way to the boathouse, and it still hadn't registered, because I always smiled contemptuously to myself over that tag. HRH for His Royal Highness, everything must emphasize the Svishtov nobility. I'd often wondered if he had embroidered crowns on his underpants. . . .

So now I knew, and I was the only person who did. I *had* to get out of here somehow. I tried until my hands and legs were scraped and sore, but it was useless. I looked hopefully for any boats to signal. There weren't many—it was suppertime for natives, and when I waved frantically, they only smiled and waved back politely. Anyway, none of them came close enough to hail urgently.

There was no ledge on either side of the cavern opening to get around beneath the rock bridge to the outside, in the hope of finding a way along the cliff face. The granite here was worn smooth without handgrips anywhere. There was no way to get up to the path; one side was blocked by an overhang and the other was nothing but loose pebbles and shale that shifted dangerously beneath my feet.

I was wondering whether I could possibly pull myself up to the highest inner ledge and survive the high tide when I heard a voice calling, "Siri?"

"Yes!" I screamed, working back to the opening as fast as possible on the wet stones. *"Don't come in!"* I was too late. Kai had already got onto the loose stuff and slid downward to the rock seats. Behind him there was a rumbling and what looked like half a ton of hillside was blocking any possible retreat. "That's torn it," I said tearfully. "Oh, Kai, why did you? Now you can't get out either."

He went rather white at that, absorbing my scratches and torn dress. "Perhaps I can, I'm taller than you." He wasn't tall enough to get a safe grip on the bridge, though, nor strong enough to pull himself out over the rock jut, and when I only caught his legs in the nick of time to get him back to the ledge, I said, "Give it up, *please,* darling—you'll ruin your hands."

"Much good they'll do me," he muttered, chafing them absently. "Well, that's me, isn't it? Kapering Kai, the Kind Protector, dashing to the rescue—and lousing up the one chance. I never managed to rescue you from anything, did I?" He sighed. "Let's have a cigarette, if I've got any, which I probably haven't."

"I've an extra pack, and this is nearly full." I extended it and rooted in the tote bag for matches, but he did have his lighter.

"This figures," he remarked. "You always had the practical essentials, and I never had anything but the useless extras."

"A lighter that works isn't useless, and you know yours always did."

"Yes." Kai chuckled. "Remember how many times I bet our bar checks on the first spin?"

I giggled involuntarily. "You never stuck anyone who couldn't well afford it," I said loyally.

"Of course not. Conduct unbecoming a gentleman in distressed circumstances." Kai exhaled and looked at the water. "Now will you tell me why Boris wishes to murder you?"

"How did you know? How did you get here?"

"I'm not in the league with him," Kai said impersonally. "It was just—he showed up with the water skis and without you. He said you'd got a bad headache, he'd taken you back to the boathouse and seen you off to Blondel. Then he decided it was quicker to take everything along by car."

"So why did you come?"

Kai shrugged. "I thought he'd made a pass at you, and you'd had to run for your life. I came to check up. Doctor Corwin said she hadn't seen you, she thought you'd gone with Boris, but the cart was there. Then I started looking." The gold flecks in his eyes gleamed. "Not like you to wander off without a word. I thought

248

you might have gone over to the clearing, or down to the lookout, to cool off.

"I didn't say much to Doctor Corwin, she was getting ready to go over to the party. I said I'd hunt you up, see if you were feeling better, and I'd bring you along with me later. But when I didn't find you anywhere, I thought you might have tried the old path this way. So here I am—and here you are—and quite obviously Boris left you here. Why?"

I shivered. "Oh, it doesn't matter now. . . ." I told him the whole story. "Sickening to think—Boris will get away with it, when I've got all Gyorgy needs."

"Hmmm. Are you in love with him?" Kai asked bluntly.

"Not really," I said after a moment. "Not like you . . . not like Anya. She really loves him, it was one of the things I wanted to tell him. I don't know if he knows. Maybe he wouldn't care, but I think he would. I wonder how they got off the track?"

"How did we?" he asked in a low voice. "What happened to us, Siri?"

"I don't know," I said helplessly. "It was . . . one cloud below heaven at first—until I lost the babies. After that, you seemed to sort of slide away from me. Would it have been different if I'd been able? I couldn't help it, Kai. It wasn't deliberate."

"I know that, Silly Siri." Kai put his hand on mine warmly. "It didn't matter. I told you at the time. I'd like a son, any man does, but I'd rather have you . . . except that suddenly I didn't have you, either."

"I don't know what you mean," I said tremulously. "You always had me, Kai."

"No." He shook his head, narrowing his eyes. "I had

a brilliant successful career woman, an outstanding hostess of the best carefully careless parties, the most desired invitation in New York, designed to put Kai Penberthy into the money class . . . all paid for by the money she earned, which took all the time she wasn't giving parties or being seen at the opera, the symphony, the newest gallery. Don't misunderstand"—he turned to me impersonally—"I know you meant to help, and you did. You got me talked about, introduced to the right people. You never put a foot wrong, you always knew who might be a good patron and who wasn't. I was proud of you. Always. Please believe me."

"But then . . . what happened? If you understood so much, why couldn't you grow up just a little bit," I asked despairingly, "instead of being—being bored and intransigent? It got so I was afraid to invite anyone, make any engagements." I caught my breath in a sob. "I was almost afraid to come home. I never knew how you'd be—if you were there at all."

"Poor Siri. I'm sorry—but I never knew how you'd be, either."

"And all those people you were cocktailing with, models and—and *nobodies,* when I worked so hard to get you into the right set."

"Yes, I know. I was a bad boy."

"But if you didn't want to follow up the opportunities, why didn't you *tell* me to quit it?"

"Why didn't I?" he mused, staring at the sea. "I suppose I wasn't aware of it, until all of a sudden I'd lost my Serendipity. I thought it was compensation for a baby and you'd straighten out when the doctor gave the green light, but you never did. You substituted a combination of me and your business career. If I'd told you that much as I appreciated your efforts, I wanted a partner rather than a mother hen masterminding my career, would you have understood?"

"I don't know," I murmured dazedly.

He shrugged. "Well, there it was. All of a sudden you were Deadly Serious Siri, you couldn't laugh with me any longer. I tried everything I could think of to get you to notice *me* instead of that coming young artist Kai Penberthy, and finally I couldn't stand any more of it. If it hadn't been Sondra, it would've been someone." He stood up abruptly, leaning against the outer rocks. "I won't apologize for Sondra, you brought it on yourself," he said in a hard voice. "Maybe I did think of marrying her, it's so long ago I can't remember, but I'd reached a stage where I was grateful for a kind word from anyone. I thought perhaps asking for a divorce would shock you into remembering me, but it was too late. You were already too absorbed into the conventional modern mores."

"Did you expect me to refuse you a divorce?" I asked hotly. "To weep and wail, beat my breast, fall down and writhe on the floor? You wanted out, you got out. All I don't understand is what took you so long."

He was silent for a moment. "I don't know. . . . I cooled off a bit after I got to Truth or Consequences. I went out into the hills and I got to painting. I sort of forgot I'd meant to get a divorce." He snorted sardonically. "I wasn't very conscious of time, I kept thinking I'd hear from you or I'd go home when I finished a couple more pictures. Typical of me, wasn't it?"

"Yes," I said baldly. "When did you remember?"

"Grandfather wrote. He said you'd gone abroad, it

251

was five months, what did I mean to do about this divorce? It wasn't fair to you, and I should either piddle or get off the pot. So I put the papers through, but"—his voice was hard again—"I wouldn't let you legally take back your name, because I was damn well going to make you remember *me*, one way or another, for the rest of your life or until you married someone else." He looked around at me coldly. "You married me, but you were never anyone but Sigrid Quain. You never used my name except for the tradesmen. I suppose it was an easier name to spell over a business telephone, and at least nobody ever called me Mr. Quain. I should be grateful for that."

Kai tossed his cigarette into the water. "That was it. I'd shot my wad. I couldn't spark any reaction from you, no matter what I did. You were never jealous, were you? You simply didn't care, so long as I wasn't underfoot."

"Not exactly," I said uncomfortably, because it was too close to the truth. "I used to be envious because you were having fun while I was stuck in the office."

"Would you rather have been with me?"

"Oh, always! But what else could I do? Everything got out of hand somehow, the bills kept piling up. . . . I did try to keep them down, but I couldn't be everywhere at once, and I got so tired I was taking taxis all the time, and not able to fight when the laundry ruined that shirt you loved."

"Which shirt?"

"The browny-yellow one." I couldn't suppress tears. "They ate holes in it with bleach and tried to say it was your paint, but it *wasn't*. You never wore that shirt in the studio. So I went back to the shop for another one, and I paid Leora extra to wash it by hand. That's why I couldn't save anything, which was the only reason I was working in the first place."

"Poor Siri, I never realized I was such an expensive luxury," he sympathized, "but it was a good ace in the hole, at least. Here you are, with a topnotch assignment, expenses paid and a vice-presidency to look forward to."

"This isn't Wells, Atherton," I choked. "It's the Aged P."

"What?"

"He wanted to make me a settlement, and I wouldn't take it, but Tubby said it was for me to get away, so I wouldn't be unstrung all the time running into you," I wept. "I only pretended about the assignment to throw Boris off the track. I mean, I have the thing, but it was only filling up time . . . and I don't want to be vice-president of anything."

"What do you want, Siri," he asked strangely, "or perhaps I mean what *did* you want?"

"I never wanted anything but whatever you wanted," I wailed, "but when I couldn't have a baby, I thought I might as well make enough money so you wouldn't be burdened when I could. I'm not very old, we could reverse things and get you solidly started while I was taking those horrid pills and exercises."

"Shhh," he murmured, mopping my eyes gently. It felt so good to have his arm around me that I went to pieces and bawled hysterically until I was as limp as overcooked spaghetti. Kai lit a cigarette and gave me occasional puffs while I calmed down.

The tide was creeping up, covering some of the jagged rocks, beginning to splash against the back of the cave. The sky was a blaze of first sunset rays. "I think we've both been very stupid," Kai stated quietly. "There isn't time to discuss it now. We have to get out of here. Can you pull together, hon?"

"Yes—but you know we're trapped."

"The one thing we hadn't thought of, the blowhole itself," he said calmly. "Come on."

We made our way carefully to the rear of the ledges, and there was enough space for him to brace securely between the two sides of the granite funnel. "Could you climb onto my shoulders and pull yourself out?"

I looked up, and the opening seemed a mile away, but if I got out . . . "The chains!" I said. "If I can just get over the smooth rock, I can link them together and let them down to you, Kai. Oh, why didn't we think before!"

"I did," he said, "but I kept hoping someone would come. It's so damn dangerous, but now I guess it's our only chance." In the dim light, Kai's eyes looked at me somberly. "I love you with all my heart and soul. If we don't meet again, remember that." He kissed me very thoroughly, let me go, and positioned himself as securely as possible. "Allez-oop!"

I wanted to kiss him again, tell him a hundred loving words, touch him, hold him . . . there wasn't time. Already the water was rushing and growling, breaking upward occasionally in tiny spurts. I climbed onto Kai's shoulders, searched and found one rough knob of granite outside the chute, and slowly pulled myself standing—to find my head and shoulders above the blowhole.

There was a ridge in the smooth rock. I braced myself on the edge of the hole to take the pressure off

Kai's shoulders, and I could just grasp the ridge. It wasn't the greatest solace in the world, only a small ridge worn slick by water and slippery with spume, but it was enough to get me out, until I was sitting on the edge of the hole, legs dangling below. I peered down and yelled, "Geronimo! I made it—back in a minute."

Actually it was nearer ten, and I never want to live any of those minutes again. I crawled inch by inch over the smooth, damp granite, pulling myself along by fingernail cracks, not daring to look back for fear I'd slip and slide inexorably down onto the very rocks that had imprisoned us until Kai gambled on me.

Kai! He was still down there, waiting with the water rising. Every impulse screamed "Hurry!" but one hasty move and I'd condemn him along with myself. I forced myself to test, to search for the ridges, to go slowly— and finally, *finally* I could feel I was over the hump. I was no longer tilted, reaching upward, but lying flat. The rocks were still slick, smooth, wet but there was no longer danger of slipping into the sea, and the chain fence was no more than a yard away. I scrambled forward, hauled myself up and went from one end of the barricade to the other, heedless of turned ankles and bruised fingers. I combined three chains end to end, hooked a fourth around my own waist, and went back across the slick rocks to the blowhole.

The growling water had increased to a roar beneath me by the time I let the chains slither down through the opening. Not possible to talk even to be heard at a yell, but I felt the chains grasped strongly . . . shaking under my hand . . . and at long last Kai's head emerged. He was pulling himself up hand over hand, by main force, because his feet were nearly useless against the smooth

255

wet stone. He was sweating with exertion, using every ounce of strength and will-power—but in another strong tug, he was out, stretched exhaustedly beside me on the rocks.

And two seconds later came the first eruption.

The water shot up in a column and crashed down on us with brutal force. I felt half-drowned, bruised and numbed, unable to move while the rivulets streamed away to the sea. Kai sat up choking and spitting, and made use of several extremely masculine words which he *says* he learned from the fences around Harvard Yard. "Come on, don't just lie there! You'll be pounded to death, come on!"

We got back to the chain pillars somehow, Kai holding me against him and puling us both together. "Sit down, I'll put the chains back while I can still see." When I got back to him, we sat limp and incapable of movement, staring dully at the spouting water. Suddenly the full horrow swept over me. If Kai hadn't come, if we hadn't got out, if we were still down in that cavern . . . by now the water would have claimed us. I buried my face against him, and I couldn't stop shuddering.

"Don't think, dear heart—it didn't happen, I've got you safe."

"Not me. I don't matter. It's *you.*"

"I don't matter either, darling." He stroked my hair and kissed me gently. "You must stop being so impressed with my puny talents, if we're going to succeed the second time around." Kai looked down at me squarely. "We are going to try, aren't we?"

"Yes, please."

"You know," he said presently, "I think we'd better start back, if you can move. It's a roundabout walk, and I'm not sure I could find the path in the dark."

In some ways that was the worst part, the walk seemed endless. We were so tired that every step was agony; we stumbled along drunkenly, already so bruised that we no longer felt the fresh bumps and scratches. Eventually we reached the clearing. Blondel was brightly lighted, but there was no sign of Maggie. "She's probably gone to the Goulenkis."

"Just as well, she'd be scared to death at the sight of us," he said wearily. "Now what do we do?"

"Stefan . . ." I pressed the button for the direct wire not once but a dozen times. There was no answer. It would have to be Paris direct, but not my voice. Kai was fast asleep on the bed beside me. I shook him awake ruthlessly. "You have to put the call through."

Yawning, he took the phone, waited for the Dresnatinko operator. She was a long while answering and sounded flustered when he said, "Where were you, Milcha? Cuddling with someone? This is Mr. Penberthy, I'd like a call to Paris."

"Oh, please—I give you operator, you make call direct?"

He opened his eyes at that. "Some sort of flap going on," he muttered. "Are the doors locked?" I sped out and closed the terrace windows, bolted the front door. He was through to Paris when I got back, holding the phone to me. "Here."

A woman's voice said, "Who is it?"

"Miss Quain for Mr. Jonas."

"He is not here, I will take a message."

"May I have the password, please?"

"Password? Oh, a thousand pardons, I forgot. Mahootma."

I said, "You *have* to reach him, or Interpol or the American Ambassador. The Swiss account numbers he wants are 1010HRH2 and 2121RPI2. All the records he needs are in a Bulgarian fairy-tale book. If it isn't somewhere in Miranda, tell him to try Philemon . . . and you have to move fast. Prince Boris has just tried to kill me."

"Oh, *mon Dieu,*" she gasped. "Release the phone, ma'amselle, and I call at once. *N'ayez pas peur,* I know what to do—but for yourself, take care!"

"I will, I'm quite safe. Don't alarm Mr. Jonas, please."

"Now what?" Kai asked sleepily.

"You take a hot bath, I go down to your cottage for dry clothes, and we plan when I get back." He was asleep again before I finished, fortunately, because I knew what I was going to do. I was going to make a try for that book, of course. I let him sleep while I changed to dry shorts and shirt, ran a bath and made him a drink to set beside the tub. Finally I got him undressed and groggily inserted into the bath.

"This isn't legal, you know," he protested while I was ruthlessly stripping off his ruined slacks. "If Maggie comes in, what will she think?"

"Nothing. You're my husband, aren't you?"

"Not officially."

"Oh, don't be New England," I said impatiently. "Get into that tub, and don't fall asleep and drown. I'll be right back."

I reconnoitered quietly from the terrace and could

see no light in Miranda. Chance I could make it to Kai's cottage and get past Vulko into Boris's study on my way back. It went like whipped cream. I grabbed an outfit for Kai, never mind if it didn't match, and returned to leave the cart strategically poised for vamoose behind the entrance bushes at Miranda. The 1010HRH2 sports car was gone. I stole up across grass and flower beds. The front door was locked, but Vulko had left the kitchen door open.

I thought sardonically that Boris was singularly unfortunate in the intelligence of his associates. No doubt he'd ordered Vulko to lock up at all times, and the man had seen no reason to adhere slavishly to such a rule—particularly if he wanted to slip back quickly after an unauthorized outing. Anyway, the door was open, the house was dark and silent. I debated, decided I could dare to make haste by turning on lights. If Boris returned, he'd think Vulko was there.

Swiftly I went to the study, and when the door opened I knew the book wasn't there. I scanned the shelves for confirmation anyway, and I was right. If it was in the secret desk compartment, I was stymied, but I had a hunch it wouldn't be anywhere in the study. Nor anything else. *If I were a horse* . . . I went upstairs, using as few lights as possible, and investigated closets. Aside from a tasty selection of female negligees in the guest room, I found nothing.

I had nearly gone downstairs again in discouragement, when I spotted a final door in the tiny hall. It was the store closet. In it sat Etelka, Boris's elephant, surrounded by traveling bags and oddments—and neatly thrust into a gaping wound in her side, secured by a couple of safety pins, was the book. The hiding

259

place was arranged to look like no more than a battered child's toy, patched together out of sentiment, and buried in the stuffing you couldn't feel an alien element. I replaced the pins tidily and stole downstairs, but there was still no sound.

I'd barely made it, though. Vulko was coming back and he was definitely no better for whatever he'd been drinking. The torch wavered along the path, and he was singing in a maudlin undertone and staggering occasionally. I retreated around the villa and listened breathlessly. Would he make a custodial tour or go directly into the kitchen? I heard the door slam faintly, a light sprang up. I didn't wait, I made tracks for the golf cart before he could turn on any lights that might catch me moving along the path.

The final hazard—meeting Boris coming back on the auto road. He must be due, or why would Vulko be here? I turned the cart, went back the full length of the road, past Kai's cottage and along the supper track until finally I got back to Blondel. I'd heard no sound of any car on the circuit road, but there seemed to be some movement in the other direction, at Dresnatinko's main courtyard. I parked the cart and dashed into the villa, to find Kai inadequately wrapped in my terrycloth bathrobe, striding back and forth anxiously.

"Where the hell have you been? What took you so long?" he demanded, angry from relief. "Why are you rushing in as though the Furies are after you?"

"I'm all right. I made it, nobody saw me . . . *and I got* it!"

"Got what?"

"The fairy-tale book, of course." I waved it at him

260

triumphantly. "Here's your clothes."

He threw them untidily on the couch and glared at me. "You mean you've been in that—that murdering bastard's house *alone?*" Kai exploded. He grasped my shoulders and shook me furiously. "Dammit, haven't you any sense? Look at you—a mass of scratches and bloody cuts, your hair like a black mat, from his first set up . . . and you calmly walk back for more! Why must you do everything yourself, why didn't you wait for me to come with you?"

"I . . . didn't think," I said in a small voice. "I'm sorry . . . but I knew where it had to be, and the house was empty. If I'd waited for you, we'd have run into the servant. He got back just as I left, and probably Boris will be back soon too. Please, Kai . . . the thing is that I've got it . . . and you're hurting my shoulders, and I'm sorry but I'm tired." I was weeping again.

Kai picked me up bodily and took me into the bedroom. "Dear, darling Silly Siri," he crooned. "Of course you're tired, and I'm a beast to yell at you, but I've only just got you back, and it'll be a long time if ever before I stop being frantic at the thought of losing you again. Understand?"

"Yes. I feel the same way. Oh, Kai, aren't we lucky?"

"Very lucky. You will now lie still while I take care of you." He padded away, drawing a tub for me, bringing me a drink . . . small accustomed sounds I hadn't heard in so long.

"It's like old times, isn't it?" I said dreamily from the depths of the tub while Kai sat hunched across the doorway. "Oh, Kai, I *have* missed you."

"And I, you," he said, eyeing me with a lascivious grin until I ducked into the water with a giggle. "Where are the rings?"

"Outside in my jewelry box on the bureau."

"Thank heavens!" He sighed. "If I had to wait until I got you home, I'd go out of my mind. I don't know what a difference a piece of paper makes, when I know every inch of you by heart, but somehow"—he exhaled a series of smoke rings—"I'd like to start from scratch. Not erasing the last five years, but calling them a trial run. D'you mind?"

"No, I'd like it that way too. Oh, Kai, how *soon?*"

"Tomorrow, perhaps." He stood up, looking away from me and tossing the lighter from hand to hand. "Siri," he said in a low voice, "I said I was through with Sondra months ago . . . but are you through with Ionascu? No, don't interrupt—let me finish. I meant to leave—I told you, remember? I knew you wanted no part of Svishtov, but I thought I was going to have to get used to seeing you with *some* other man. Then I got the impression you were scared.

"All the time we were at Tekirdag I couldn't get it out of my mind, and I suppose it was silly, but finally I worked it around to: you didn't have anyone to turn to yet, I ought to be around until you got settled. So I came back." He smiled faintly. "Funny, in a way it was—encouraging to feel you might need me, even in the offing. But after the day at Delos, I . . . well, I didn't know who he was, then"—Kai's jaw tightened—"but I knew he was real. For you. And I knew I wasn't going to be able to take the real one."

"Anya's—an exceptional person," he said quietly. "She knew I was divorced, not too happy about it. She didn't know it was you, but she's been a magnificent friend all along. When I said I was getting out of here at

262

once, she asked no questions. She said she'd drive me to Tekirdag next day, if I liked. I didn't care where I went. We went there. It didn't do much good. I couldn't get my mind onto anything. She tried to help, said perhaps I needed a new scene. Her husband had a place at Mytilene and relatives in Izmir—why not go there?"

"Then one day I ran across a picture in a photograph album. She said it was her husband." Kai was silent for a moment. "Sorry, Siri, but it has to be said. I thought I had the picture: you were scared because your lover's wife was on the scene. It didn't sound like *you* to be making this sort of mud pie," he went on impersonally, "but I wasn't sure I knew what you'd do these days.

"Anyway, I knew Anya was eating her heart out for her husband. She'd been damned decent to me all summer. We knew you were here all the time, of course; she called Dresnatinko every day—hoping for word from him, I suppose. But when I found your 'guide' was actually her husband—well, I trumped up an excuse and made her come back. I don't know what I meant to do, except get hold of you, see if you knew what you were doing.

"So now, it goes the other way, too," he said steadily. "Do you know what you're doing, Siri? Do you really want to give up Ionascu for me?"

I laughed! I couldn't help it, it was all so absurd. "Bless you, darling, I don't have him to give up. I never did, never likely to. Nothing like that at all."

"Don't feel you have to tell me anything," he said quickly. "I mean, this past year never happened."

"Yes, it did, and you have to know exactly how dull it was," I said firmly. "Gyorgy was the only bright spot, and you have to understand about him, because I won't

263

let him go. We met at the Granets', and we . . . meshed mentally. Then we met by accident—I told you about that, before Germond's window—and we still meshed, but I'd got involved in his affairs without either of us knowing it. The third time was on Delos. That's all.

"I don't say I didn't think about . . . later"—my voice trembled—"but only for getting adjusted to starting over. He'd have been *kind,* if it didn't work out, but it isn't . . . I mean, we sort of love each other, but it's *simpatico,* not 'let's go!'"

He nodded silently. "Are you going to mind about Sondra?"

"No. You put it the right way," I said. "It was my own fault."

"Well . . ." Kai drew a long breath. "That's that, thank goodness." He grinned at me. "We'll get married tomorrow if we can—but first we have to finish Boris. It's nearly an hour since you called Paris, oughtn't there to be some word by now?"

"I don't know," I said helplessly. "If we could only get hold of Stefan—Gyorgy trusts him implicitly."

"I've been trying the direct line off and on, there's still no answer. We ought to have some food, too." Kai pondered. "I think: you get dressed. I'll get a car and take you to Athens for dinner. Then you call Paris again, and we play the rest by ear. The book can go to the American Embassy, you either stay there all night or we go to a hotel—wear your rings, in case. Leave word for Maggie. She's the only one who'd worry."

"All right. See if there's anything to nibble in the kitchenette, while I dress."

He came back with crackers and cheese. "Something's up. I see lights moving in the woods toward the sea. I think I'll investigate. Lock the doors and don't open for anything but Chiri-biri-bim," he ordered. "Not even Stefan or Ionascu himself."

"They have keys."

"If there's no answer, they won't search. Stand in the closet. I won't be long, I just want to get close enough to know what's going on. I'm not sure it's you. I think it's too soon. If Paris reached Ionascu, he knows you're safe. Blondel's the first place anyone would look before starting a search—on the chance you'd come back."

"If you think it's part of Boris's plans, for God's sake be careful! Oh, I'd rather you didn't go at all," I pleaded. "I've only just got you back, too."

"I'm probably safe, even if seen. He's no reason to suppose I know anything, and it'd be quite logical for me to be wandering around there, coming back to my cottage." He kissed me and departed.

I locked the door behind him and stuck the fairytale book under the mattress in Maggie's room. Then I got dressed very slowly, stopping constantly to listen. Twice I heard cars dashing along the back road and stood with pounding heart, but they didn't stop. The party must be over, one of those cars would be Boris. Would he verify the safety of his book? Not unless he needed it tonight—but if he found it gone, he'd come here at once, however incredulous he might be at my escape. I was trembling uncontrollably when I heard Kai's whistle. I opened the door and fell against him, limp with relief. "Boris is back, I heard two cars going toward Miranda."

Kai was breathing hard. "They weren't Boris," he said. "He's at the main house—sorry, let me get my breath, I ran back." He pushed me into the bedroom.

"Finish dressing, hon, and be quick. Everybody's there, the place is crawling with people. The lights were search parties for you, that's probably why we couldn't raise Stefan. There's a police car, too." Kai narrowed his eyes. "Wear your red evening dress," he said suddenly. "We'll say I met you at the lookout, I took you to Athens for dinner, and we've just got back . . . depending on how it goes. He may go to pieces when he sees you."

"What do I say if he doesn't fall apart?"

"Expurgated truth," Kai decided. "Boris left you, you thought something must have happened to him when he didn't come back, so you crawled up to the smugglers' road and came home."

"He knows I couldn't."

"Let him worry over it. Do you, or do you not, realize he meant to kill you? He'll have enough to explain why he said you went home with a headache, when you say you fooled around the shore in the boat for a half hour before he left you at the cave. Where's the book?"

"Under Maggie's mattress. Should I get it?"

"No," he said slowly. "Play ignorant—you don't know why he pulled this stunt. He won't try anything more in the midst of people, but it's better for Ionascu to have the book without Boris's knowing."

The telephone rang. "Don't answer!" Kai said sharply. "Come on." We ducked out to the golf cart. Dresnatinko was ablaze with lights. The courtyard was full of cars, including Maggie's Karmann Ghia. The police car was at one side. Kai ran us into the lee of some bushes, just as another police car whirled into the yard, followed by a sports car. Gyorgy leaped out and strode to the house, policemen falling in behind him. "No, don't call him," Kai muttered. "Let him handle it his own way, Siri. He knows you're safe, he's heading for the showdown. Slip along the poolside in the shadows and reconnoiter . . . see what develops. It may be better for you to fade away entirely and let him play it on the basis you're dead."

"Yes, but he has to have the book."

"I can phone later, or leave a note."

We sidled along quietly in the shadows, but the scene within the salon was so tense that they wouldn't have heard a brass band. Zaro was on the telephone. Boris was pacing back and forth, stopping to peer anxiously from the farther windows, occasionally closing his eyes faintly and rubbing his forehead, turning to make agonized comments. It was a beautiful act. Maggie and Anya sat white-faced on a couch, holding each other's hands. Rosa was sitting comfortably in an easy chair, wearing an expression of sadness and restoring her shattered nerves with a snifter of brandy. Everybody was talking Greek, Anya translating to Maggie. Zaro put down the phone. "The coast police have started. They will report every fifteen minutes," he said in English.

"You *must* find her," Maggie said, rigidly controlled. "I'm responsible for the girl."

"No," said Gyorgy's voice. "Since she is the guest of Dresnatinko, Miss Quain is my responsibility."

The reactions to his entrance were revealing. Anya sat up, her eyes sparkling as Gyorgy walked forward. Zaro exclaimed, "Gyorgy, it is providential you have come! I suppose the servants have told you?"

"Yes, what has been done to find the girl?" he asked.

"Anya, my dear." He held her hand to his lips conventionally, and her eyes went dull. She said, "Zaro has done everything possible, but it is good you are here, Gyorgy. Doctor Corwin, may I present my husband?"

Maggie's eyes were sparkling too. "I am happy to see you, Mr. Ionascu. Prince Svishtov appears to have misplaced my traveling companion."

"How careless of him," Gyorgy murmured smoothly, turning to Boris, who was standing speechless, transfixed, in the farther window. "What has happened, exactly?"

Boris came forward rapidly. "We were all to have gone by boat to the Goulenkis' water party," he said, "but Mama—you know she and Rosa do not care for boats—at the last moment, she decided to drive, and when Siri reached the dock, she tells me she has a bad headache and does not wish to go at all. So I put away the boat." He shrugged. "I didn't feel like a solitary trip. I transferred the skis to my car and followed Mama. The last I saw, Siri was returning to Blondel in the golf cart—and now it appears she reached the villa—the cart was there, but she has wandered off somewhere. Doctor Corwin became alarmed when she got no answer to the phone for over an hour, and Stefan has mobilized a search of the grounds. Now Zaro has informed the police and the sea patrol." Boris groaned, closing his eyes and rubbing his head distractedly. "We fear she may have gone down to the lookout, or along one of the sea paths, and fallen in a spell of dizziness. Now we are waiting for word. That's all at the moment."

"Not quite," said Gyorgy, deadly soft. "May I ask

why *Prince Svishtov* allowed a young woman suffering from migraine to be unescorted? Surely the merest tinge of *noblesse oblige* would have required you to take her back to her villa, to see her safely in the hands of Doctor Corwin. Why didn't you?"

Boris drew in his chin and glared arrogantly at Gyorgy. "She didn't wish it, she said she was quite able to go alone—and obviously she *was* able, because the cart was there."

"Why didn't she wish it?" Gyorgy asked silkily. "Was it because she found your attentions disgusting? To the point that she ran away?"

"*My* attentions?" Boris went purple with affronted incredulity. "To an American *clerk?* I have given her simply the politeness due anyone on your estate, and you accuse *me—Svishtov—*of making improper advances?"

"It's exactly the sort of thing you're most likely to do," Zaro roared. "You've been making a play for that girl every time I've seen you, Boris. By God, Gyorgy's right! You pulled something this afternoon, and for once you put both feet in it."

"I pulled nothing," Boris snorted contemptuously. "My interest in Siri is obviously nil compared to Gyorgy's. I know when to keep out of the way of my revered stepfather's arrangements, I assure you." Boris made a show of taking a cigarette from his case and lighting it.

"Then why," Anya inquired, "did you tell me to go by car this afternoon, so that you could be alone with Siri? I must tell you, Boris, that I do not care for your insinuations."

He hadn't expected her to let him down. He whirled

on her and said something incomprehensible that widened Zaro's eyes with a shocked "I say!" and made Gyorgy's hands clench, but Anya refused to back down.

"No, the game is over. I did not object to paying your debts, but this time you have gone too far. Let us have the truth—what have you done with Siri, where is she?"

Kai nudged me. "Entrance!"

I stepped through the French windows. "I'm right here," I said. "I'm so sorry you were worried, it was terribly thoughtless of me. Please, can you forgive me?"

There was a terrific babble. Maggie said, "I'll forgive anything, so long as you're safe. Oh, my dear, I was so worried!" Zaro picked up the phone, yelled excitedly to the operator, "It's all right, Miss Quain is found—tell everyone, Milcha." I was aware of Anya, smiling with tragic eyes, and Rosa leaping up from her comfortable chair, the contented-cat expression wiped from her face—"Siri, how could you worry us so!" Most of all I was aware of Boris, whirling toward me, aghast . . . incredulous. I *couldn't* be there, but there I was.

He was sheet-white but still trying. "Siri! Oh, thank God! I have been out of my mind, *duzhka*. What happened, where have you been?" He plunged across the room, arms outstretched, sobbing dramatically . . . and Kai swiftly stepped in front of me.

"She's been exactly where you left her, Svishtov—in the blowhole cave," he said evenly. There was a horror-stricken silence, an indrawn breath. Boris stopped short, protesting, "No, no—it is not so, the girl's mad!"

Kai walked forward, panther-footed. "You tried to kill my woman," he said softly, "and now I am going to kill you."

270

Boris recoiled and his hand made an infinitesimal gesture that produced a wickedly glinting six inches of blade. "Kai, watch out, he's got a knife!" I screamed.

"I see it," Kai said calmly. "The navy taught us how to deal with ordure like this." After which everything happened very suddenly. Kai picked up the nearest object and threw it like greased lightning. It later proved to be a priceless Ming vase, which shattered against Boris's ankles, and before he'd regained balance, Kai dived forward and brought him crashing to the ground. The knife went flying to the side and slid along the floor to my feet. Rosa dashed for it, but I'd got there first, and when she was inclined to scratch, I kicked her.

Everybody else was occupied in getting out of the way, and the living room was a shambles in five seconds. There wasn't anything to do about it, either. Several policemen rushed through the windows, but nobody could get close enough to Kai and Boris to pull them apart. Rosa was whimpering behind me; Anya was hanging on to Maggie, both of them silent and set-jawed. Gyorgy simply watched—impassively, impervious to the holocaust.

It was a perfectly *sensational* fight. Chairs and tables went flying in every direction, smashed like matchsticks. Lamps, bibelots, ashtrays . . . the glass in the breakfront desk . . . the rug saked with overturned flower vases. Kai took Boris apart and literally *thrashed* him, until Boris picked up a broken glass vase. . . .

"Hah, would you, you—?" In another five seconds he had Boris in some sort of death grip. Then Gyorgy snapped out an order, and the policemen closed in to

271

pull Kai away. It took three of them. Boris was as good as dead, but Kai wasn't much better. He stood swaying groggily, his clothes torn, a bleeding cut over one eye, holding one hand painfully in the other.

I rushed forward. "Oh, darling, your hands! Sit down, hon." I pushed him onto the couch, mopping away the blood with my chiffon skirts and cuddling him. He rested against me exhaustedly, "I *could* have killed him, I should have—why wouldn't they let me?"

"Oh, yes, darling—you were magnificent, but don't talk . . . you need a doctor," I said distractedly. "Please, somebody get a doctor. . . ."

"Be all ri' in a moment," he mumbled, and fainted in an untidy sideways heap.

"Here's some water," Maggie said quietly. "Bathe your husband's face while I get the police doctor." I was so startled that I spilled half the water. Maggie smiled wickedly. "Oh, I've known all along, my dear. Marcus Kai Penberthy is a Radcliffe trustee."

So *that* was the letter I wasn't to see? "Why, you deceitful old woman!"

"Look who's talking!" She went away and presently came back with a doctor, who clucked at sight of Kai.

"The cut is not bad; he will have a black eye, but there is no need for stitches." He slapped some gauze and tape over it, dabbed antiseptic on various scratches. He was less happy over Kai's hand. "Oh, yes, definitely broken bones—no, no, they will mend. Do not be alarmed, madame." Kai groaned involuntarily and fainted again while the doctor was setting the bones. He was amazingly deft and quick. "I shall be through before he revives, you will see. It will be over and he will have felt nothing. It must have been a

272

splendid encounter," he said admiringly. "You should see the other one."

I had no desire to see the other one, ever again! I sat on the floor beside the couch, holding Kai's good hand and feeling stunned. Who would have dreamed Kai was capable of such fury? And such possessiveness! "*My* woman," he'd said, and fought for me! I fingered the silver cuff gently, and his hand closed over mine. "My Kind Protector," I murmured.

"I'm more wounded hero than protector," he said disgustedly. "If I can't take that little dust-up, I'd better join a gym class."

"The doctor says we should see the other guy."

"Cut him up a bit, did I?" Kai sounded modestly pleased.

"He'll never be the same, and neither will I. Oh, Kai, your poor hand! The doctor says it will mend, but . . ."

"It will," he assured me cheerfully, "and that will teach you not to become involved with unsavory characters, Serendipity." He fell asleep with the suddenness of a baby, and I sat on the floor beside him, hearing auto engines in the distance.

Maggie came in. "I'm going home to bed, unless you want me for anything," she said.

"Bed?" It rang a bell dimly. "Oh, good heavens! Maggie—there's a book under your mattress. Tell Mr. Ionascu. . . ."

"A book under my mattress," she repeated. "Tell Mr. Ionascu. Very well, I'll tell him. Will he want to read it there?"

"No, of course not," I giggled softly. "Just give it to him before you go to bed, or we'll have to wake you up later."

273

"You can wake me any time," she assured me, "particularly if you're going to tell me what this is all about. I thought you said you weren't a spy—were you lying?"

"No, it was all accidental. I didn't know what was going on myself until I met Gyorgy on Delos."

She nodded. "I like his looks, but this one's better. Siri—are you really all right?"

"Yes. I won't tell you about it, Maggie. It's over." I snorted grimly. "This one he can't settle with a dozen pairs of stockings."

Vaguely, when she'd gone, I wondered what they'd do with Boris . . . and the next thing I knew, Gyorgy was bending over me, gently pulling me to my feet. "Leave him to sleep," he said softly. "Stefan will look after him. Are you too tired to talk for only a little while, Siri?"

I stretched out the kinks gingerly, but the nap had done me good. "No, I don't think so," I said doubtfully. "I'm mostly hungry. I missed dinner because we were in that damned cave."

"Good heavens!" he muttered, leading me out to the pool patio and snapping his fingers imperiously. A servant rushed forward. "Get Miss Quain some dinner as quickly as possible." There were a couple of men sitting at the end of the pool, rising politely as Gyorgy brought me forward. One was Interpol, one was Greek police; I couldn't pronounce their names even if I remembered them. "It is only to tell us exactly what happened this evening," Gyorgy said quietly. "I'm sorry to distress you, Siri, but Boris will admit nothing."

"I suppose he's playing for time hoping the shipment

274

n slip through. Did Maggie give you the book?"

"Yes, but it will take time to identify the maps. Aside from the license numbers, the code is only helpful, if we find it in use. To immobilize Boris, we need your story."

"Well, he didn't expect to find anyone at Dresnatinko, and he was mad as hops with Anya for coming back from Tekirdag." I went along slowly, remembering the pool conversation, explaining why it had taken me so long to realize the importance of the book. At some point food arrived and I was talking with my mouth full. "I didn't particularly want to go in the boat with him, but he sort of undermined me by promising not to make any passes . . . and he didn't. He was—quite decent company, talking about impersonal things. Finally he said he'd forgotten the tow lines for the water skis, for me to wait while he ran back for them."

"And that was it," I finished simply. "He never came back. I suppose he got the golf cart back to Blondel easily enough. Maggie was working at the typewriter, she wouldn't have heard a herd of elephants. Then he went to the Goulenkis' by car and said I had a headache. Kai didn't like the sound of it somehow. He suspected Boris had . . . upset me, so he came back to see. When I wasn't at Blondel, he thought I might have beat it into the woods to get away. Finally, he came along the path and found me in the cave."

"A horrifying experience, Miss Quain," the Interpol man said hastily, "but all's well that ends well."

"Yes, but you don't know the half of it." I held my voice even. "Kai got down to the cave before I could stop him, which caused a rock slide, and then we both

275

couldn't get out."

"My God," somebody muttered.

"But you are here," Gyorgy said after a moment. "How did you accomplish this?"

"Kai boosted me up through the blowhole, and I got across the rocks, unhooked the chains, and let them down for him," I said simply. "After a while we got back to the villa. I couldn't get Stefan, so I called Paris. The girl said she knew what to do. Then we waited to see what developed. Kai had a bath, I went over to his cottage for clothing, and on the way back—Miranda was deserted, so I went in and found the book."

"Where was it?"

"Buried in the stuffing of a nursery elephant. I expect you'd have found it eventually, but I had a hunch where to look. Kai was dreadfully angry," I confessed, "but I figured Boris would keep everyone at the Goulenkis' as long as possible, to prevent realization of my disappearance, so it seemed too good an opportunity to miss."

There was a slight pause. "Two carloads of us tore Miranda and Philemon apart," the Interpol man remarked, "and I saw the elephant myself. It didn't look as though it'd ever been disturbed."

"I know. I wonder where he got the rusted pins." I felt apologetic. "I put them back in the same holes, in case he looked. I'm sorry you had so much trouble. We were going to telephone again from Athens, except you were all here before we got there."

"After you returned to Blondel with the book?" Gyorgy prompted, with suppressed amusement.

"We didn't know what to do. Kai saw the lights and prowled around while I had a bath and dressed. He back saying the search was on. So we went over to how much damage we could do . . . and I'm afraid was rather a lot," I said in a small voice. "I never dreamed Kai would go berserk like that. I'm sorry, Gyorgy."

Gyorgy laughed. "I'm not. He deserved his revenge, every punch of it, and I shared his satisfaction. I have rarely enjoyed anything more than the sight of your husband beating up Anya's whelp. A Ming vase is a small price to pay, my dear. Well, gentlemen," he said, turning to the others. "I think that's all you need? Better than we expected, in fact. No matter how Boris changes his story, you have an independent witness to the fact that Miss Quain was still in the cave and unable to get out while Svishtov was stating she'd returned to Blondel."

"How could he change his story?" I asked.

"Oh, he has now said that he did take you to the cave and that he was a bit delayed in finding the tow lines. When he returned you had gone. He supposed you'd walked up to the smugglers' road, and he put away the boat and ran the cart back to Blondel, hoping for a chance to apologize. He confesses he did attempt to make love to you and was rejected, that his original story was only covering his humiliation at the repulse—which did not, of course, lessen his determination to win you for Princess Svishtov," Gyorgy stated dryly. "However, he cannot understand your accusation of intent to murder. This he feels is too much anger for his merely being carried away by your beauty, and he has no doubt that you will soften toward him when you have had time to consider."

"Good Lord!" I murmured, awed.

"Yes, it's a clever story, isn't it?" Gyorgy agreed. "␣ has not been told of Mr. Penberthy's connection wi␣ you, Siri. That is what will trap him. He's genuinely startled at being attacked physically, can only explain it as a summer romance between Americans, although he is wounded that you could not say your affections were engaged." Gyorgy smiled at me. "Finish the coffee while I send our friends on their way."

Kai was still sleeping; I went to peek. At the far end of the salon, Marko was quietly sweeping together the shattered fragments of china and glass. Stefan was setting chairs and tables in place. He smiled at me. "I'm happy to see you, Miss Quain."

"I'm happy to see me, too. It's a mess, isn't it?" I glanced around uneasily. "I'm so sorry."

Stefan's shoulders quivered silently. "So are not we, Miss Quain. The staff only regrets its nonparticipation. I fear service may be slightly disrupted tomorrow. They have been drinking Mr. Penberthy's health for an hour."

"Oh, dear," I said helplessly, hovering over Kai anxiously, but his breathing and color seemed all right. "He was rather a wowser, wasn't he?" I murmured proudly. "Did you see any of it?"

"I am happy to say I did. Very heartwarming! Mr. Ionascu has returned." Stefan led me away from the couch. "I shall be here—but Mr. Penberthy will probably sleep for some time. Don't worry."

Gyorgy took both my hands and kissed them one after the other. "I shall have an iron grating fixed across the cave entrance tomorrow," he said conversationally, filling two brandy glasses and handing one to me. "If he'd succeeded," he murmured grimly, "I would

278

had him killed, Siri. Unfortunately I'm too old to ⟨d⟩it personally, but it would have been done." He ⟨pa⟩ssed off the brandy at a gulp and refilled the glass.

"It isn't really over, is it?" I asked, troubled. "What about Rosa—and Anya? What will happen to Boris?"

Gyorgy twisted the glass absently. "He will go to prison," he said slowly, "but the length of sentence will depend on how much can be determined of his activities. I fear we will find he played a lone hand as much as possible. Zaro will get whatever Rosa knows, in view of what he learned in Chamonix and Montreux (thank you, my dear!), but she will know nothing helpful, you will see. She allowed Boris to invest her money in cargoes, she'll admit she suspected they were illegal, but she will know nothing." Gyorgy smiled. "By the time Zaro gets through with her, I assure you she'll wish she did know something!"

He sighed. "But it will be like that everywhere—the few who know anything will be so implicated that they'll reveal nothing until caught by independent evidence; the others will have nothing concrete. We can hold Boris on your charge of attempted murder, we can hope this may flush something." He shrugged. "A request for instructions, perhaps, but otherwise . . ."

"How discouraging!" I sipped my brandy and looked absently at the softly lit pool. "Why did he have to be *here?*" I asked suddenly. "I mean at Dresnatinko, not merely on the property."

"I wish I knew," Gyorgy muttered. "There's no place for loading a major cargo."

"It isn't that, it's something here—in the house itself. That was what threw him when he found Anya and Kai were here. He counted on being alone and unobserved

279

in this house," I said slowly. "Servants wouldn't bot[her] him, Anya did . . . because he couldn't shut a door [in] *her* face or say, 'None of your business.' He improvise[d] fairly well—commissioning Kai to do a portrait of me. He probably thought Anya would sit in . . . but that would only cover daylight hours. What could he need to use here that a servant wouldn't question but Anya would wonder about? The switchboard? Is there a telegraph here, Gyorgy, or a ham radio? Something to send and receive messages, but in a location Anya would notice?"

Gyorgy sprang to his feet. "Zaro once had a radio room!" he exclaimed incredulously, walking across to lean heavily on the bell. "Years ago . . . it didn't work very satisfactorily, he lost interest. . . ."

"But it is still there, and Boris has made it work much better," I said, while Gyorgy was telling the servant, "Ask Mr. Zaro to come here at once, please. If he is in bed, wake him up." He walked back and forth, eagerly pounding his hands together. "Siri, if you're right—it will be another link. We'll have him!"

It wasn't quite that easy. When we got up to the radio room, the place looked dusty and unused, and the set didn't work. "He's disconnected something very simple and quick to replace when he needs it," I said. "One of our friends used to do that with his amplifier, because the maid *would* try to use the phonograph and ruined one of his collector's items. Look around behind, for a clean spot." Zaro found it in two seconds, and instantly all the tubes lit up. He wasn't dumb, either. He looked at the set and touched nothing.

"It's on a different beam," he muttered. "Now, has Boris left it ready to transmit or altered at random to event recognition if I happened to examine it?"

"The former," said Gyorgy authoritatively. "Give me the setting, Zaro, and switch over to receive. We can't send until we know what and where, but with luck we'll get a message in his code. Siri, keep Zaro company, if you please, while I call Interpol."

"Hadn't you better know which Ionascu ships will be within range tonight or tomorrow?" I asked doubtfully, "or will this set reach anywhere?"

"Only from Istanbul to Rhodes, once in a while Cairo."

Gyorgy sighed. "Thank you, Siri." He went away to a phone in the next room. I could hear him barking away in Greek, while we sat silent before the equally silent set. Eventually he came back. "They'll alert at once. The devil of it is, I haven't any idea which ship it might be and no way to check before tomorrow morning."

"Who's the captain from the old days whom you'd most distrust?"

"Berriet," Gyorgy said instantly.

"What's his ship?"

"He was given the newest . . . oh, *boze moy!*" Gyorgy yelled. "The *Etelka!*" He raced for the phone again—and suddenly the radio set chattered. Zaro said, "Get paper!" and twiddled dials while I ran out to the desk, found pad and pencils, ran back while Zaro was saying something. "I acknowledged," he said tensely, and twiddled again. Gyorgy was back then, and the message came through—slowly enough for Zaro to get it down. "Now what?" he asked. "It's code. Do I acknowledge or ignore?"

"Say Berriet received, again one hour," Gyorgy took

the paper to the phone. Zaro twiddled and fiddle[d]
spoke tersely, received an equally terse bark, an[d]
finally said, "That's it. Shall I stay here, on the chance?"

"No, we've got what's needed, if he didn't question
the name Berriet. Turn the set off and go back to bed."
He clapped Zaro on the back. "Thanks! Come, Siri, it's
time you were in bed too."

"But shouldn't someone get the message an hour
from now?"

Gyorgy shook his head. "We won't have a coded
reply ready for him that soon. Better for him to suspect
difficulty, hang around for instructions, than *know* it's
all over. He might jettison the cargo. As it is, he'll give it
a few hours on the chance it's only a minor delay here.
By then we'll have spotted the ship. She'll be coming
down from the Dardanelles, lying about off the coast
by now and heading for Suez."

He led me out of the radio room, and I could see at
once why Boris needed Anya gone from Dresnatinko—the door opened onto the same large square
upper hall that served Anya's suite with the "lovely
view." Gyorgy said, "Shall we tuck you into a guest
room here, Siri, or would you rather go back to Blondel?"

"Blondel, please."

"I must wait a few minutes on the chance of a call.
Will you wait with me, or shall Stefan take you at
once?"

"I'll wait." While he went into a downstairs study, I
stole into the living room again, but Kai was still
asleep. The place was in perfect order once more, if a
bit sparse on *objets d'art*. By the looks of him, Kai was
going to sleep till Gabriel tooted, but the couch was

g and he appeared quite comfortable.

When's the wedding?" Gyorgy's voice was amused.

"Tomorrow, if we can arrange it," I said calmly.
Would you care to give the bride away?"

"I'd be honored." He laughed softly and reached for
my hand with a long sigh. "I'm glad there's a happy
ending for you."

I looked at his ugly face turned toward the lights of
the sea. In the dim patio lights, it was filled with
indescribable sadness. "Why not a happy ending for
you, as well?" I asked, holding on to my courage with
both hands. "In the cave tonight with Kai, I discovered
how terribly easy it is to misunderstand, to get lost for
lack of the right word, to think you're doing what's
wanted when all the time it's misinterpretation."

"What are you trying to say, Siri?" he asked after a
moment.

"That Anya loves you very dearly. I don't know if
you know that. Perhaps you don't care, or it's even a
nuisance to be loved when you're so busy," I faltered,
"but that's why she's here this summer. She thought
you'd be more likely to come here if you had any free
time, and she hadn't seen you in months, so she came
on the chance. I'm sorry if I'm impertinent."

"Did she tell you this?"

"Only about hoping you'd be here, when she showed
me the portrait. She talked about her lovely balcony
view, how she sits there alone at night, and somehow I
knew. Kai knows it too," I said. "It's all in his portrait
of her."

"Ah? I have not seen it. Is she pleased?"

"Yes. She said she'd been painted many times, but
this is her. I wanted her to lend it to Germond's

exhibition, and she said she couldn't without y~~
approval."

He nodded. "Anya is always very careful i~
consulting me about small conventional matters," he
murmured absently. He sat silent for some time,
holding my hand lightly. He was evidently *thinking,*
but of what, I couldn't tell. "I owe Boris a score for this,
too," he said presently. "You were right that he held a
club over her head, but as you said once—it looks
different once you have the missing piece to the puzzle.
I saw only a foolishly doting mother, but tonight he
was spiteful, lashing out to harm anyone he could. . . ."

"Because, when the chips were down, she protected
you," I murmured. "Whatever the secret was, she knew
damn well he'd tell you . . . but she still wouldn't let
him blacken you."

"Yes." He smiled mischievously. "You are a most
persuasive advocate—but this I had already concluded
for myself."

"I'm sorry; I'm being very rude, I'm afraid."

"No, I think you have been right to box my ears," he
murmured. "I might still not have reflected. . . . It was
that Anya knew I expected children and married me
when she knew she could have no more. Several years
later she apparently had the operation, but in fact it
had already been done long before. Heaven knows how
Boris learned this, but he threatened to tell me,
believing I would divorce his mother on the grounds of
fraud."

"Would you?"

"No, never," he said quietly. "I should probably have
been very angry for a little while—until she coaxed me

284

of it." Gyorgy smiled and stood up. "Come, I must ᵉ you back to the villa. The call is evidently not ᵒming through, and you should be in bed." He helped ᵉ to my feet and clasped my arms lightly. "I shall ᵒrgive Sidonie Granet all her stupidities, which are too numerous to mention," he remarked, "for the one brilliant stroke that put you next to me at dinner that night!"

"Hallo," said Kai's voice. "What are you doing still up?"

"I am about to kiss your wife," Gyorgy returned calmly, "and you had better not object, or I shall refuse to give her away to you at your wedding tomorrow."

"In that case," said Kai, "I will turn my back. . . ."

They nabbed the *Etelka* the next day, carrying a full load of oil from Constanta bound for Rhodesia, and the captain was persuaded to turn state's evidence. There were three other ships in the deal, but all were caught before they made port. Gyorgy duly gave me away at the American Embassy, after which he went to Geneva to overhaul Boris's operations. Anya went with him, her eyes sparkling like a child at a Christmas tree. Kai kissed her goodbye at the airport. "No arguments," he told Gyorgy, poker-faced. "You owe me one."

We honeymooned at Dresnatinko by special request of everyone, including the staff. Maggie revised her book—it later was condensed in a magazine prepublication, but it didn't sell to the movies. It still made enough money for jubilation. I finished up the work for Wells, Atherton and sent in my resignation, which

produced transatlantic telephone protests of suffi[cient]
volume that they could probably have been hea[rd]
without the phone lines.

"Would you like to go back to them?" Kai asked. "[I]
could take it now, if you'd like it."

"I wouldn't like it. I have decided to become a
cordon bleu, so you have to make enough money for us
to live in Paris for a while."

"Savarin Siri? It has rather a pleasant ring to it—but
don't let them teach you how to make codfish cakes. I
hate them."

Kai bought a camera and took arty photographs
until his hand mended. Zaro duly got his divorce and
married Mademoiselle Rouget the next day. They
honeymooned at Dresnatinko too, but that was later.
The new Madame Zaro was a comfortably cozy little
woman, rather alarmingly pregnant at the moment,
but obviously adoring Zaro, who adored her equally.
He would hardly allow her to set foot to the ground or
exert herself to raise cigarette to mouth. Kai did an
enchanting portrait of her, fat tummy and all, as a
wedding present. Anya's portrait went to Germond's
exhibit and produced an immediate commission from
Sidonie Granet!

I was for leaving by the next plane, but Kai said,
"No, she can wait until fall."

"But we can't stay here forever, delightful as it is."

"No," he agreed, "although Ionascu said to plan on
staying all year."

"All *year?* What would we do with ourselves?"

"I don't know what you'll do. I shall be painting a
picture of my wife." He grinned at my stupefaction.

t—why *now,* when you've a commission?"

Because now is when I finally know you well
ough to paint you. Did you think I didn't *want* to
aint you?" Kai put his hands on my cheeks, held my
ace gently. "I *couldn't* paint you, dear heart. In the
beginning, there was too much of you; you were too
new and wonderful for any perspective, I couldn't put
all of you on canvas and I couldn't decide what parts of
you to choose.

"There was too much of you," he said again. "Then
for a while there wasn't enough of you . . . but now it's
just right, and I don't want to miss the perfect
moment. . . ."

It was a magical, dreamlike summer of lazy days and
pleasant company that made those first weeks seem
totally unreal. There were reminders that brought an
occasional jolt. Boris was in prison, where Foucald
joined him as soon as Gyorgy'd dug into the shipping
affairs. Miranda was closed and abandoned. Zaro's
price for allowing Rosa to avoid a public scandal was
every fur and jewel she owned. She still had her
marriage settlement, it was an irrevocable trust
entailed for Rosa's children by Zaro and dissoluble
only at her death. "What a pity," said Maggie.

One day we were invited for a private run on the
Ariadne, and sailing up to Stylos we passed
Dresnatinko. Gyorgy'd been good as his word—a
barrier of iron crossbars was fixed across the blowhole
cavern. After the first glance, I couldn't look at it—it
looked like a medieval picture of the mouth of hell. We
went to a water party near Larimna, and the ski tow
ropes gave me a nasty jolt, so that I dumped both Kai

and myself, but otherwise life was heavenly. We did some of the sightseeing Maggie had planned Vravroun, Sounion, Thermopylae—but we never d get to Thessalonike.

"I don't suppose I'd have liked it if we'd gone," Maggie said philosophically—and we went to the Goulenkis' instead.